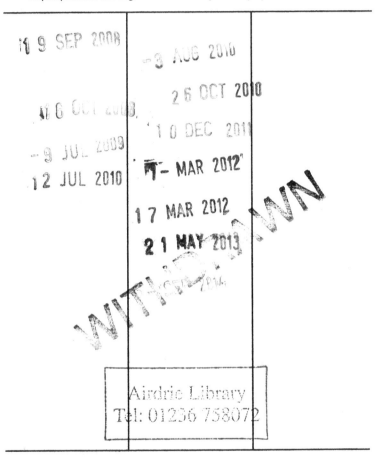

Force of Nature

Also by Sue Cook and available from Headline Review

On Dangerous Ground

Force of Nature

Sue Cook

headline
review

First published in 2008 by Headline Review
An imprint of HEADLINE PUBLISHING GROUP

1

Cataloguing in Publication Data is available from the British Library

Hardback ISBN 978 0 7553 2235 0

Typeset in Giovanni by Avon DataSet Ltd,
Bidford on Avon, Warwickshire

Printed and bound in Great Britain by
Mackays of Chatham plc, Chatham, Kent

Headline's policy is to use papers that are natural, renewable and
recyclable products and made from wood grown in sustainable
forests. The logging and manufacturing processes are expected to
conform to the environmental regulations of the country of origin.

HEADLINE PUBLISHING GROUP
An Hachette Livre UK Company
338 Euston Road
London NW1 3BH

www.headline.co.uk
www.hachettelivre.co.uk

For my friend, Jill

Acknowledgements

The author's thanks go to the following:

Dr Timothy Appleton, Cell Biologist, Fertility Counsellor and author of numerous books, CDs and papers about the miracle of IVF and the ethics involved.

Scott Galloway, Consultant Clinical Psychologist, BSc, MSc.

Liz Railton, CBE, former Honorary Secretary, Association of Directors of Social Services, and current Director of *Together for Children*, working with local authorities across the country to help them deliver the Government's Sure Start Children's Centres.

Andrea Berkeley, Education Consultant and former Headteacher.

Former Chief Superintendent David Hatcher and his Detective son Nick, for attention to detail with the law enforcement procedures encountered by the characters in this novel.

Part One

Chapter One

Mark Elfick lay in the darkness trying to hold on to reality. He was careering through space, out of control, frantically trying to dodge a continuous stream of debris flying past him. They'd do some serious damage if they hit him.

He wanted to cry out, 'Help me. I'm in trouble here. For God's sake!' But he mustn't wake Jenny. She'd only just got back to sleep, having got up to comfort Chloe after one of her night terrors.

Maybe his daughter was having the same kind of nightmares as he was. At nearly two years old, she couldn't explain of course what was causing her to wake screaming almost every night between three and four in the morning.

'She'll grow out of it,' everyone said.

But the sleep deprivation was beginning to take its toll.

Chilled after her visit to Chloe's bedroom, Jenny nestled close against him, her breasts pressed into his shoulder blades, knees crooked in the bend of his, the cool draught of her breath playing on the back of his neck.

Hang on, Jenny. Their survival was all down to him now.

Another unwieldy chunk of detritus came somersaulting out of the blackness and beyond it, were the shapes of dozens more. It was as if the entire contents of the

3

builders' skip in the street a few doors down had risen up to assault him.

After their elderly next-door neighbour died last February, a couple of young city types had bought the place on a three-month bridging loan, preferring to wait until the house had been gutted, fumigated and redecorated before they took possession.

The skip stood now overflowing with items of furniture that had once been the old lady's life: a chintz armchair with wads of horsehair spilling from its sides, a scratched mahogany-veneered coffee table with a leg missing, a splintered pine piano stool, a 1960s standard lamp, piled senselessly on top of each other, all draped in ribbons of yellowed floral wallpaper.

Adrift in the bleak, dark no-man's land between sleeping and waking, it came to him what the flying missiles were. They were the furniture of his own existence: icons of his thoughts and feelings, once ordered and rational, now reduced to crazy, disjointed, terror-inducing fragments.

Where everything had once seemed so clear and predictable, now none of it made sense. Nothing added up. There were no reference points any more. Nothing to hold on to.

He could either go on like this, losing his sanity little by little, or he could take control. Shape his destiny; probably for the first time in his life. At the moment destiny was shaping him – and making a total pig's ear of it.

Tomorrow he would confront it.

There might be repercussions. Shock waves. But there was no alternative. He could see that now.

Jenny considered leaving the phone to ring. She wanted to keep track of Mark. He seemed to be getting ready to go out.

Watched by Chloe, still in her high chair, dunking her Little Pony in the soggy remains of her cereal ('Pony's in the field. He's getting all muddy'), he'd cleared away the breakfast things and had sat down at the dining table to lace up his trainers.

Damn. She'd been hoping to persuade him to come shopping with her. There was a new Sunday farmers' market in the station car park she wanted to investigate. She'd planned on a bit of a browse around, maybe taking Chloe for an early lunch at The Bakery restaurant. It would have to be early as it was usually too crowded to get the buggy in there after about twelve thirty on a weekend.

She and Mark had always been such great companions. For years they'd done almost everything together. But this last couple of months he'd seemed increasingly distant. Absent-minded. Preoccupied.

When he wasn't at work, he'd be glued to the computer in the study.

She picked up the burbling handset, peered at the caller display and pressed the button.

'Hi, Annabel.'

'Hello, darling. And what's wrong with you this morning?'

'Nothing.'

'Something is. I know you too well.'

'Oh I don't know.' Glancing over her shoulder, she retreated into the kitchen and lowered her voice. 'It's Mark. He's not his usual self. Hasn't been for weeks really. I'm beginning to think he might be having an affair or something.'

'Not Mark, darling. That's ridiculous. He adores you. He always has.'

'He's in a world of his own most of the time. We hardly even make eye contact. It never used to be like this.'

'Maybe it's money worries. How's the antiques business going lately?'

'It's been a bit slow since January. Not so many Americans.

Sue Cook

But he's still got a good solid client base. It can't be the business. He'd tell me. He tells me everything. Well, he used to.'

'Perhaps you're just a bit too wrapped up in Chloe. She's quite demanding sometimes, isn't she? Utterly adorable, but a handful.'

'Look, I know what you're trying to say, Bels, and it's not that. I don't cut him out at all. I let him read the bedtime story last night.'

'Let him?'

'Well, she usually insists on it being me. He's back too late from work most nights anyway. He used to make it a rule that he never saw clients out of normal working hours unless it was a mega-big deal. Now he does it quite a lot.'

'Don't let things drift, then. Talk to him. Cook him a really nice meal, open some wine, sit down together and talk. Find out what's eating him.'

'I cook him a meal and open some wine most evenings.'

'Then make it an extra-special one. You know what I mean.'

'You're not talking candles and frilly negligées I hope. He'd just fall about laughing.'

'Don't be silly. I'm serious. Just make time to have a proper talk to him, that's all I'm saying.' Glancing out towards the hall, she could see Mark wriggling into his Barbour jacket.

'Bels, I've got to go. Call you back later.' She almost threw the phone on to the worktop. 'Mark! You're not going out!'

'Sorry, Jen. It's a new client. This morning is the only time he can manage to see me.'

'It's *Sunday*!'

'I know. I know,' he shrugged helplessly, 'but I've got to go for it. This guy represents a Belgian customer who is so rich I'm not even allowed to know his name.'

'You might have said.'

'I'd been hoping to get out of it, but I just got a call on the mobey. Apparently there's no other time I can see him.'

6

'Where is it?'

'Oh, down Sevenoaks way. I shouldn't be there too long. I'll be back by two, three maybe, at the latest.'

He peeled back his sleeve to look at his watch. Was his hand shaking? She must have imagined it.

'I was looking forward to a gentle Sunday morning together. Like we used to.' He raked his fingers through his curly brown hair as he usually did when he felt uncomfortable.

'I'm sorry, Jen. Really. Next Sunday. I promise.' Jenny followed him as he strode back into the living room to plant a kiss on Chloe's forehead. Everywhere else on her chubby little face was covered in milky bits of food.

She trailed ineffectually behind him again as he headed back towards the front door. He glanced at her guiltily.

'When I get back we could go for a walk on the heath with Chloe, if you like. If it's not too cold.'

She shrugged. 'I don't think so. The forecast said rain this afternoon. It'll be dark by four anyway.'

'I'll be as quick as I can. It's just making contact really. See you later.'

By the open car door, he reached out to hook his elbow behind her head to kiss her goodbye. Seeming not to notice her pointed reluctance to kiss him back, he shoved his oversized black work case across on to the passenger seat of the Peugeot estate, climbed in after it and turned the engine over. The door slammed, his face disconcertingly becoming a reflection of her own until the window slid down.

'I'll make it up to you,' he called, clunking the car into reverse.

He'd rehearsed this drive so often in his head. From Wordsworth Grove, Blackheath to Simmonds Road, Fulrow Green, twenty-seven point one miles. Front door to front door. The AA route finder on the net said it would take forty-seven minutes but he was sure he could do it in less. They always overestimated the time factor, probably because he found it impossible not to sneak over the speed limit.

The detective work hadn't been as difficult as he'd expected, once he'd made the decision to try to find the address. He had taken afternoons off work whenever he could, shutting up the shop at lunchtime and driving across London to the Family Records Office in Islington where he would spend hours at a time, trawling through the enormous leather-bound registers before heading back south again.

True, the business had suffered a little. He'd lost a couple of sales he knew he could have clinched if he'd been his usual assiduous self. But it was a matter of priorities. He'd make up for it eventually.

It had been such a thrill, by a process of diligent elimination, getting closer and closer. He'd known for nearly a month now. The address and the phone number. The knowledge at first smouldering slowly at the back of his brain, then increasing in intensity, branding his very being.

With trembling fingers he'd picked out the digits on his office phone nearly a dozen times, making sure to dial 141 first to ensure anonymity. The first couple of times he'd hung up as soon as it began to ring. Then he forced himself to wait until someone answered, but hung up on the first syllable.

After that, he'd pushed himself further. He waited to hear the voice at the other end.

'Hello . . . Hello? Who's there? Hel-*lo*. Who do you want to speak to?'

The voice was relaxed, warm. Quite deep for a woman. He hoped she wasn't a smoker. She sounded approachable though; puzzled rather than angry or intimidated by this silent phone caller.

Once, his heart thumping in his chest, he actually spoke.

'Sorry. Wrong number,' he'd managed.

It had taken him half an hour to stop shaking. This was getting ridiculous. Furtive, obsessive behaviour. He wasn't a furtive or obsessive type of person. He was a straightforward, rational human being; above average intelligence, expensive education behind him . . . a good, well-paid job. Not just a job but a reputation. An antiques dealer specialising in fine silverware, who knew what was what, whose judgement could be trusted absolutely and whose contacts in his field, he liked to think, were second to none.

This agonising had gone on too long. He was in danger of making himself ill.

There was nothing else for it but to go and look at the house. What harm could that do? It was no big deal anyway. A quick trip out on a Sunday morning to satisfy his understandable curiosity.

Why then were his hands trembling on the steering wheel? It must be this cold February weather. Annoyed with himself, he rubbed them vigorously on his dark brown cord jeans and turned the heating up a notch.

Jenny closed the front door before the car had left the drive, the morning now yawning ahead of her. At least during the week she had Thora, their Norwegian au pair, around the house each afternoon; a pale, lumpy girl whose cleaning and ironing skills were perfunctory but whose redemption was a ready smile and a love of giving manicures and finding creative new ways of styling Jenny's unruly auburn hair.

Perhaps it was time to resurrect Jenny Elfick Interiors. Mark had discouraged her from working during the pregnancy. He'd been an anxious wreck throughout the whole nine months, but she had understood why and gone along with it. The pregnancy had been so very hard won. A miscarriage halfway through would have been unendurable.

Even after Chloe's birth, he'd still wanted Jenny at home, watching the new baby twenty-four/seven. There'd been the hysterectomy to recover from too. That had been psychological more than physical.

Coming to terms with the hard fact that any chance of a second child was gone for good would take time. Going back to working again might make her feel less . . . unproductive. Chloe wasn't so much of a baby now. She'd recently started attending nursery school a couple of mornings a week. And Jenny still had her old business cards and headed notepaper.

There'd be some house visits of course, but she had the phone and the internet; she could base herself at home and start off slowly with just one or two clients. And if she had buying trips or visits to make in the afternoons, she could either take the baby with her or Thora could look after her.

It would take a while to get back on the radar screen of course but . . .

'Mama.' Chloe was holding out her arms beseechingly. 'Gehout.'

Unclipping the sludge-spattered pelican bib from her daughter's neck, Jenny lifted the child out of the high chair and placed her on the floor near the play-tent she and Mark had bought her for Christmas.

Chloe had sat watching her parents intently while they pored over the assembly instructions, trying to make sense of the elastic-corded aluminium poles and multicoloured nylon panels.

After nearly an hour of struggle, they'd finally succeeded in getting the construction to look like the picture on the leaflet.

Chloe had regarded their handiwork thoughtfully for a

moment then set off, bum-shuffling on her nappy across the floor, straight past the new tent, to the discarded cardboard box, where she crawled in and sat sucking happily on her thumb, looking out at them both.

Jenny loved being with Chloe. 'My little miracle', as she called her, was the most precious thing in her life. But it wasn't the same as adult company. And not at all the same as the company of the man she'd always thought of as her best friend in the world.

Was he having an affair? Weren't women supposed to have an instinct about these things? There was certainly something gnawing at him. But if it was an affair, she had to congratulate him on his sexual stamina.

His need to make love to her had gone into overdrive in the last six months or so. While they'd been trying so hard for a baby, they'd reached a point where sex became something they'd both have preferred to avoid. It was a chore. Something they had to do. And to a timetable. A means to an end, rather than the exuberant indulgence in each other's bodies it had once been.

Now, suddenly, he had started wanting her more than he ever had. It was almost obsessive. Most nights before they went to sleep she'd feel his erection nudging at her, his hands cupping her breasts, his mouth searching in the darkness for her nipples. Often in the small hours he'd wake her, wanting her again. But now it was a quiet, serious, urgent business. He wasn't violent, not entirely inconsiderate, and sometimes, if she tried hard, she could match his pace and climax with him. Most times, though, there was only enough time to play along and she was left wide awake, feeling used and resentful.

She still loved him of course. She wouldn't want life without him. This was a phase, she was sure.

At first she'd thought this renewed sexual enthusiasm was the sheer relief of being able to make love without that constant, desperate pressure of wanting to conceive. But it couldn't be that, because sometimes he would cry quietly afterwards. She knew that because she had felt his warm tears on her neck, tasted their saltiness on her lips, and she was shattered to the core.

She had tried to talk to him about it but he always deflected her.

'I'm fine. Really. I think it's after holding everything together for so long while we were trying, you know? Four years of hanging in there. And seeing you suffer and having to be strong for both our sakes. It's just a huge emotional release, that's all. Nature taking its course. All you need to know is I love you. OK?'

The subject was firmly closed. She could have pursued things further, perhaps tried to probe a little deeper. But she didn't.

It was cowardice really. What if he were to tell her he wept because of the inescapable truth – that she could never now give him another baby? That after every frantic climax there followed an equivalent anticlimax? Like scratching a mosquito bite until it stopped itching, just to make it hurt instead. If that were the truth, how could she live with that?

Mark had so much wanted a second child, but even the skills of their IVF specialist, Lionel Lockhart, were useless to them now.

They'd discussed and rejected the idea of adopting, or finding a surrogate mother to incubate their leftover embryos, and in the afterglow of Chloe's birth, watching her grow, learning to walk, staggering like a miniature drunkard, babbling her baby language, gradually discovering her own little personality, Jenny had thought they'd both come to terms with the situation. Chloe was so beautiful. So perfect. How could they possibly want more?

But this weeping in secret, this private, covert burden he seemed to be carrying around. It was illogical, she knew, but she felt to blame. And somewhere, way down in her psyche, she wondered: if anyone were weeping, shouldn't it be her?

From various parts of the house, Jenny rounded up Chloe's pale pink sheepskin coat, her little tasselled hat, mittens and red shoes with the appliquéd butterflies.

'We're going to see the market, Chloe. That'll be fun won't it?' She remembered the old rhyme her own mother used to chant.

'To market, to market to buy a fat pig.
Home again, home again jiggety jig.'

Chloe chuckled with delight, inexpertly clapping her hands. 'Again! Mummy sing again.'

The traffic was light on the A20. Most people would be enjoying their Sunday morning sleep-ins.

Mark scanned through the presets on the radio. Capital Gold was his usual station of choice – they played some great oldies over the weekends, but something classical might be better this morning, to help him relax.

A half-familiar requiem drifted into the car. Bach was it? Verdi? Who cared. He breathed out slowly, making a conscious effort to lower his shoulders. Jenny had looked so crestfallen when he'd said he was going out. He hated lying to her.

For the first time it occurred to him that the burden of this deceit, this unspoken secret, had been driving an insidious wedge between them for nearly five months.

More than once she'd asked him, 'Is anything wrong?'

And he hoped she believed his assurances that everything was absolutely fine. It put a stop to further questioning but he knew in his heart that she wasn't convinced. They'd known each other too long and he'd always been hopeless at deception. His shoulders had been stooping, probably literally, under the strain of this enormous but invisible weight and Jenny could hardly have failed to notice.

He hadn't asked for this burden. Far from it. But he had been offered the fruit of the tree of knowledge and found it impossible to resist. It had been only the tiniest taste, but enough to blight every aspect of his life. And worse, he was hooked. He had an unavoidable need now to sample a little bit more of that deadly fruit. Just one more bite. Then he would push it away.

He hadn't told Jenny because he didn't want her poisoned too. What she didn't know couldn't hurt her. She was right, though. He couldn't remember how long it was since they spent an easy relaxed Sunday morning together.

He'd always been so scathing about people – usually men – who let the demands of work take precedence over quality time with their family. Now it must look to Jenny as if that was exactly what he had begun to do himself. He must try harder to hide his feelings. None of this was her fault. Her body had let her down, that was all.

It should have been the easiest, most natural thing in the world to get pregnant. Some people seemed to fall for a baby at the drop of a hat. Quite often the baby wasn't wanted. Sometimes they'd even have abortions. How unfair.

For him and Jenny the whole process had been agony, mental and physical. Not to mention expensive. Nearly five years – half a decade – on a white-knuckle rollercoaster ride of hopes raised and dashed and raised and then dashed yet again.

All those IVF attempts. Four of them. It seemed like more than that, looking back on all those early appointments at Lionel Lockhart's smart Greenwich clinic. Endless, repeated tests on just about every fluid in both their bodies.

The first stage had been to try to conceive nature's way, to a timetable. Keeping careful records.

After nearly a year of that with no luck, Lionel Lockhart's consultations had become more 'hands on', injecting Mark's sperm directly into Jenny's uterus. Intrauterine insemination. That hadn't worked either.

There was nothing else for it but to go for IVF.

It had begun with the prolonged and painful business of stimulating Jenny's ovaries with hormone injections to produce as many eggs as possible. They'd then be fertilised with Mark's sperm in the lab to turn them into viable embryos, ready to plant in Jenny's uterus to begin the job, they all fervently hoped, of growing into a baby.

Poor Jenny. She'd been so squeamish about giving herself those injections every morning. He'd always done it for her, pinching the soft flesh of her inner upper thigh, grasping the syringe like a dart, briskly stabbing the needle up to its hilt into the pinch and slowly depressing the plunger until all the medication had gone in. Alternate thighs, one day the left one, next day the right.

He remembered the bruising. He'd felt like a torturer. And all the medication she'd had to swallow. Her stomach had bloated. She felt sick every morning. It seemed the treatment itself was mocking her inability to conceive by giving her the symptoms of pregnancy without the baby to go with it.

He'd bought her a little seven-day pill organiser and loaded it for her every Sunday night so they could both keep track of what she'd taken.

He'd drawn up an elaborate multicoloured chart to record every visit to the clinic – every lab test date and ultrasound appointment, the daily hormone levels, the dosage of every drug, the precise time of every morning's injection, when she'd felt sick

15

and when she'd actually thrown up – and Blu-Tacked it inside the door of the bathroom cabinet. He made sure he updated it every evening before they went to bed with a selection of felt pens he kept in a pot beside the washbasin.

He'd shopped every day on the way home from work for something fresh and preferably organic for supper, usually chicken or fish or lean mince, and vegetables that contained phytoestrogens to promote healthy hormone balance – soy beans, chick peas, celery, fennel.

He'd never before taken much interest in cooking. Now he bought cookery books with titles like *Eating for Life – Foods to boost your Fertility* and *The Infertility Diet*.

He had put himself on constant alert for new ways to make dishes with lentils and brown rice interesting. Well, as interesting as possible. He banned coffee and alcohol from the house, absolutely. (Which didn't stop him keeping his own supply at the shop of course.)

He'd felt a pang of guilt sometimes when he called in for a pint or two at the pub across the road from the shop when things were quiet, or took a client out for an expensive lunch and a bottle of good claret; he should be suffering along with her for moral support – not that it was *his* body that wasn't playing ball, as it were.

All the same, if he could have changed places with Jenny he honestly would have. He would far rather have shouldered all the indignities, discomfort and misery himself than watch her suffering.

Next – and at long last – it was Egg Retrieval day. ER as they called it at the clinic. Everything to do with infertility treatment was cheerfully referred to in terms of initials, by staff and patients alike.

AF was Aunt Flo, which meant the monthly period. BMS was

Baby-Making Sex. He'd even been reduced to an acronym himself. Partners seemed to be referred to as Dear Husband whether couples were married or not.

'Your appointment is ten thirty next Wednesday,' Jenny would be informed, 'and you'll need to bring your DH in with you.'

On ER day, Lionel had harvested a bumper crop: a triumphant fifteen eggs from Jenny's drug-stimulated ovaries which were whisked off to the laboratory to be introduced to Mark's sperm in little glass Petri dishes.

Mark felt somehow he and Jenny should have been present for this intimate ritual, but it was all down to the people in white coats now.

The two of them went home to crack open a bottle of pink champagne and wait for a call from Angie, the practice nurse, to tell them how their fuckless conception had gone.

And the result was eleven. Eleven of the fifteen fertilised successfully. He and Jenny were the proud parents of eleven embryos. Eleven microscopic potential Elficks.

Jenny had always attached huge significance to the number eleven. She said it represented a mystical gateway or something. She was forever glancing at the digital clock in the bedroom, or on the computer taskbar, or the DVD machine just at the moment when it read 11:11. It happened far too often, she said, for it to be mere coincidence. The strange thing was, once she'd pointed it out, he had begun to notice it himself. Perhaps it would have been the same with any given set of numbers.

All the same, to have produced eleven healthy embryos had seemed like a wonderful omen.

Two embryos were selected from the eleven. The remainder would go into the clinic's freezer – cryogenically preserved for the next time. (They'd tried not to contemplate the possibility of a next time.)

Before the Embryo Transfer procedure began, Mark and Jenny had been allowed to see their two little clusters of cells via a camera and microscope in the laboratory. His heart constricted again at the memory. Two tiny living Elfick seeds, smaller than pinheads to the naked eye, there on the little monitor screen. His children!

What a rare, extraordinary privilege to be able to see them at this, the very beginning of their road to life. It was a chance 'normal' parents never had.

He hadn't realised tears were trickling down his cheeks until a drop of water splashed, star-shaped, on to the embryologist's workbench.

Jenny, too, had been shedding quiet tears.

Half an hour later, in the little candlelit operating theatre, gentle New Age music tootled and burbled around them as Jenny lay on the couch, Lionel Lockhart carefully placing the embryos inside her womb, while Mark held her hand.

Fourteen days later, Mark had been queuing fretfully at the chemist's counter for a pregnancy testing kit.

In fact he'd bought two. Belt and braces. The first one, and then the second one registered nothing. BFN. Big Fat Negative.

Mark went back to the chemist and bought two more. These, too, remained resolutely negative.

Life's road he'd been so sure had begun, had turned out to be a cul-de-sac.

There had been so many tears. So many times they'd sat the other side of Lionel Lockhart's leather-topped desk at his consulting rooms in Greenwich, planning the next assault (which is what it had begun to feel like) surrounded on all sides by framed pictures of lusty, bouncing toddlers and their radiant parents; Lionel's personal success story, which even Lionel himself was beginning to believe the Elficks would never be part of.

*

A week or so after that first failure, they made a determined effort to pick their spirits up with the consolation that at least they had nine more precious embryos still waiting in their liquid nitrogen cylinders for their chance at life.

Three months later, Jenny was on the operating table once again, Mark stroking her hair and forehead, listening to the boops and beeps of the clinic's daft *Dreams of Dawn* CD, Lockhart frowning intently down at the business end.

Two 'Dotties in a Dish', as they'd taken to calling them, had been successfully thawed and were being placed in the dark, pink warmth of Jenny's womb.

Once again, the agonising wait before the pregnancy test.

Once again the result: BFN. Or BFBN as Mark described it.

Big Fat Bloody Nothing.

'Get straight back on that cycle,' said Lionel, enjoying his own pun. 'You've got seven left. Seven is just as magical as eleven.'

So another three months later, there they were again. This time, Mark had spent days compiling a cassette tape of his own: an eclectic mixture of Ennio Morricone, Neil Diamond, Nina Simone, Simon and Garfunkel (Jenny had always said he looked a bit like Art Garfunkel with his beginning-to-recede curly brown hair and stockyish frame), Erik Satie and a couple of Afro-American lullabies. He could hardly bear to listen to any of them now. They brought back too many memories of despair and uncertainty in magnolia-painted clinic anterooms.

Another BFN.

More grieving for two more embryonic children whose lives had started but then fallen at the first fence. And then there were five.

A month or so later, the fourth attempt, and more fervent prayers muttered mantra-like to a God neither of them believed in.

Mark even took to dropping in at a little chapel in Blackheath on his way into work to send out 'vibes' to the tiny growing thing inside his wife.

Maybe that was what finally did it.

Fourteen days later, the pregnancy test had showed positive. They went through several testing kits again, hardly daring to believe it possible that Jenny was actually pregnant at last.

But it was true. One of the embryos had 'taken'. To their almost incredulous joy, Mark and Jenny were having a baby at last! Chloe Leonora Elfick was on her way.

For nine months, Mark wrapped Jenny in proverbial cotton wool, hardly letting her leave the house. He'd hired an au pair to take over the housework and had taken huge amounts of time off work, to take as much care of his wife and precious unborn child as possible.

He thought now of Chloe's infectious baby giggle, the way she shook her fine, copper-coloured curls vehemently when she didn't want to do something, how she clung to his neck like a koala cub when she was tired, thumb plugged firmly into her mouth, and that little 'golly golly golly' sound she made around it.

He caught himself smiling foolishly. It had been such a long and painful journey – especially for Jenny – but so worth it. So bloody worth it.

Registering the sign to Hastings almost too late, he wrenched the Peugeot across the hard shoulder and on to the A21 slip road, just missing the grass verge.

He was unlikely to need it, but he leaned across to the shelf under the glove compartment and took out the AA road atlas. Just in case.

It fell open at the right page automatically now, so often had he stared at this map, willing the street to somehow take shape on the page, trying to imagine what the house was like.

This next turning ought to be it. Yes. Simmons Road. He indicated right and steered into a suburban residential street full of small, red-brick, post-war, semi-detached houses.

He pulled up at the kerb. He needed to steady his nerves before he pulled up outside number 115. What if he was wrong? He half hoped he *was* wrong. Then at least that would be the end of it. He wouldn't be able to take things any further.

For a moment he thought he was going to be sick. He opened the car door and leaned out over the gutter. The moment passed.

He'd thought through what he would do. He would drive past the house, do a U-turn fifty yards or so further on, then park up on the opposite side of the road a couple of doors away. Then he'd have a good view of the house and any comings and goings.

He let out the handbrake and cruised along the street in second gear.

The front doors in Simmons Road were black, maroon or bottle green, except for number 115's, which was a vivid, pillar-box red. It also had by far the tidiest front garden.

Even this early in the season, the tiny lawn was green and close-cropped. Purple crocuses and snowdrops pushed up amongst the grass. In the narrow, weedless border beside the concrete path, clusters of daffodil leaves speared upwards promisingly amongst clumps of ornamental grasses and manicured, calf-high shrubs.

Above a low brick wall, a geometrically square privet hedge looked as though it had been trimmed with a pair of nail scissors. The garden gate, neatly latched, was the same colour as the front door.

The house itself, pebble-dashed, seemed as well maintained as its little garden, the ground-floor bay window edged on either side by green velvet curtains. Panels of cream lace (Jenny was always so scathing about net curtains) precluded him from seeing inside.

Mark had read an article only yesterday about house prices in the South-East having risen nearly twenty per cent in the three years between 1995 and now. Little semis like these would be going for about a hundred grand now.

So the family wasn't hugely well off but they'd be comfortable enough. That was good. One thing was for sure, though, it was dull as ditchwater round here. He looked in his rear-view mirror. The street was as quiet behind as it was in front of him. Was *everyone* still in bed?

A grey-permed woman in a tan-coloured coat and shabby sheepskin ankle boots padded past the Range Rover, making him jump. The overweight spaniel plodding along beside her matched the colour of her coat exactly. It threw him an indifferent glance over its shoulder.

A few minutes later, two teenage boys meandered past on bikes that looked several sizes too small for them, hands hanging behind their backs. A ginger cat mooched along the pavement hugging the garden walls, before launching itself across the road, spooked by something Mark couldn't see, disappearing under the gate at number 111.

Then everything was quiet again.

He opened the *Independent* at the sports pages, keeping watch on the scarlet front door from the corner of his eye. He'd give it an hour or so. See if anyone made an appearance.

*

It was nearly four o'clock in the afternoon by the time an irritable Mark got back to Blackheath.

Jenny was peeling potatoes in the kitchen. She had resolved to hide her hurt feelings. She needed him to open up, not bring down the barriers.

'Since Sunday lunch seems off the agenda these days,' she began airily, 'we're having Sunday supper instead. Roast chicken.'

It was no use, she had sounded peeved.

'There's a bottle of wine in the fridge. Perhaps you'd like to open it.'

That sounded peeved too, dammit. Oh, what the heck. She dropped the potato she'd finished peeling into the sink and turned to face him.

'Mark, why can't you at least keep your mobile switched on if you're going to go AWOL on a Sunday?'

He was rummaging through the kitchen drawer for the corkscrew.

'Look. OK. If it pisses you off so much that I am working my socks off, trying to build the business for the benefit of all three of us, well . . . fine. I'll stick to nine to five like a good little suburban husband.'

'That's not fair. I'm not asking for that, and you know I'm not. But I *would* like more than five minutes' notice on a weekend in future. And I don't think it's asking too much to keep your phone on. If you're worried about upsetting your client, keep it in your pocket on vibrate. What if I needed you for something? If I had a problem with Chloe . . .'

'OK, OK. You're right. I'm just in a foul mood and I shouldn't take it out on you.'

'It didn't go well, the meeting, then.'

'It was useful up to a point. I think it'll come to something in

23

the future. But nothing definite today.' Well that was true. 'These things take time. Softly, softly catchee monkey and all that.'

A wet potato in one hand and peeler in the other, Jenny put her arms round his neck.

'Let's not get snippy with each other. We've both got a bit preoccupied and we used to be such good mates; such a good team. Weren't we? I feel I'm losing you sometimes.'

She tried to fix a casual smile on her face, preparing for an irritable denial of such nonsense. But instead of pulling away as she'd expected, he was looking her full in the eyes for the first time in weeks.

He wound a stray strand of her hair behind her ear. An old habit.

'I'm sorry, Jenny. I really am. Sometimes we forget to nurture each other properly in all the daily routine and things. And it's my fault more than yours, I do realise that. I love you to pieces.'

He kissed her gently on the mouth. She kissed him back. Restorative, reaffirming. Everything was going to be fine. Thank God.

She turned quickly back to the sink to finish the potatoes. She didn't want him to see her eyes filling with warm tears of relief.

Chapter Two

It was disappointing. She'd really thought there'd been a bit of a breakthrough in the kitchen the other evening. But he'd been, if anything, even more distracted and irritable. He hardly seemed to hear anything she said to him.

As ever, it was only in the dead of night that their bodies would connect in an intimacy that simply didn't exist in the light of day.

It wasn't that he was ignoring her on purpose, she was almost sure of that. He didn't seem angry with her, and yet somehow she'd lost him. And because he wouldn't acknowledge there was a problem, there seemed nothing she could do to get him back. She felt utterly bereaved.

What made it harder to bear was that the more this distance grew between the two of them, the more infatuated he seemed to become with their daughter.

Jenny had seen him gazing wistfully at Chloe as she scrambled around the floor with her toys. He'd bend down beside her and touch her hair, constantly wanting contact, to stroke and cuddle her.

But Chloe was a live wire, a bundle of energy most of the time, and she'd rarely put up with the burden of these attentions for more than a minute or so before squirming free, leaving him looking hurt and rejected.

The other night, he'd managed to get home by six, like the old days. He'd volunteered for 'bath and bed duty', and on her way back from a visit to the loo Jenny had paused outside Chloe's bedroom door, really just to take pleasure in hearing father and daughter enjoying the bedtime story together.

What she'd heard jolted Jenny's world on its axis – a deep, anguished sigh, then a whispered, 'Night night, sweet dreams, my precious angel . . . You're Daddy's reason for living, you know.'

Once upon a time, Jenny had been his reason for living. He'd said it to her often. She felt an almost physical stab of pain. Like that terrible needle.

Grasping the banister rail, she was assaulted by the memory of the daily ordeal the two of them had shared just three years ago.

She'd avert her eyes from the syringe, fastening her gaze above the mantelpiece, trying to will herself into the huge oil painting they'd bought on a holiday in Crete together in 1993; a rustic old whitewashed village house, its rounded edges outlined against a luminous, sapphire-blue sky . . . warm Greek sunshine . . . the rhythmic sound of the blue, eternal ocean.

He'd hated having to do it, Jenny knew that, but it was the only way they'd stood any chance of having their longed-for child. From the corner of her eye she'd see Mark's arm lifting, aiming determinedly at her soft, white, exposed, inner thigh; his usual gentle demeanour disfigured by grim deter-mination.

As she stood now at the top of the stairs, her memory recalled the image and distorted it, turning his set expression in her mind to one of cold, emotionless cruelty and placing in his hand not a syringe, but a long stiletto which he was smashing down towards her chest.

She ran from the vision, down the stairs to the kitchen where she set about re-polishing the cooker and the already-cleaned surfaces, trying to regain a sense of normality before he came down to join her.

If only, if only they could have been granted a second child. Just one more before her womb had rebelled for good.

This concentration on Chloe wasn't healthy. A second child would have meant him having to share his attentions. A younger sister or brother would have brought about an entirely different family dynamic.

They'd had three 'Dotties in Dishes' left over of course, so surrogacy had been an option. They'd had several counselling sessions and talked it all through, but in the end Jenny simply couldn't countenance the idea of another woman pregnant with her and Mark's child, radiant and smiling through the experience she couldn't physically manage to achieve herself.

Was it jealousy? She had tried to tell herself to be bigger than that. Jealousy is such a petty emotion. Certainly she felt inadequate.

The sound of the kitchen door opening made her jump violently.

Chloe had finally dropped off to sleep, thumb in mouth as usual, and Mark had crept down the stairs to find Jenny standing stock still at the sink, staring out of the window.

She really ought to say something to him. What though? Where to start? How about: 'Mark, do you think Chloe is your *only* reason for living, because I heard what you said and that's what it sounded like?'

Or perhaps 'Mark, do you think we should have found a surrogate mother after all?'

A profound physical exhaustion swept over her. She had to hold on to the kitchen table to stop her legs buckling under her.

She lurched towards the door, just finding enough strength to say, 'Going up for a bath. Knackered.'

He'd made progress this week. On the Tuesday after work, he'd watched the little house all evening from around half past six until ten.

Lights had gone off and on in various rooms but still Mark hadn't seen any of its occupants.

He resolved to get there earlier next time.

On Thursday he had been there by four o'clock.

There was still some light in the sky, and this time he'd seen the husband.

Shortly before six o'clock, a green and black Transit van had turned into Simmons Road and drawn up outside the house.

On the side of the van was painted a giant tap, a droplet of water hanging from its lip.

Underneath were painted the words 'DeeKay – at your service' with smaller lettering below that; DON'T SLEEP WITH A DRIP, CALL THE PLUMBER! and a phone number.

The artwork didn't look too professional.

The driver's door rasped open and out had bounded a cappuccino-coloured puppy – all legs and paws and floppy ears – the sort that grows from cute pup to fair-sized dog inside eight weeks.

It was followed by a tall, ponytailed man in jeans and a black T-shirt.

Mark couldn't easily guess his age with forty or so yards between them and the light fading fast, but he'd looked about ten years younger than himself, mid to late thirties.

Man and dog had loped round the side of the house and disappeared.

'Daddy's reason for living.' Jenny couldn't get that line out of her head. Obviously he didn't love her like he used to. She felt neglected. Superfluous. Sidelined.

She told herself to hang in there; to have faith that he'd get whatever was bugging him out of his system.

But every time he told her about another newly discovered silverware collector he just had to go and see, a tiny bit more of her love and trust in him seemed to shrivel and die.

And each time there were the apologetic promises that this was an untypical phase the business was going through; that soon he'd have had all the introductory meetings he needed with this new batch of clients he'd been chasing.

Maybe they weren't excuses. Maybe it was all true.

So off he'd driven on Saturday morning, leaving her alone for most of the day with the bibs and the baby food and the toys and the Teletubbies.

She remembered now, Yvonne Allitsen, the 'unashamedly directional' counsellor they'd had some sessions with after Chloe's birth, had warned them that the bumpy ride Mark and Jenny had been through as a couple wouldn't just suddenly stop.

'It's like throwing a rock in a pond,' she'd said (Yvonne loved her analogies). 'It takes a while before the ripples disappear. They get smaller and smaller and less and less significant, but do be aware there could well be one or two more little ups and downs ahead of you. For five years, you were living night and day with a yearning for what you couldn't have. An enormous proportion of your time together was bound up with the attainment of this goal – the measurements, the injections, the medication, dates ringed on calendars . . . And you succeeded. But there'll be a vacuum where all that was. You'll almost miss all that focus and ritual.'

Jenny had pointed out that they had their wonderful, miraculous little baby who was doing a great job of filling that vacuum. But Yvonne had smiled knowingly.

'You've been the centre of each other's universes for so long. Now another little being will be taking up all your energies – emotional and physical. You wanted her so much, you didn't even think about any downsides of parenthood. You'll be jostling for position in each other's lives and priorities for a while. It's a very different dynamic. Give yourselves time and space. Cut each other some slack.'

Jenny hadn't attached too much significance to her words at the time. They'd only gone for half a dozen meetings with her. She had seemed a nice, wise woman but once she'd helped them decide how they were going to use their leftover embryos, there hadn't seemed to be a lot of point in seeing any more of her.

Now Jenny came to think of it, Mark had seemed more inclined to continue the sessions than she had.

Why, she wondered?

Perhaps Yvonne would have some insights on what might be going on in his head. Jenny ran to her writing desk and rifled frantically through the top drawer. Had she kept the counsellor's business card? Good. She had.

She rang the number and made an appointment. There'd been a cancellation the following Tuesday morning.

Tiny specks of dust hung glittering in a shaft of early spring sunshine that had found its way into Yvonne Allitsen's consulting room between the branches of a magnolia tree in her back garden.

When Jenny and Mark had seen Yvonne before, it had been in

one of a suite of rooms adjoining Lionel's clinic.

This seemed to be the Allitsen family's sitting room: cosy and cluttered, the walls covered with bookshelves or framed watercolour landscapes, two big squashy sofas set at right angles to each other against the walls, heavy gold-coloured drapes at the French windows.

Outside, Jenny could see a paved terrace covered in terracotta pots containing various plants and shrubs and an almost meadow-sized lawn beyond.

Only this morning, looking down from the bathroom window as she cleaned her teeth, she had noticed her own garden was beginning to look rather neglected.

The euphorbia had become more of a tree than a shrub. The camellia was getting that way too. The forsythia was wafting loose, straggling branches all over the place and, for the first time ever, the normally vibrant-berried skimmia had failed to produce its fruit. Even its leaves looked reluctant to make an appearance, which didn't bode well for its future. She used to trim them all back severely every autumn. They'd seemed to thrive on it.

But it was a couple of years since she'd last pruned them.

It occurred to her she had developed a fear of killing them. Why? She had never let that bother her before.

The irony dawned on her; when she'd been harsh and drastic with them they'd thrived, and now that she was trying to be kind to them, they had become drab and sorry for themselves.

They were ceasing to flourish. Like her marriage to Mark.

The more careful she was trying to be, the more out of control they were becoming.

It wasn't neglect though. Not deliberate neglect. It was . . . misplaced respect.

It was just that the result looked like neglect.

*

Yvonne Allitsen was small and blonde and bird-like. Jenny towered a good six inches above her as she was ushered into the hallway of the counsellor's Edwardian terraced house in Richmond.

Yvonne's face was tiny too, heart-shaped, but with generous features which, strangely, didn't seem out of proportion. A largeish nose, a wide, generous mouth and reassuringly alert, intelligent brown eyes, the lashes almost too long and dark to be natural.

The straight, chin-length blond hair was shiny and well groomed.

Framed school photos seemed to indicate that she was a mother of two children, a girl of around thirteen and a younger boy.

Two straight-backed dining-room chairs had been set facing each other about six feet apart. The comfy sofas were off limits then.

Clipboard on lap, Yvonne had seated herself on the one with its back against the bookcase. Jenny sat stiffly on the other, in the middle of the room, feeling bulky and exposed. Her only protection, to her right, was a low occasional table, on which was a box of man-sized tissues, carefully positioned, one tissue poking out in her direction; an indication of how the conversation over the next forty minutes was expected to go.

A small digital timer was Blu-Tacked to the top of the counsellor's clipboard so that she could glance at it during the session from time to time without the client noticing.

But Jenny *did* notice it. It made her feel pathetic that she had to come here for timed, paid-for conversations with a stranger.

Shouldn't she have friends she could talk to about her worries? Annabel. Her mother maybe?

But they'd only want to leap to her defence and jump to

conclusions – almost certainly the wrong ones. The objective view of a stranger was what she needed.

Characteristically, the counsellor dispensed with the niceties.

'So, Jenny. Why do you think your marriage is in trouble?'

'Mark and I are losing contact with each other. I just know something is wrong. Last week I heard him telling Chloe she was his reason for living.'

'Isn't that just something a doting dad might say on the spur of the moment?'

'I don't know. He just sounded so . . . intense. And for months now, Chloe's been waking up terrified and sobbing at three or four in the morning, saying monsters are chasing her.'

'So you think she's sensing an uneasy atmosphere between the two of you?'

'Yes I do. I'm so worried about Mark. I think he's heading for some kind of meltdown.'

'Why though? What makes you think that?'

'He's not his normal self any more. I really think he's ill. He's hardly sleeping. He's got bags under his eyes. His hair has got long and fluffy and all over the place. He's like a different person.'

Yvonne regarded the woman in front of her quietly for a moment or two. Attractive and well dressed, in tailored black trousers, jade-green cashmere button-through jumper and amber pendant. Not plump, but the sort of figure lingerie departments called 'curvy'.

She suspected the shoulder-length auburn hair had been treated to a few copper highlights. A woman used to looking after herself. But her face was pale beneath the carefully applied make-up and there was a strained expression behind the hazel eyes. She looked in need of a decent night's sleep herself.

'Have you talked to him about things?'

'I have tried. Several times. But he just fobs me off. He won't admit there's anything wrong. We used to be each other's best friends, and now . . . I don't know if it's something I've done or if it's something else.' She paused. 'Or someone else.'

'So if he's not confiding in you any more, who else might he feel able to open up to?'

'Well, no one that I can think of. He's one of those men who doesn't have any really close friends. A lot of acquaintances . . . business associates, but not best friends in the way women tend to have best friends.'

'What about his parents?'

'His father died of a heart attack when he was fifty. His mother is very old now. She retired to Spain a few years ago now, to be near Mark's aunt, her sister. He talks to her every couple of weeks on the phone, but it's difficult. She's quite hard of hearing, which doesn't help.'

'He always had a good relationship with them both though?'

'Yes. In fact, he tended to idealise them a bit, I always thought. And he was devastated when his dad died. But he was never actually that close to them. They travelled abroad a lot when he was a child. His father was a civil servant with the Foreign Office. Mark was sent away to school at the age of eight. Sometimes he had to stay up at school over the holidays as well. Or go and stay with a classmate's family. I feel quite sad on his behalf whenever I think about it. Poor little kid.'

'So,' Yvonne recapped, 'he's withdrawn and preoccupied, sleeping badly, doesn't confide in anyone, not that we know of anyway. What about your sex life?'

'Well, the strange thing is, he's got very . . . keen. I think it might be his way of dealing with the insomnia. But it doesn't really feel like making love any more, not like it used to.'

Yvonne cast her mind back two years to when the couple had

just had their baby and they'd come to her seeking advice on what to do with their remaining embryos.

She could still picture Mark quite clearly: the brown curly hair and the little-boy-lost look about him. He'd struck her as highly intelligent, gentle, but emotionally insecure. She'd found him quite sexy actually; something about the way he had of looking intently into your eyes when you talked to him, as if he were searching for the answer to something there.

She'd decided he was a bit of a hypochondriac as well. When she'd asked him why he kept burying his right hand in his left armpit beneath his jacket, he'd said it had become a habit after the death of his father. Both his father and grandfather had had heart attacks in their early fifties and he had convinced himself that he, too, would go the same way.

'I'm just making sure it's still beating,' she remembered him saying.

Well, he'd be just about forty now but it sounded like he was on course to fulfil his own prophecy. She took a deep breath.

'I think your husband might be suffering from post-natal depression, Jenny. You know, it happens to nearly twenty per cent of men. People don't realise that. They think it's a woman thing.'

'I don't really see why. It's not *their* bodies that have been racked with hormonal upheavals.'

'It's to do with feeling out of control I think. It's the mother who's at the centre of things, carrying the baby for nine months, giving birth, doing the feeding, the nurturing, the bonding . . . The man has to stand back while the woman takes the driving seat. Some men are fine with that and some hate it. They feel inadequate.'

'But how can Mark, of all people, have post-natal depression when we – he even more than me – wanted a child so much?'

'I think the infertility treatment the two of you went through for all that time might have made it more difficult for him . . .'

'But I was the one—'

'Absolutely. It was toughest on you, I know, physically and emotionally. But perhaps he felt helpless, you know; powerless to relieve you of all the discomfort and burden and everything that went with five years of IVF.'

'I don't agree he felt helpless. He took control of my life those three years. I think he thought it was all down to him that she was born at all.'

'Do you think you're being entirely fair to him? Certainly I think it's true that he would have gone through the pregnancy for you if he'd had the chance. That's the problem. That's why he's suffering. Try to see it from his point of view.'

'But that's what I'm bending over backwards trying to do.' Jenny knew her irritation was showing, but she couldn't help it. 'That's why I'm here. To try and work out what is wrong and how to make it right again. And I think what *I've* been through deserves a little consideration too. Never mind him.'

'I know.' Yvonne smiled gently, and waited.

Probably as intended, Jenny felt shamed.

'I'm sorry. I realise now how angry he's been making me feel. This withdrawn behaviour; cutting me out of his life. It isn't fair. I think I've been through enough. All that IVF and then the hysterectomy . . .'

Furious with herself, she snatched at the tissue sticking out of its box. The hot tears she'd been struggling to contain had finally spilled over her lower eyelids and down her cheeks, turning cold as they reached her jaw line. She blotted them out of existence.

'We never used to be angry with each other. We used to sit across the table from each other in restaurants and congratulate ourselves on what perfect soul mates we were. How lucky, to have friendship and admiration, love and lust; to be so much on the same wavelength. And now we seem to be on different planets.'

'You've both had a lot to readjust to. First of all, life without the tyranny of all that infertility treatment and without your dependence on him. I remember warning you about that when I first saw the two of you. Then when the baby arrived, this new little person took over both your lives completely. It's a shock to discover how deeply and strongly you can fall in love with your new baby – particularly sometimes with fathers and daughters. He has to reassess how everything fits into place in this life of his. You, Chloe, his work . . . He'll be processing all these new experiences and feelings.'

'Doesn't every new parent have to adjust to all that?'

'Some find it easier than others. And from my memory of your husband, he seems to be a particularly sensitive man.'

'He's always been a worrier, that's true. Very sensitive – too sensitive to what people think of him. He does like to be liked. To be thought well of. Don't we all, I suppose.'

'So he needs to get back to his work. Where he's in charge. Where he can achieve something. Could that be why he's taken to staying late so much?'

'I hadn't thought of that. Yes, you could be right.'

'And he's always been a loving husband, hasn't he?'

'Yes. I think so.' Jenny opened the tissue out in her fingers, turning it over, looking for a dry patch. She was determined not to have to take a second one. 'You don't think he's having an affair then?'

Yvonne swivelled to put her clipboard on one of the shelves behind her.

'You're the one living with him so it's your instincts that

count. But from where I sit, I would say it is highly unlikely that he's having an affair.'

Jenny let out a slow, juddering sigh.

'Hang in there. You'll have the old Mark back again. I'm sure of it. But see if you can get him to talk to someone. It really sounds as though he needs to. He's welcome to contact me. I'd be more than happy to see him. Or the people at the clinic would be able to recommend someone else.'

'I'm not sure that I'll tell him I've seen you today. I don't want him to think I've been worrying and complaining about him.'

Yvonne inclined her head. 'That's up to you, of course. But keeping things from each other builds up barriers. And how can he object? You want to fix things. To understand him better.'

'I'll think about it.' Jenny stuffed the soggy tissue into her handbag and stood up, 'Thank you for seeing me.'

'Good luck. You know where I am. Oh – and get some Omega 3 tablets. They boost serotonin. Good for helping depression. And Vitamin B complex is good for mental health too!'

'I'll get him some on the way home.' Jenny smiled ruefully from the doorway. 'I'll try anything.'

'Not just for Mark. You need them too.'

Chapter Three

Mark could hardly contain his excitement. If only there were someone he could talk to.

Jenny was normally the person he could turn to when he needed a friend. But how would she react to what he'd been doing these last few months? She'd be shaken to the core, he was sure. It hardly bore thinking about.

It wouldn't be long now, though. Then he could put all this behind him. He was so close. First he'd seen the husband. And now he'd seen all three of them.

Under cover of the *Independent*, he'd watched mother, child and dog emerge from down the side of number 115 Simmons Road and make their way along the pavement towards the main road, the exuberant puppy bouncing and straining against the lead which was wrapped around the buggy's handle and the woman's wrist.

For a moment or two he was paralysed. Could hardly even breathe.

Elinor Keegan's hair was long and fine, reaching halfway down her back, loosely tied at the nape of her neck with one of those scrunchie things.

Like Jenny, she was a redhead, but a paler, ginger colour.

Jenny's was a darker, more chestnut red, and much thicker and curlier. Elinor was smaller than Jenny, and very slender. Too thin really. He liked women to be more rounded.

She was wearing an olive-green trench coat, belted in tight, collar turned up against the cold over a green woollen scarf.

Perhaps, like Jenny, she had a penchant for the colour green. It set off the hair colour so well.

She disappeared round the corner and he managed to pull himself together. Controlling his trembling fingers enough to turn the ignition key, he drove slowly to the end of the street.

She'd progressed a few hundred yards along the main road, and he was just in time to see her steering dog and buggy through a wide gateway to an area of parkland, identified by a large wooden sign that said 'Priory Gardens'.

Heart thumping inside his ribcage, he coasted quietly behind her through the gates and into the car park. Thank God, there was one space remaining.

As he rooted clumsily in his jeans pockets for coins to put in the Pay and Display machine, he lost sight of her behind the high brick walls that surrounded the gardens on all sides.

Forcing his legs into action, he approached the park.

It was a pretty little public garden; formal flower beds just inside the entrance were filled with primulas and early spring bulbs, themed purple, yellow and white. Beyond them a group of trees – hawthorn, oaks, birches, and a newly budding willow tree – gave shelter to half a dozen wooden benches overlooking a duck pond.

Elinor Keegan was making unhurried progress towards it. He followed at an angle roughly thirty degrees to the line she was taking, and stopped at a bench about a hundred yards from the one she was preparing to settle herself on.

She released the catch on the dog's extendable lead and tied it to the arm of the seat. The puppy shot off, bounding excitedly around the bushes, rooting out exciting new smells.

Now she was fumbling with the straps of the buggy. She seemed to be making quite a meal of the job. Her hands would be cold. It seemed an unusually chilly day for March. He wished he'd brought something warmer to wear himself. He couldn't stop shivering.

At last Elinor lifted the baby clear of its complicated harness and held it aloft with both hands; a miniature Michelin figure, swathed from head to foot in an orange jumpsuit, its mitten-ended arms sticking out almost perpendicular to its body.

Hardly able to breathe, he watched her waggling the infant from side to side above her head, babbling daft baby language. The child chortled and giggled in response.

Chloe had loved that kind of thing too when she was that age. The more vigorously he'd swung her about the more she'd loved it. Was it really nearly two years ago?

Elinor sat the baby on her lap like a doll, while she bent forward to rummage in the tray beneath the buggy and fished out a supermarket carrier bag. Four ducks waddled hopefully towards her. Elinor opened the bag and scattered small square-cut chunks of bread on to the ground at their feet.

The ducks tossed and pecked. More arrived, informed by some kind of avian telepathic grapevine, soon followed by half a dozen pigeons and a couple of seagulls.

The child waved its stiff little arms in delight and Elinor's face was wreathed in smiles.

Mark couldn't look any more. Somehow he managed to get to his feet and stumble blindly back to the car. He should have found a way of speaking to her. But he was trembling all over and his throat was constricted. His voice wouldn't have worked.

He had to go home and think. Plan what to do next.

Chapter Four

Mark's night-time wakefulness was more disruptive than ever. He'd drift off for an hour and then there'd be the customary crazy, falling-through-space nightmare and he'd wake wide-eyed, feeling motion-sick.

It didn't help that Chloe was still waking up in the small hours almost every night. He and Jenny had got to the point where, by some innate parental instinct, they would wake up just before the first whimper. That was if he'd managed to get to sleep in the first place.

They usually took it in turns now to go to her room and lean into the cot to soothe her back to sleep – a task that could take as long as half an hour.

Sometimes it necessitated picking her up, holding her quiet and close, and walking up and down the room in the dark while she sucked her thumb and gradually settled down. It would be his turn tonight.

The digital clock showed eleven minutes past three. In the distance he could hear the familiar, distant throb of his next-door neighbour's Kawasaki motorbike coming down the street. Jamie Broughton arriving home after his regular late shift on the *Guardian*.

How the man kept on working such unsocial hours was beyond Mark. It hadn't done his marriage much good. Still, he evidently thrived on it.

The other day, over the garden fence, he'd told Mark he'd applied for promotion to senior sub-editor and had high hopes of getting it. It would still be the late hours though. Still the relentless nightly neurosis of bringing out a national daily paper.

Oh well. Each to his own.

Across the landing, the familiar whimper sounded from his daughter's bedroom. He was almost relieved. Something to do, at least.

Quickly, he slid out of bed and padded barefoot across the landing. The sooner he could get to Chloe's side, the less thoroughly she would wake herself up.

Softly humming the tune of 'Rock-a-bye-baby', he stroked the little flannelette-flowered back and shoulders with gentle circular motions until, slowly, she relaxed, her eyelids stopped fluttering and she drifted off again.

Back in bed, he turned over and closed his eyes, trying to remember the breathing method in the book on insomnia that Jenny had bought him. But the little tableau on the park bench was back centre-stage in his thoughts again.

She hadn't looked at all like her voice on the phone. The voice was firm and warm . . . while her body was pale and slender, fragile.

He needed to hear her voice again, to connect it with the person he'd seen in the park.

He'd called again, a few hours after he got back home that Saturday, but this time a man's voice had answered. The husband had come back from work. Damn.

Tomorrow was a Monday, so he'd call again then.

He put out a hand and gently followed the smooth curve of Jenny's back until his fingers found what they were looking for and burrowed in.

She turned sleepily towards him. She knew what he wanted.

This must be what it was like to be a drug addict. To feel that needle pushing into your body, deep, and sharp and hard . . . until at last, here it came, merciful relief . . . surging, rushing through every fibre of your being and the unbearable pain of reality turned to sublime, extraplanetary bliss.

For now. Until the pain came back.

When he made the call next morning, that soft, warm voice answered. It wasn't so much the voice of a stranger now, somehow. He put the phone down quickly.

He had to get closer to her. Talk to her. See the baby. Find out more about her life.

Then he would let go.

At least then he would have some pictures in his head to treasure.

Then he would get on with his life. Find his way back to Jenny and Chloe.

His main hope was that the walk to the park was a regular Saturday morning thing. Next time he'd be prepared. There wouldn't be the rush of emotion blocking his powers of speech. But how to start up a conversation . . .

He had a brainwave. He'd borrow Jamie Broughton's dog. He or Jenny quite often took it for walks when Jamie had to work at weekends.

Jamie's marriage had broken up two years ago when Pamela left him for an older but richer man and Jamie had replaced her a few weeks later with a cute little Westie puppy.

45

He called it Babe, short for Babe Magnet, which was Jamie's main purpose in buying her. And certainly, whenever Mark took Babe to the common, women would stop him all the time, aah-ing and coo-ing, and Babe would wag her white carrot-shaped tail, fix their faces with her black button eyes and turn over on to her back for them to tickle her soft pink tummy.

The trouble was, Babe was just *too* cute. Jamie had goofed on that front. Women were far too taken with the puppy to take any interest in who was at the other end of the lead.

Elinor couldn't fail to notice her. And even if she wasn't beguiled, Mark was sure her mad puppy would come bounding up to make Babe's acquaintance.

Jamie had been only too delighted to lend Babe the following Saturday.

In fact, could the Elficks have the dog for the whole weekend? It would save him the kennel fees. He was off to a two-day 'Technology in Media' conference at the NEC in Birmingham.

So that was settled.

Chapter Five

As it turned out, the Elficks had a second house guest that weekend.

Shortly after eight o'clock on Saturday morning, Jamie arrived on the doorstep to hand Babe over along with her tartan quilt-lined basket and bag of dog food, just as Jenny answered a distraught phone call from her friend Annabel.

'Annabel's bedroom ceiling has just fallen in,' Jenny informed Mark a few minutes later, coming back into the living room where Chloe was trying to clip her bib round Babe's neck. 'A leak in the flat above apparently. She woke up to this almighty crash about an hour ago. It just missed her bed. She could have been killed. It doesn't bear thinking about. Her dressing table was smashed to matchwood.'

'She's probably exaggerating. You know what a drama queen she is.'

'Don't be mean. It must have been such a shock. Actually she's amazingly philosophical about it. She said she'd been intending to redecorate the room for ages and now she can get it done on the insurance.'

'Where's she going to sleep in the meantime? Not her living room, surely? It's full of tatty old easels and junk and half-dried-up oil paints.'

'I've told her she can stay with us. At least for the weekend. She'll be here in about half an hour. I'll go and make up the spare room.'

Ideal, thought Mark. While she's chatting away to Annabel, I can slide off in the car with Babe.

'You won't miss me if I go off for a quick client visit then.'

'Another one?'

'Well, it's the same one I went to see in Kent a while ago. I think he's going to come up trumps. He's furnishing this great country mansion for his mystery rich client. From scratch. It could be worth a fortune.'

This wasn't quite the elaborate lie it sounded, as Anthony, a highly camp client of his who specialised in interior design for the rich and famous, had called him the previous week to say he'd been commissioned to furnish the home of an exceedingly wealthy record company executive who'd come back from a lucrative stint in California and wanted his estate stuffed with antiques and statuary, inside and out. It was in Berkshire rather than Kent, but still . . . the facts were accurate enough for him to clothe the fib with conviction.

'So you're taking him some pieces to try out?'

'Not yet. Anthony just wants to give me a thorough guided tour of the place so that I can come up with some appropriate pieces for him to choose from.'

Jenny stopped herself from saying 'And it has to be a Saturday again, does it?' Perhaps he read her mind anyway though, because he added: 'And Jenny – the best news of all is that this should be the last time I have to give up my time at the weekend. After today – I hope – we'll have our family time back again.'

'I'll believe that when it happens,' said Jenny as the doorbell rang.

Annabel arrived in a flurry of perfumed hugs and air-kisses

48

and a jangle of pendants and bangles. Chloe loved Annabel. Festooned with all that jewellery, she was way more fun than any activity toy.

'Darlings! Thank you so much for taking me in. My flat's a bombsite. Soggy rubble all over my bedroom floor. I'm still in a state of shock.'

Jenny's oldest friend, Annabel was a one-woman house party. No moment of silence was allowed to go beyond five seconds unfilled. She was a bit too much for Mark, who preferred quieter, more thoughtful people. He was naturally quietly spoken and to get a word in edgeways it was necessary to shout. Since he didn't like shouting, he tended to take a back seat in any conversations she was part of.

Today, though, he was grateful for a bit of drama to take his mind off what he was about to do. He'd been trying hard not to think about it too much.

Long, deep breath. Lower the shoulders. It was vital that he seem cool and casual. He absolutely must not get tongue-tied like last time.

'So how's life treating you then, Mark? You look tired, darling.'

'I'm good thanks.'

'Too much bloody work,' chipped in Jenny.

'Work. Ugh. Invention of the devil.'

'Coffee, Bels?'

'Coffee! I guess, OK, in the absence of anything stronger . . . I need something for the shock.'

'There's some Scotch in the cupboard, I think,' said Mark. 'Anyway, I'll leave you girls to it.'

'Where are you off to then?'

'Client visit,' Jenny answered for him again.

'On a lovely sunny Saturday morning with the scent of spring in the air? You're mad. No wonder you look pale and wan.'

49

'Thank you for those kind words. I shall do my best to survive the morning and see you later. I assume you'll be here when I get back?'

'Don't count on it, sunshine.' Annabel grinned. 'We may have found something much more exciting to do than stick around here.'

Mark left them, Annabel sitting at the kitchen table, Jenny balancing Chloe on her hip as she fetched two china mugs down from the cupboard.

'So do you still reckon he's playing away?' hissed Annabel when the door shut behind him.

'Oh Bels, I don't know what to think. To be honest I'm feeling almost too tired to care.'

'You look worn out. And so does he.'

Summoning Babe, Mark clipped on her lead and headed for the front door. Perhaps he'd better mention that he was taking the dog, in case they thought they'd lost her or something.

He put his head back round the kitchen door.

Two pairs of mascara-fringed eyes turned to look at him.

'I'm taking your remarks about the spring sunshine to heart and taking the dog with me. She can have a run in the grounds of this mansion I'm going to.'

Before they could question him, he shut the door and made for the garage.

Annabel ran through to the living room at the front of the house and peered out of the window. Mark was fumbling with the key in the garage door. She ducked back out of his sight.

'Is this a regular thing these days then, this working at weekends?'

'This last few weeks it seems to be, yes. It never used to be.'

'It's a bit weird, isn't it? And taking the next-door neighbour's dog with him as well?'

'That is unusual,' agreed Jenny. 'He's not done that before.'

'I know where you can hire a private detective if you want.'

'Oh Annabel. I couldn't do that. What if he found out . . . that I didn't trust him any more? Anyway, people do that in novels, not real life.'

'But you don't, though, do you? Trust him, I mean.'

'Of course I do. I don't know. No, maybe I don't really. I just don't know what to think, that's the truth of it.'

'So it's time we found out.' Annabel snatched up her handbag. 'Bring Chloe. Come on.' They heard the slam of a car door and the Peugeot starting up.

'What?'

'Get Chloe's car seat thing. Quick! We'll take my car.'

'You don't mean . . . We can't follow him!'

'Do you, or do you not, want to know if you can trust him?'

Jenny hesitated. Impulsive behaviour didn't come as easily to her as it once did. Was it parenthood that had changed her, or had she just fallen out of practice?

'What the hell. OK. Let's do it.'

The Peugeot was disappearing round the corner as they locked the front door and ran to a silver Vauxhall Corsa parked at the kerb.

'I thought you had a trendy sporty job? A Honda something-or-other?'

'It's in the garage. Gasket went. Get Chloe strapped in. Come *on*! We'll lose him.'

Trying to keep her fingers from shaking, Jenny slotted the seat belt into the clips on Chloe's car seat, finally managed to click the straps into place, and threw herself into the passenger seat. Annabel had already started the engine.

'Go-go-go!' yelled Jenny and then got the giggles. 'I can't believe we're doing this.'

'Go-go-go,' squeaked Chloe's baby voice from the back.

'I don't want to end up following the wrong car,' murmured Annabel. 'Dark blue estate cars are ten a penny. Why couldn't he have a nice bright colour?'

'Just because your Honda's a vivid lime green. Mark's not a lime green kind of man.'

'I was cursing this boring courtesy car. So un-me. But at least it's inconspicuous. And it goes like a bomb.'

At the end of the road, Annabel stopped and looked right and left. There was no sign of the Peugeot.

'Damn,' she cursed. 'Where do you think he might be heading?'

'I think he said Sevenoaks area – if it's the same client.'

'So he'll be making for the A20, I expect.' She swung the wheel to the left and accelerated towards the traffic lights a couple of hundred yards further on, which changed conveniently to green as they approached. Annabel swung left again, just in time to see the Peugeot 406 waiting to turn right at the next crossroads.

'There he is!' squeaked Jenny. 'Hang back a bit, Bels.'

'I've always wanted to do this.' Annabel smiled. 'Do you remember we decided we wanted to be private eyes when we were at school? And the stupid careers officer told me to grow up and had I thought about dentistry. And she didn't mean becoming a dentist. She meant a dental *receptionist*. Patronising old bag. Just because she had teeth like a row of tombstones.'

'Don't get too close, Annabel,' Jenny managed to say through her giggles. 'I'm terrified he'll see us.'

'If he does notice us, which he almost certainly won't,' grinned Annabel, 'we'll say Chloe was inconsolable when he took the dog away and so we thought we'd take a run out to the country and see if we could help him keep it amused.'

'What if he *is* having an affair?' Jenny stopped laughing abruptly, her eyes fixed on Mark's back bumper as he slowed down for some traffic lights near Kidbrooke station a couple of hundred yards ahead. 'To be honest, Annabel, I'd rather stay in ignorance than discover something I really don't think I could cope with.'

'You can't change your destiny if you don't know what it is,' stated Annabel firmly. 'I'm a great believer in knowing what you're up against in this life. No use putting your head in the sand.'

She twitched the wheel to tuck the car neatly into the inside lane. There were half a dozen cars now between them and the Peugeot.

'Anyway, we'll probably find out that he's doing exactly what he said he was going to do and we'll creep away and find a country pub or something and have some lunch and a nice glass of wine.'

Jenny looked behind her to check on Chloe who, uncharacteristically, had had very little to say about the unexpected outing. She smiled mischievously at her mother around her thumb, her bare toes wiggling with pleasure.

'Damn. I forgot to put her shoes on.'

Chapter Six

Annabel kept him in her sights most of the way; along the A20, on to the M25, off again, now on the A21 towards Hastings.

There was just the right amount of traffic. Too much and they might have lost sight of him or been left behind at traffic lights. Too little and they'd have been too conspicuous. Mark might have noticed the silver car behind him taking all the same twists and turns he was.

Once he had turned off the A21 on to the smaller roads, they hung back a little more.

'I'm sure he won't see us anyway,' said Annabel. 'He's a bit vague, your Mark, at times, isn't he? And the last thing he'll be expecting is us following him.'

Then, just as they passed a road sign marking their arrival at Fulrow Green, the Peugeot slowed down and swung left into a residential street. Annabel carried on past the turning and pulled up at the kerb thirty yards further on.

'Better not follow him down there straight away.'

'Doesn't look the sort of street where you'd find a country mansion exactly,' commented Jenny.

'I'll hang a U-ey and drive past slowly. If he's out of sight we'll turn down there and follow him.'

Jenny slid a little lower in her seat. They both peered down into Simmons Road.

'He's turned the car round and parked up.'

'Doesn't seem to be getting out, though.'

'What do you think he's doing?'

'Maybe he's waiting for someone,' suggested Annabel. 'Or perhaps he's stopped to make a call.'

'So now what do we do?'

'Sit here and wait, I guess.'

'This is ridiculous.'

'Dickiless,' echoed Chloe cheerfully.

Mark didn't drive up as far as number 115 this time, but parked nearer to the beginning of Simmons Road. He'd turned the car round so that he could see the road stretching behind him in the rear-view mirror.

He kept the engine running so that as soon as he saw her emerge from her house, he could move off and get to the park ahead of her.

The street was livelier than he'd seen it before: cars coming and going, couples, families, young teenagers in groups of three and four, the woman with the old spaniel again . . . The sunny start to the day must have brought everyone out and about.

He just prayed that Elinor was intending to take her Saturday morning walk today. He couldn't go through much more of this.

Mercifully for the state of his nerves, he didn't have to wait too long before he caught a glimpse of her green raincoat and there she was with the buggy and the dog heading in his direction.

Heart thudding, he put the car into gear and set off towards the park. He kept his speed as low as he feasibly could to keep an eye on her in the mirror.

*

'Shall we give up on this and go back home?' said Jenny. 'Chloe will be getting hungry soon.' Annabel's eyes were fixed on the rear-view mirror. 'We'll just give it another couple of – ah – here we go! He's coming out. He's coming towards us.'

Instinctively, Jenny shrank even further down in her seat, putting her hand up to hide her face.

A second or two later the Peugeot crawled past them.

'Why is he going so slowly? What is he playing at?' wondered Annabel.

Jenny peeped through her fingers at the Peugeot in front of them. 'Oh God. Do you think he saw us?'

'No, I'm sure he didn't. He seemed to be looking very intently into his rear-view mirror as he passed us.'

She put the car into gear and released the handbrake. As she began to move forward, the Peugeot indicated left.

'I think that's a park he's driving into,' said Annabel. 'Maybe he's going to take the dog for a run before he goes on to his meeting.'

'I guess. He's never bothered much with that dog before though. I don't get it.'

Annabel pulled up again. 'We'll wait here for a minute.'

A woman in a green raincoat walked past, pushing a child in a buggy, struggling to keep it going in a straight line, while trying to control a boisterous puppy on a lead. Behind her strolled a traffic warden, studying his electronic handset.

'Oh hell. I'll have to move on. Bloody traffic warden about to pounce. The buggers seem to have some kind of sixth sense. I'll drive up to that roundabout up there and come back. Then we'll go into the park ourselves. See what he's up to.'

*

57

Mark turned into Priory Gardens and found a space at the end of the car park nearest the little gate.

Scenting grass and space and other dogs, Babe whimpered with excitement. This man had never taken her anywhere more exciting than the local newspaper shop in the past.

Her eager black eyes scanned his face with new-dawning affection.

When Annabel drove in through the entrance to Priory Gardens a few minutes later, Mark's Peugeot was parked towards the end of the little car park, but there was no sign of him or the dog.

'Shall I look after Chloe while you go and take a peek in the park?' she suggested.

'I don't think I dare. He might see me. You go, Annabel. Please. You're not as familiar to him as I am. Wrap your scarf round your head. Like the Queen.'

'Great. I'll look like a right idiot. The things you do for friendship!'

Knotting her red, yellow and turquoise scarf under her chin, Annabel clambered out of the car.

'Keep an eye out for wardens, Jen. Or better still, stick some money in the Pay and Display over there. Wish me luck!'

Looking around exaggeratedly from left to right and back again, Annabel tiptoed to the wall and flattened herself against it.

After more over-the-top peering about, she began to creep slowly along the wall to the park gate where she paused for a final comic-furtive look in Jenny's direction before disappearing round the corner. Jenny had to laugh.

Thank goodness there was no one around to see that embarrassing pantomime.

She found a pound coin in her purse and crossed the car park to feed it into the ticket machine, praying that Mark wouldn't choose that moment to come back to his car. She'd have to confess they had tailed him. She was hopeless at lying.

Back in the Corsa, Chloe was beginning to fidget. The fun had stopped now that Annabel had gone off somewhere.

'I hungry, Mummy,' she stated plaintively.

Jenny had some chocolate in the chaotic depths of her bag somewhere. It took her a while to find it. She didn't approve of giving Chloe sweets usually, but this was a special case.

Annabel appeared suddenly at the window.

'Well?'

'He's talking to some woman.'

Jenny clapped her hand to her mouth. 'Oh God. What do you mean, "talking"? How talking? Casual chatting? Passing the time of day? Or is it more . . . intimate than that?'

'It's hard to tell really. There's a child in a buggy he's taking a lot of notice of. And she's got a brown dog. The two dogs are getting *very* pally, that's for sure.'

'Did he see you?'

'Of course he didn't see me. You're talking to a professional private detective manqué.'

'Is she nice-looking?'

'I don't know. Quite nice, I think.'

'But what did you think? Is this an assignation – a pre-arranged secret tryst – or just a chance meeting? Oh Annabel, I can't bear it!'

'I honestly haven't a clue. They are smiling at each other a lot. You go and have a look. I'll stay with Chlo-Chlo.'

'I don't believe this is happening. This is awful. I can't. But I've got to, haven't I? I've got to know!'

'That is why we're here, isn't it?'

59

'He might see me.'

'He won't see you. He doesn't know you're here so he won't be looking out for you. They are over on the other side of the park, a couple of hundred yards away. Over by the lake. Take the disguise.'

She untied the scarf from her head and threw it across on to her friend's lap.

'Have you got anything a bit . . . quieter?'

'I don't do quiet. You know me!'

Heart banging inside her ribcage, Jenny slung the colourful piece of fabric over her head, shoved her hands deep into her coat pockets and affected a relaxed saunter towards the park.

She found herself in a network of carefully tended flower beds. She looked around anxiously. She needed some cover.

A couple of hundred yards away was a less manicured area and a copse of higgledy-piggeldy trees and shrubs. Instinctively she struck out towards it.

Drawing closer, she could see some wooden seats lined up at regular intervals alongside a partially algae-covered pond.

Her husband was sharing one of these benches with a woman in a green raincoat, her long, pale hair blowing loosely in the breeze. In front of her was parked a buggy with a child in a bright orange all-in-one suit strapped into it.

On the bench, between Mark and the woman, was a carrier bag, which they were taking it in turns to dip their hands into, pulling out chunks of white bread and flinging them at a jostling group of mallards and pigeons.

As Jenny watched, Mark took the child's hand, prising the little fingers open gently, and put a piece of bread into it. Then he and the woman burst out laughing as the child stuffed the bread into its own mouth.

Left to their own blissful devices, Babe and the woman's mongrel puppy were chasing each other round the tree trunks, taking it in turns to be chaser and chased. To anyone who didn't know different, it looked like a normal, Saturday morning family scene in the park.

Stopping furtively by the mottled trunk of a plane tree, Jenny attempted to assess the situation. It was most unlike Mark to strike up a conversation with a stranger. He was usually quite shy. And what was he doing in this little park miles from home? He surely hadn't just happened on the place. This must be a pre-arranged meeting.

What should she do now? Go up and confront them? Risk a scene? Or go home, wait until he got back and then tackle him?

Coming from the car park in the distance she heard a thin wail of complaint. Unmistakeably Chloe. It was past her lunchtime. A pause, and then the wail was repeated, but for three significant seconds longer.

It was now or not at all. Annabel could cope with Chloe. Jenny tried to take a deep breath for the mental strength she was going to need in the next few minutes, but her lungs seemed to have stopped working. So had her legs. Her body was using all its available energy sending her heartbeat into overdrive.

Forcing herself into action at last, she set off at a run towards the pond.

A moment later, flushed and breathless, she had planted herself in front of the bench, and was looking down at the two of them.

'Hello, Mark.'

The two faces looked up in surprise; Mark's turning a terrible greyish white.

'Jenny! What on earth . . . How on earth . . . ?' He turned to his companion. 'Um, this is my wife, Jenny.' He turned back to

Jenny. 'I . . . I'm sorry . . . I'd introduce you but we've only just met . . .'

The woman glanced uncertainly from Mark to Jenny and back again. Struggling to disguise her agitation, Jenny put out her hand. 'How do you do? I'm *Mrs* Jenny Elfick.'

Out of involuntary politeness the woman briefly touched the proffered hand. 'And I'm Mrs Keegan,' she said. 'Elinor Keegan.'

'I hope I'm not interrupting anything?' Jenny loaded her voice with as much irony as she could muster.

Elinor stood up abruptly. 'Well, I'll leave you to it and carry on with my morning.' She looked over towards the trees. 'Boot! Come on, boy.'

Mark stood up too. 'I'm sorry. Forgive me, Mrs Keegan.'

But the woman had her back turned to him, letting out the brake on the buggy.

'Come on, Leonie, let's go and find some pretty flowers.'

Mark glared at Jenny, lowering his voice in the ominous way he had on the rare occasions he was angry with her.

'Jenny, I came here to take Babe for a quick run and Mrs Keegan and I had literally only just got chatting. Now, I've got work to do, I'm afraid, so I've got to get going too. What have you done with Chloe?'

Had she just made a complete fool of herself?

'Annabel's looking after her,' she said weakly, 'in the car park. We just saw you in the distance.' She remembered Annabel's earlier suggestion for an excuse if Mark were to catch them following him. 'Chloe wanted to play with the dog. She loves Babe. But you took her. So we came after you to get her back.'

Who was she trying to kid?

'Well take Babe then, by all means. Here. Take the lead.' He took the lead from round his neck and thrust it into her hands. 'I'm going to my meeting.'

He turned towards Elinor who was now emptying the last few crumbs out of the carrier bag on to the ground. His tense features barely relaxed, despite a game attempt at a polite smile.

'Well . . . I'm sorry . . . It was good to meet you, Elinor, Mrs Keegan. And little Leonie. Maybe see you again one day.'

'Right.' Elinor had started to wheel the buggy away from the bench. She looked none too keen on the idea of seeing Mark again. Or his crazy wife. 'Come *here*, Boot. Boot!'

The puppy came shambling up to her, tongue lolling out stupidly from the side of its mouth.

'I'll see *you* at home, Jenny.' And Mark was striding away, leaving Jenny to round up Babe.

Walking unsteadily back to the car park, it occurred to her that she'd been swathed in Annabel's ridiculous multicoloured scarf throughout the whole encounter.

Chapter Seven

'So what the hell was all that about?' Mark had settled on attack as the best form of defence.

'You bloody tell me!' Jenny had decided on the same approach, having gratefully accepted Annabel's offer to take Chloe off to see her eccentric mother in Pimlico for tea, to give the pair of them some time to talk things through. 'You give me all this crap about important clients and business meetings on Saturdays and Sundays and most evenings of the week and I'm supposed to buy this total pack of lies.'

'It's not lies.' That didn't sound too convincing. 'I've had a lot on my mind and some very important business to attend to.'

'Perhaps it's time to tell me what this important business is and with whom, exactly.'

Actually, Mark realised suddenly, it would be a relief to tell her the truth at last. He'd carried this burden alone for too long.

He was sitting at the kitchen table, fiddling with the pink nylon mane on one of Chloe's toy ponies. Jenny was pacing backwards and forwards in front of the work surface, ostensibly making a pot of tea, waiting for the kettle to boil.

'Jenny. Stop being angry. I'll tell you the whole story. But just stop being angry.'

'Why wouldn't I be angry when you lie to me? You say you're seeing important clients and then I find you chatting up some woman in a park.'

'I could be just as angry with you. How dare you follow me? What does that say about our relationship that you trust me so little?'

'My point exactly. What *does* it say about us? It says that you've been acting so weird lately that you're not the man I married any more. And yes, you're damn right. I *have* stopped trusting you. You used to tell me everything. We were best friends, and now you're furtive and secretive and . . . you know what, Mark? I'm not going to live like this any more. I'm really not. Either you tell me what's going on with you or let's just . . . call it a day.'

She could see that she'd shocked Mark even more than she had herself.

'For Christ's sake . . . Jenny . . .' Mark could only breathe in a series of gasps. This was frightening. The thought of splitting up had never occurred to him. It was unthinkable. 'Let's pour ourselves a drink and have a proper talk. Sit down. Forget tea. I'll open some wine.'

'There's some open already. Annabel and I had some when we got back this afternoon.' She banged a half-empty bottle of red wine down on the table in front of him. 'I needed it.'

She seized two upturned wine glasses off the draining board and put them next to the bottle.

Mark filled both glasses almost to the brim.

'Now, Jenny, sit down.'

Jenny pulled a chair out from under the table opposite her husband and sat herself down.

She was amazed how in control she felt now. It was liberating to let her feelings out at last; not to have to bottle up all that resentment any more.

Mark slid one of the glasses over to her.

They sat facing each other.

'Go on then. Talk. First of all who was that woman in the park?'

'If you want first of all, I'm going to have to start at the beginning of all this. Ten months ago.'

He was fiddling with Chloe's toy pony again.

In one movement, Jenny reached across the table, snatched it out of his hands and flung it across the room. Ricocheting off one of the kitchen cupboard doorknobs, it came to rest on top of the fridge.

'Are you or are you not having an affair?'

Mark had never seen Jenny so livid.

'What? Of *course* I'm not having an affair!'

'Well *something*'s going on, that's for sure.'

'Oh God. I should have told you from the start. I so wish I had now.' He also wished he hadn't filled the glasses so full. His hand was shaking so much as he tried to get his to his lips that he slopped wine down his front.

Cursing, he stood up. 'Why is it always red stuff I spill on myself!'

Jenny was nearer the sink. She reached round the back of her chair, snatched up a soggy dishcloth and threw it at him. He caught it and sat down again, dabbing ineffectually at his favourite blue Timberland shirt.

'I'm waiting. *What* should you have told me from the start?'

'I should have told you what Lionel told me.'

'And what did Lionel tell you? Jesus, this is like pulling teeth.'

'You know we decided to donate our leftover embryos to help other childless couples?'

Suddenly Jenny had an idea where this might be going. She fought an instinct to cover her ears and run out of the room.

'Well, Chloe's got a sibling.'

He might just as well have pulled the pin from a hand grenade and dropped it on to the table in front of them.

For a moment, Jenny wasn't sure she was still conscious. Everything seemed to go dark and far away. She was sinking, drowning, in a deep, black, slurry-filled pit. She made a gasping bid for the surface.

'That child . . . in the park . . . that was . . . *our* child.'

'Yes.'

'My God.'

Slowly, colour began returning to her brain in small amoebic blobs.

'Does she look like Chloe?'

'Yes. A lot like Chloe when she was that age. Her name's Leonie.'

'Why didn't you tell me?'

'I couldn't. I just . . .' Tears were running down his face. He dabbed at them with the wine-stained dishcloth.

'Did that woman know who we were?'

'No. At least, she didn't. You blundering in on my carefully planned accidentally-on-purpose meeting wasn't helpful though. I just hope she didn't twig.'

'You could get us into deep trouble making contact like that. We signed legal guarantees. And it was Lionel who told you!'

'He didn't mean to tell me. He kind of let it slip out by mistake. We were at Lord's. The Australia match.'

'What was he thinking, for God's sake? How can information as important as that just slip out? It's dynamite.'

'I don't know. We'd been sitting around in the stands waiting for the rain to stop for the third or fourth time. And we got to philosophising about life and things . . . and I was saying I was a bit fed up with work and everything . . . you know, things weren't going very well around then . . . and I was feeling like a bit of a waste of space. He was trying to cheer me up really. He said I should be happy because I'd done a good thing. Something to be proud of. I'll never forget that moment. It's on a permanent sort of video loop in my brain.' He imitated Lionel's well rounded, polished tones. '"You've made a real life-changing difference in the world, Elfick," he said. It took me a few seconds to work out what he was hinting at. We were a bit drunk. I sobered up after that though. The thought that someone was having our child. Chloe's sister or brother. Chloe's *twin*, technically. It hit me like a thunderbolt.'

'Pretty much how I'm feeling now,' murmured Jenny.

'I couldn't get it out of my head after that. A couple of times at the squash club on Tuesday nights, I casually asked him if everything was going OK. And he always said, "Yes, fine. It's all going fine", and that was that. Then one evening when I asked, he said the child had just been born. "Lovely healthy baby," was all he said. "Got all its fingers and toes. The couple are over the moon." And he said again something like I could rest assured that we – you and I – did a wonderful thing. And then he changed the subject. He wouldn't answer any more questions. Point blank refused.'

'So then what?'

'Well, I tried to put it out of my mind of course. But it started eating away at me, Jenny. I couldn't stop thinking about it. I kept wondering things. Did the baby have the same coppery curls and big blue eyes that turned to that amazing grey-green colour a few weeks later I wondered if it had a little constellation of moles on its back . . . you know . . . like Chloe has. I caught myself peering into buggies in the street to see if the baby inside looked like Chloe. And I thought how supportive we could be to the parents if they could talk to us, you know, compare notes. Things like, you remember how worried we got when Chloe went through that phase of screaming at six o'clock every evening and we found out it was colic and the health visitor recommended that herbal stuff? We could reassure them if they were having the same problem. I used to wonder whether the mother was breast-feeding, for example, because I thought maybe if she's infertile she might not be able to produce her own milk and she'd have to bottle-feed and that wouldn't be so good for the baby because the experts always say that breast is best. Oh Jenny, do you think I'm crazy?'

Jenny gave him a short, unconvinced shake of the head. Maybe he was. But would she have felt the same?

'All I wanted was to know that our child was well and happy. That the parents were good people, you know? That's all. I couldn't just forget about it. It wouldn't have been natural if I had, would it? My – our – flesh and blood. I didn't even know if it was a boy or a girl. So I decided to find out for myself. I had to.'

'So did Lionel tell you where they lived?'

'No. He wouldn't have done that. I found out for myself.'

'How did you manage that? You didn't even know the date of birth, did you?'

'It had to be within six days at the most of Lionel telling me it had been born, or he'd have mentioned it at the squash club the previous Tuesday. So it had to have been between the eleventh and seventeenth of November. And I was ninety-nine per cent certain it was the couple he'd told us about, do you remember – patients of his at West Kent General?'

'Yes I do.'

'So I looked up all the babies that had been born in Kent between the eleventh and seventeenth of November.'

'Did you do that online?'

'No, I tried that, but I wasn't sure it was comprehensive

enough. So I went to the Family Records Office in Islington. Every single birth in England and Wales is registered there.'

'How long did it take you?'

'A while. It meant a lot of trips backwards and forwards to Islington, but it had become a real challenge, you know . . . All these huge, heavy, red books. I worked my way systematically through the babies born that week in November and registered in the Kent area. There must have been getting on for a hundred of them.'

'So all those evenings and weekends you said you were working late, you were at the Family Records Office.'

'Well, they closed at five most nights. Seven on Tuesdays and Thursdays. So I went there in the afternoons and put in time at the shop in the evenings and some weekends instead; phoning clients, visiting them at home and all that. So I really was working late.'

'But I still don't know how you could possibly tell out of a hundred of them which was . . . ours?'

'I was counting on one thing. You remember he told us that most of his patients named their babies after him in some way, like we did, with Chloe Leonora? I was just keeping everything crossed that this couple had done the same. If they hadn't, that would have been the end of it. But I found one called Leonie. Leonie Saffron Keegan. None of the others had anything like Lionel in their names. So I thought that had to be the one. I was so excited. It could have been coincidence of course, though. I had to be absolutely sure. So the next thing was to, you know, see the child.'

'Because if she looked like Chloe . . .'

'Yes. If she looked like Chloe, then I'd know. After that, I just needed to satisfy myself that she was happy and well looked after. Then I could get peace of mind.' He slumped back in his chair. He looked exhausted. 'So now you know.'

'It explains so much. I just wish you'd told me, Mark. I've been going through hell. I even went to see our counsellor. I thought you were . . . I thought . . .'

'Oh Jenny. I'm so sorry. I didn't tell you because . . . well, mostly because I just couldn't do it to you. It was bad enough one of us having sleepless nights. It was doing *my* head in. I didn't want you going half crazy as well. We'd have made it worse for each other. With just me knowing, I could quietly get on with my detective work, find out what I needed to know and no one need get upset. And, I suppose, to be honest, I was also scared you might tell me to back off. I knew I couldn't do that. Not until I'd found out what I needed to know.' He looked across at her. 'Do you understand?'

Hardly aware of what she was doing, Jenny got to her feet, dragged her chair across the kitchen to the fridge, climbed on to it and then on to the kitchen worktop to reach up and retrieve Chloe's toy pony. How the world had changed since she'd thrown it there twenty minutes ago.

'Well, do you?' he pleaded.

'I don't know. I honestly don't know. I feel completely numb.' She gazed absently at the still-jaunty Little Pony, teasing its tangled, pink mane between her fingers. 'I need some time to think about it.'

She scrambled back down to ground level, repositioned the chair at the table and stood facing Mark from behind it.

'Look, Mark. We've got our little miracle. We went through hell and high water to have Chloe in our lives. We're so lucky. It's just plain ungrateful to ask for more than that.'

The phone warbled on the table, making them both jump.

Mark looked at the caller display. 'Annabel.' He handed it across to Jenny.

'Hi, Bels.'

'Is it safe to come back yet? Are you OK?'

'Yes, fine. Sure. Absolutely.'

'Is Mark there with you?'

'Yes.'

'So you're OK, then.'

'Yes, Annabel. We're OK. How's Chloe?'

'She's wonderful. We had a sing-a-thon. She's spark-out in the car seat now. Can I come back now?'

'Yes, of course.'

'See you in about twenty minutes then.'

Jenny put the phone back on the table and sat down again.

'You found out where the family lived from the Births Register then?'

'No, I had to get hold of a copy of the actual birth certificate. And that wasn't as easy as I thought it would be. I applied for one online, with the reference number from the register and everything, but they wrote back saying my application had to include the parents' Christian names. Only parents' surnames are in the register. So for a while I thought I was stymied. Then I had a brainwave. If the couple were married, they'd be in the Marriages Register. The father's surname was Keegan and the mother's was Roberts, so I just had to find a Keegan marrying a Roberts. So I went back to the Family Records Office again.'

'They might not have been married.'

'I know. I just had to hope they were. Given that they had been having fertility treatment themselves, I guessed they must have been together at least five years before the baby was born. So I decided to go back ten years and work my way forward from then. And when I got to 1990, there they were. Daniel Keegan marrying Elinor Roberts in Maidstone. August 1990. And when a copy of Leonie's birth certificate arrived in the post a few days later, I had the address. One hundred and fifteen Simmons Road,

Fulrow Green. I drove there a few times to check it out. I saw the father first. Long, lanky guy. Looks like a roadie for a rock group. And then I saw the mother with the child in a buggy but I couldn't get a good enough look at the baby. I saw her going to the park to feed the ducks last Saturday, so I decided to be there this Saturday and see if she turned up there again. I wasn't going to say who I was or anything. Just get talking to her. See what she was like. And see what the baby looked like. Then you came along.'

'And? She does look like Chloe?'

'It's amazing, Jenny. I wish you'd got a proper look at her. It's like Chloe all over again.'

'I saw her putting the ducks' bread in her mouth. Just like Chloe used to.'

Mark was relieved to see Jenny smile at last. 'She's got exactly the same hair, Jen, the same bluey-grey-green eyes. Same cheeky grin.'

'But that's it now, Mark. It has to be. If they find out who you are, we could end up with an injunction or maybe worse. You have to let go. Apart from anything else, you've been driving yourself nuts. You said so yourself. When did you last have a haircut? Or buy yourself a new pair of trousers?'

'What's that got to do with anything?'

'A lot. You used to be so meticulous about how you looked. Have you seen yourself in the mirror lately? You look like a dandelion clock.'

'Come on.' He combed both hands back through his hair, in a futile effort to smooth it down. 'It's not that bad, is it?'

'Darling Mark, you have to promise me to give this up. I know it won't be easy. *I've* got a lot of thinking to do as well now. But I know what comes first – us. You, me and Chloe. This other child . . . Leonie . . . well, we have to make ourselves accept that

74

she's not ours. She may be our genetic material but that woman in the green raincoat gave birth to her. As far as she is concerned, she is *her* daughter. Completely. That is the deal we all agreed to. If you don't let go now, you'll go mad. We both will. I won't let that happen. And what about Chloe? It's not fair on her. You love Chloe to pieces, don't you?'

'Of course I do. That's what's made it worse somehow. Knowing that there was another perfect, wonderful child like Chloe in the world. The same flesh and blood as us. And how great it would be for little Chlo to have a sister . . . It tears me up. Just tears me up.'

The doorbell rang.

'Annabel.' Jenny stood up. 'Chloe will need her tea. She'll have had goodness knows how many sweets and cakes, but nothing nourishing, I wouldn't mind betting. We'll talk more about this later. Or maybe tomorrow. I need time for all this to sink in.'

The doorbell rang again.

Jenny started towards the front door. 'This may sound harsh, Mark, but you've got to let this go. You've absolutely got to. For all our sakes.'

He was gazing unseeingly across the table, out of the window into the garden beyond.

'Did you hear me?'

'Yes, I heard you.'

'Promise me!'

The doorbell shrilled again. Annabel was leaning on it now.

'I said *promise* me.'

'I promise. OK. I really will try.'

Chapter Eight

Patience was not Annabel's strong point, so the rest of Saturday evening and the whole of Sunday were almost beyond her endurance.

They'd managed a few hissed interchanges; later that Saturday evening when Mark had left the room for a moment or two:

'Who was that woman then?'

'I'll tell you later.'

'Has he been having an affair with her?'

'No.'

'So you're not going to split up or anything?'

'No.'

And next morning when Mark took Babe for a stroll to the paper shop:

'You've forgiven him then?'

'It's not a matter of forgiveness.'

'But he was telling you porkies. All that guff about new clients.'

'Yes I know. He had his reasons though.'

'Is he going to start behaving himself?'

'Things are certainly going to change.'

'I hope you told him enough was enough.'

'Annabel, I can't tell you everything in five-minute bursts. It's complicated. I'll explain things properly tomorrow when Mark's gone to work.'

She was grateful not to have to talk about it yet. She needed time to think. It had all been such a shock.

Now it was her turn to lie awake at night, buffeted by a maelstrom of emotions. Trying to weigh expediency against wishful thinking. Logic against instinct. She'd stood less than a yard away from her own child. If only she'd known.

Somehow she *should* have known. If she could just have looked into her daughter's eyes, soul might have seen into soul. Something would have passed between them. She was sure of that. She ached for a second chance. But it must never be.

And the mother. How she wished she'd had a proper look at her, too. Inside this other woman's swelling belly, Jenny's biological daughter had spent nine months growing. She pictured the still-slippery infant sucking at her breast for the first time and her entrails ached where her own womb had been. Hollow and dark. Convulsed with envy and a profound sense of loss.

Beside her, Mark lay wrapped in peaceful slumber for the first time in months.

'A trouble shared is obviously a trouble halved as far as he's concerned,' she thought, resentful and yet indescribably relieved to have seen the beginnings of the old Mark returning; the lines across his brow relaxing, a glimmer of that once-so-easy boyish smile that could still make her heart contract after all these years together.

Even Chloe slept right through both Saturday and Sunday nights.

Evidently it was Jenny's turn now to fall victim to the gremlins of the night.

'At last!' crowed Annabel as Mark's car reversed away down the drive and Thora the au pair was installing Chloe in her buggy ready for a childminder's coffee morning at La Violetta Café on the common.

All Jenny's friends had known about the IVF of course. Some of them who had fallen pregnant with consummate ease had felt embarrassed about it, but Jenny had always been at pains to reassure them that she wasn't jealous at all. That she loved being a kind of surrogate auntie to all her friends' offspring.

This hadn't been strictly true. She'd tried her very best to share their family joy. They were her friends. But inside, she had to admit she sometimes found it painful to see her friends playing happy families, children snuggling up to parents on laps, mouths straining open in highchairs for spoonfuls of gunky-looking food. Little dresses and dungarees pegged on clothes lines, cute-faced teddies and unlikely coloured fluffy animals ranked on endless toyshop shelves begging to be bought and cuddled . . .

Annabel, on the other hand, had always been mystified by the whole thing.

'What's the big deal? Who wants snotty kids anyway? For what? You lose your figure for a start. Stretch marks and lumpy bits . . . Spontaneity goes out the window – no more late-night parties, no more carefree holidays lounging around in the sun reading books and getting squiffy on cocktails. For years you'll never be able to go anywhere without lugging jars of baby food, great packets of nappies, boxes of tissues and evil-smelling creams along with you. You couldn't aspire to a two-seater drop-head for at *least* ten years – if ever. No romantic dinners *à deux* without the baby alarm shrieking at you every time things start getting cosy. Trails of dried-up sick down the back of your best cashmere, your brand new lipstick smooshed into the stair carpet . . . You must be completely off your trolley. And then the school-runs . . . and the dreadful screaming birthday parties with inane songs and out-of-work actors trying to be clowns. And then it gets even worse! You're sharing your life with hulking great self-centred, charmless things called teenagers cluttering up every available place to loll around in your living room . . . pizza boxes and half-empty beer cans all over the place . . . demanding expensive gifts they can't possibly live without, like, iPods and digital cameras, mobile phones and computers, portable DVD players . . . You shell out thousands on some college course they may or may not bother to finish. And then what do they do? After all that, they bugger off without so much as a backward glance. And you're at least fifty by then with arthritis and Alzheimer's waiting for you just around the corner. Far too late to pick up the threads of the decent life you were living when the little sods first put in an appearance. Not for me thanks. And you should listen to what your body is trying to tell you, Jenny Elfick. It's obviously got more sense than your brain. It's saying keep your life your own. You and Mark enjoy each other. Have fun, for goodness' sake.'

It was an entertaining tirade, and almost convincing sometimes, if a little tactless. Unfortunately, it didn't make Jenny and Mark any the less keen to embark on the years of purgatory Annabel was so fond of describing.

'So for Christ's sake spill the beans.'

'I'm not supposed to tell you, Annabel.'

'Jenny! I'm your best friend. We've always told each other everything.'

'I know but—'

'Have I ever, ever betrayed a confidence in all the years we've been friends?'

'I can tell you the basics, I suppose, in general terms, but no details. Nothing specific. And you've got to promise me you won't tell another living soul.'

'Cross my heart and hope to die.'

'I'm not joking, Annabel. This is serious.'

'I know, I can see that. Just tell me what you can then.'

'The child in the park on Saturday was . . . is . . . technically Mark's and my child.'

'What? I don't get it. What do you mean by "technically"?'

'When we were having IVF treatment, I don't know if you were aware, but it involved stimulating my ovaries to release as many eggs as possible. That's what all those injections were about.'

'I know. I remember. How could I not?'

'And after Chloe was born, we had some embryos left over, which we decided to donate to the clinic for childless couples.'

'Ah.'

'Yes. Ah.'

'But isn't it supposed to be anonymous? You aren't supposed to know what happens to them, are you?'

'No. We had to sign legal papers revoking all our rights to our embryos and undertaking not to seek or claim any connection to any resulting children.'

'But . . . Mark found out,' said Annabel quietly.

'Our fertility doctor "let it slip", as Mark put it.'

'No! How unprofessional can you get?'

'I know. I just don't get it. He always seemed such a pillar of integrity. I think maybe the trouble was that he and Mark got too friendly. He meant well, I'm sure. We wouldn't have had Chloe without him. He was wonderful.'

'What was he playing at though?'

Sue Cook

'I'll be asking him that very thing, I can assure you. I'm going to phone him in a minute.'

'You could sue him, you know. Get him struck off.'

'What good would it do?' Jenny shrugged miserably. 'Once you know something, you can't go back and un-know it. We're into damage limitation now.'

Chapter Nine

'Hello, Angie, it's Jenny Elfick here.'

'Mrs Elfick. How are you? It's been a couple of years. How's your lovely baby?'

'She's just great, thank you.'

'Chloe, isn't it?'

'That's right. Good memory.'

'Bring her in to see us sometime. I can take another photo of her for our noticeboard.'

'Great. Yes, I'll do that. Angie, is Mr Lockhart in his office?'

'I'm afraid he's got wall-to-wall patients today. He might get a moment to call you at the end of his morning session.'

'I need to see him actually.'

'Oh?'

'I don't need a formal appointment but it's important that I talk to him as soon as possible. Maybe after he's finished this evening?'

'Oh dear, I'm sorry, Mrs Elfick. I really couldn't commit him to that. He's got a long enough day as it is today.'

'If he knew what I had to say I think he'd want to see me as soon as possible.'

'Can you tell me what it's about?'

'I'm afraid it's confidential. Just tell him it's to do with the embryos we donated. And something he said to Mark. I think he'll see the urgency.'

'All right, I'll see what I can do. Let me put you on hold for a moment, Mrs Elfick.'

As Jenny sat looking out at her front garden, the phone at her ear treating her to sounds remarkably similar to the music that had accompanied her first two embryo transfer procedures, she could hear Annabel on the landing upstairs shouting into her mobile.

'I could have been *killed*. The plumbing in that upstairs flat has been *nothing* but trouble ever since they supposedly refurbished it . . . Yes of *course* I'm insured, but you're the freeholder. You need to sort this out. I can't be doing any longer with these *constant* leaks. I shall expect you or the people upstairs to pay my five hundred pounds excess *plus* compensation for being driven out of my own home for three days. Not to *mention* the disruption of trying to get on with my work at home with plasterers and decorators in and out of my flat for the next two weeks. Just think yourself lucky I'm not suing you for *criminal negligence.*'

'Mrs Elfick?'

'Yes, hello.'

'Sorry to have kept you waiting. Mr Lockhart can see you tonight at six.'

Lionel's office hadn't changed much in two years. There were a few more baby photos around the walls, including the one of herself and Mark smiling almost incredulously down at their tiny newborn Chloe, cradled in Jenny's arms.

Lionel was as dapper as ever, wearing one of his signature beautifully cut, muted pinstripe navy suits with bottle-green velvet bow tie. Perhaps there was a little more grey now in his neatly swept-back dark hair. He stood up as she entered the room, leaning across the familiar heavy oak desk to grasp her hand. She thought she detected a hint of watchfulness in the blue-grey eyes.

'Jenny, my dear. How nice to see you again.' He indicated the two small leather armchairs in front of him with a sweep of his hand.

Automatically, Jenny chose the one she'd always sat in when she and Mark had come to discuss the next stage in their struggle to achieve a child.

'I hear that little Chloe is thriving. You'll have to bring her in one day. I love to watch my babies growing up.'

'Thank you for seeing me so quickly.'

'Well, I'm up to my eyes as usual but I've always got time for you, my dear. Where's Mark this evening? Working no doubt.'

'He doesn't know I've come to see you. I will tell him, but I wanted to see you alone first.'

The doctor studied her over his spectacles. 'I see. So what can I do for you?'

'Lionel, we've been going through hell, Mark and I.'

'Oh dear. I'm sorry. What's been happening?'

'You can guess, surely.'

'I'm not sure I can. You'd better tell me.'

'You must have had some inkling of what Mark's been going through this last ten months. After what you told him.'

'No. What has he been going through? He's always seemed fine at the squash club.'

'You haven't noticed how tired he looks?'

'I suppose he has been looking a bit haggard, yes. I told him he was working too hard.'

'It's not the work. It's the information you gave him. It's what you told him about our . . . biological child.'

He raised an eyebrow. 'Well, Jenny, I dropped a hint that your embryo donation had had a successful outcome, if that's what you mean. It can hardly have been a big surprise. It was always going to be on the cards, wasn't it? Why donate otherwise?'

'You told us yourself that anonymity was a fundamental element of donation.'

'And anonymous it is.'

'No it isn't. Mark's seen the little girl. He's talked to the mother.'

'*What?*' Lionel looked shattered. 'He can't have!'

'Elinor Keegan. You gave him enough information to track them down.'

'I certainly did not! I told him nothing beyond the fact that your donation had been a worthwhile thing to do. I didn't give him a name or an area. No clue to their identity whatsoever. I wouldn't have dreamed of it. He showed very little reaction anyway. I remember he seemed quite pleased and that was that.'

'He reacted all right. He spent months checking through all the recorded births in Kent in the second week of November.'

'I'm speechless. I cannot for the life of me work out how he's found out where she is.'

'The clue was the name. They named her after you.'

'Oh my Lord,' Lionel groaned. 'Oh my Lord.'

'You obviously underestimated Mark's capacity for dogged determination.'

'So it would seem.' Lionel closed his eyes for a second or two, pressing his thumbs into his temples.

'What do we do now?' demanded Jenny. 'We're in this terrible situation because of you. What are you going to do about it?'

'So if Mark's met the Keegans, they know who he is too, do they?'

'I'm not sure. I don't think they do.' Jenny decided to withhold, for the moment, the information that she'd followed Mark to his encounter in the park at Fulrow Green last Saturday. If the couple did have any suspicions now, it was partly her fault.

Lionel's frown relaxed a little. 'Let's pray that they don't or we're all in trouble. You signed legal guarantees, you know.'

'I know that. Of course I do. I only found out about this on Saturday. Mark and I had a long talk. He told me everything for the first time. You can imagine the shock . . .'

'Indeed.'

'. . . mixed with relief. I thought he'd been having an affair. I've asked him to promise me he'll leave these people alone, put them out of his mind. Now that he's seen they look like reasonable parents and the child seems happy, I hope he'll be able to do that. But I don't think he'll find it that easy. He's been obsessed for so long.'

'Look, Jenny. It's vital these people don't find out about you two. Absolutely vital.'

'You should have thought of that before you told Mark they existed. You, of all people, must have been aware of the implications.'

'I'll talk to Mark. Tell him I'll call him first thing in the morning.'

Jenny got to her feet.

'Jenny. I'm so sorry. It was such a small piece of information while we were having a man-to-man chat one day.'

'Careless talk costs lives,' remarked Jenny on her way to the door.

'Jenny?'

She paused, her hand on the brass handle.

'Are you all right?'

'I'm not sure yet. It's still sinking in. Knowing in theory that you *might* have another genetic child somewhere in the world is one thing. It's very different knowing for *sure* that you have one.'

'I can't apologise enough . . .' He couldn't think what else to say. It didn't matter anyway. The door had closed. She'd gone. With another groan, he dropped his head in his hands.

Chapter Ten

The garage doors slid open. Lionel Lockhart tossed the remote control handset back in the glove box and slammed it shut. He was rattled now. No two ways about it. And it took a lot to get under his skin. He prided himself on his unflappable temperament. He needed it in his profession, with so many raw emotions flying about. You do what you can for people, you bend over backwards. You think you've thought it all through for them, you've explained everything, you've nannied them, you've befriended them . . . you've been on the end of a phone for them day and night for months . . . years very often.

Usually, it had to be said, he got it right, but there had to be the occasional one. This was the first time he could remember, though, that he'd had trouble when the treatment was well over. The child must be getting on for two years old now. The jubilation when she'd been born . . . He loved that moment. Every time it was like the couple were the first people ever to have given birth to a child.

So grateful had the Elficks been that they'd sent him a present on the baby's first birthday. A Georgian silver salver. He rather treasured it actually. He'd liked this couple more than most. This latest development was all most upsetting.

The Mercedes flashed its lights goodnight and he pushed open the door between the garage and the kitchen.

'I'm home,' he called.

'Hi, darling. I'm on the phone,' his wife's voice called from upstairs. 'Down in a minute.' He could smell baking. Illuminated behind the oven's glass door, something delicious was browning; bubbling and glistening in an oval glass dish.

He breathed slowly in and out again. He could handle this. There was bound to be the odd occasion when things went a bit awry.

Almost by definition the patients he dealt with were in an emotional soup of some sort – a mixture of hope and despair most of the time – and eventually if – when – things went right, euphoria. It was the euphoria he lived for. That moment when the mother and her partner would fling their arms around his neck, weeping tears of joy and gratitude. He was Superman. He was the Great Creator . . .

He'd brought forty-four babies into the world now. Forty-four little individuals who would never have made it on to the planet had it not been for him. He'd have a lavish party when the fiftieth arrived. Make sure the press knew about it too. His legacy to the world. His reason for being. His footprints in the sand.

In the sitting room he poured himself a dry sherry from the decanter on the sideboard.

He shouldn't have got so friendly with Mark Elfick. It had been difficult not to though. They'd been at Chadwick together. Elfick had spotted an old school photo on the wall in his office. Lionel hadn't been sure he remembered him at all at first. He'd been four years ahead of Mark. But the shared background . . . it was hard to explain, but there was a bond there. Something understood between them.

There were differences too, of course. Elfick had come from

quite a poor background as far as he could gather. What he called a bootstrap kid. A scholarship boy. And scholarship boys tended not to mix with the fee payers. It was a money thing really, he supposed. The backgrounds were too different. Still, the old school thing never really left you.

When the Elfick family became his patients – or clients as they were supposed to be called these days – he was in a position of power from the start. Not just because he was the man who could – if anyone could – give Elfick the family the pair of them wanted so much, but also because he was historically Mark's senior from schooldays.

He rather enjoyed the paternalistic role it gave him. He'd taken him under his wing. Got him membership of his exclusive rackets club at Greenwich – most people had to go on the waiting list for at least two years. As an MCC member, he took Mark along to the occasional cricket match at Lord's. They had shared some enjoyable afternoons over the last three summers. And this was what he got in return. Frankly, he felt let down.

Chapter Eleven

Mark was in defensive mood when he arrived at the rackets club. Jenny had told him of her visit to Lionel's office and he was expecting a showdown. Not that the situation was his fault, he reasoned. Lionel should have kept his mouth shut. But he knew in his heart the doctor had meant well.

Jenny had described how appalled Lionel was to discover that Mark had managed to track the Keegans down. His main concern now was to hang on to the friendship with Lionel. He'd been such a tower of strength for him and Jenny throughout all those fertility treatments and he'd enjoyed maintaining contact with the man after Chloe was born. He could be an egotistical so-and-so, no doubt about that, but Mark had learned to take his boasting with a pinch of salt.

From time to time he and Jenny had spent evenings at the theatre with Lionel and his ex-dancer wife Alice. They had shared dinner parties at each other's houses. Most of all, Mark had taken enormous pleasure in the days out at Lord's and the regular workouts on the squash court. Ironically it had been these sporting outings with Lionel that had helped save his sanity; first of all throughout the years of IVF treatment and then during these last few months while he'd been so obsessed with finding the parents of his biological daughter.

He just hoped he hadn't blown it.

Lionel was leaning on the fireplace in the lounge quaffing some kind of high-energy sports drink from a can and engaged in bantering conversation with three or four other club members, already changed into his sports gear.

He looked up as Mark walked in with his squash bag; brow furrowed in his habitual expression of vague anxiety.

'Ah, Elfick. We're ringing the changes tonight. It's me and Clive against you and Peter.'

There'd be no bonding on the court then. Confrontation from the start.

'Hurry up, we'll see you on court.'

As he struggled into his shorts, Mark could hear the ball thwacking around the court as the other three warmed up.

He was shoving his bag into his locker when the door squeaked open and Lionel's neatly coiffed head appeared around it.

'And when Clive and I have whopped your arses, we need to talk. The bar'll be empty by eight. They'll all be in the TV room in front of the Six Nations final.'

To Mark's resigned irritation, Lionel's prediction for the outcome of their match turned out to be accurate. He and Peter seemed to get weaker and slower as Lionel and Clive grew faster and furiouser and more devious. They lost in forty-seven minutes. A humiliating 9–7, 9–4, 9–2.

Flushed, but damp and refreshed after their showers, Mark and Lionel were alone in the changing room stuffing their sweaty kit back into their bags. Peter and Clive had sprinted off to watch the rugby.

'I bet you a tenner France gets through,' ventured Mark.

'I'm not a betting man,' replied Lionel coolly. 'I'm happier with certainties in my life. Things that don't pretend to be other than they seem.'

'Jenny tells me she's been to see you.'

Lionel crossed to the mirror to smooth a comb through his hair. 'I had hoped for a chance to talk before we met on the squash court tonight, but it's turning into one of those weeks. In fact it's been one of those months so far. For two pins I could chuck it all in and whisk Alice off to the Caymans for good.'

'Things are that bad, are they?' Mark asked Lionel's mirror image.

'Thanks to you, Elfick, yes. Things are that bad.'

It didn't look as though they were going to make it as far as the bar. Mark sat down heavily on the bench and waited for the onslaught, which wasn't long in coming.

'I'm not at all happy with you, old man. I had you down as a reliable, grounded sort of chap but it turns out you're a loose cannon.'

'That isn't fair, Lionel. I don't see why I should be made to feel guilty. You shouldn't have given me the information you did.'

'Damn right I shouldn't. My mistake was not realising how flaky you could be. Not that I gave you much in the way of information anyway. Out of sheer friendship, all I wanted to do was drop a hint that you'd done a worthwhile thing and brought joy and happiness to a sweet and deserving couple. I thought you'd be pleased by that. And you gave me every reason to *think* you were pleased. But you were thoroughly disingenuous, Elfick. You strung me along, every so often asking innocent-sounding questions, hoping to tempt me into telling you more. I hadn't the slightest inkling you were trying to track these people down. I'd have been horrified. When I think of the emotional chaos you could have caused! What if that family had found out what you were doing?'

'They didn't though. I was careful.'

'I don't call it careful, hanging around outside the family's house, watching the comings and goings, following the woman to the park with the child. Actually *talking* to her. I don't call that careful at all.'

'They weren't to know who I was.'

'Mainly because you'd be the last person they'd expect to see; because my team and I did our job and promised – erroneously as it turned out – that they would never know who had donated the embryo they adopted and neither would their identity be revealed.'

'I still don't know why *I* should be made to feel bad when you're the one who was out of order, telling me this baby existed.'

'That's because the last thing I expected from you was this obsessive behaviour. How far were you going to go? What was next? More apparently chance meetings in the park? Strike up some kind of spurious friendship perhaps? How long would it have been before you found yourself telling them who you were; your relationship to their child? It doesn't bear thinking about.'

'I had no intention of doing that. I hadn't actually thought of anything beyond wanting to know that my own flesh and blood was being well cared for.'

'So now that you've seen the family and observed that she *is* well cared for, that's it, is it? Or will you need to make more surreptitious little inspections? What school are they sending her to? What are they dressing her in? Where are they taking her on holiday? What time's her bedtime? What TV programmes are they letting her watch?'

'Look, Lionel, obviously I can't let myself go there, can I? But you opened the door a chink and what else could I do but push it open and have a peep inside? Do you usually give people the information that their donations have been successful?'

'I'm not usually seduced into thinking they're my friends.'

'So it's my fault for being your friend. That's weak, Lionel.'

'Well I've certainly learned my lesson, I can tell you. My concern now is that the Keegans are left alone to get on with their lives without having you peeping through their keyhole all the time. Will you let them do that, Mark?'

Mark stood up and slotted his racket into its case. 'You don't need to worry. I won't be making contact again. Now I can picture the kind of family they are . . . I'd have preferred them to be a little better off, but I can see the mother adores her . . .'

Abruptly, Lionel stood up too, 'And that's exactly why I'm concerned. You want perfection for that child in *your* terms.' He zipped his racket case and swung it across his shoulder. 'I strongly advise you to see a counsellor, Mark. I can recommend a couple of good people for you to see. Or you can find one yourself. Ask your GP to recommend one. But the two people I have in mind are experts on the implications of sperm, egg and embryo donations. They're both terrific.'

'Thank you, but I'll be fine.'

'You really believe you can now nip this fixation in the bud and leave it behind? Get on with your life?'

'Yes, I do. Absolutely. Talking to Jenny about it made a big difference. I feel so much better now that she knows everything. I'm not carrying the burden round on my own any more. It's brought us closer together again. We're both much happier. I'm even managing to get a decent night's sleep.'

'Well I still reckon you need professional help. I'll get Angie to send you the details of the counsellors I mentioned.'

'OK, I'll think about it. Can I buy you a drink?'

'I don't think so. I'll go and check on the rugby score and then get off home. As I said, I've got a lot on my plate at work at the moment.'

'Maybe next Tuesday then?'

'I won't be here next week. I've got a conference in Athens.'

'Another time then?'

'Sure. 'Bye, Mark.'

''Bye Lionel.'

Part Two
2007

Chapter Twelve

'Da-ad? Is there any chance of getting my own pony for my birthday?'

'Chloe, no. We've been through this a hundred times. There's nowhere to keep it for a start. It's out of the question. You *know* that.'

Chloe could fairly be called pony mad. Ponies were her reason for getting out of bed each day. Every two or three weeks, on a Saturday morning, a school friend and her mother would take her to a riding centre a few miles away. The mother had tried to persuade Jenny to come with them at first, but Jenny always said she had work to catch up on.

The truth she couldn't bring herself to admit to Chloe was that horses frightened her. On the rare occasions she had to get close to one, it would invariably sense her trepidation, roll its eyes, stamp its hooves and lunge its head at her; and no matter how hard she tried to stand her ground, her nerve would crack and she'd have to dodge out of range, trying to look as casual as possible. It was particularly humiliating in the light of her daughter's passion for the creatures.

'Well she's a normal twelve-year-old girl,' Jenny's mother had commented more than once. 'It's usually horses or ballet; one or the other. You were a strange one; you didn't like either of them. You could never be bothered with dolls either.'

Cycling had been Jenny's thing. Bikes, climbing trees and, after the age of eleven, hockey.

Posters and photographs of horses and ponies lined the walls of Chloe's bedroom.

Books with titles like *Getting to Know Your Pony* and *My First Book of Riding and Pony Care* filled her bookshelves.

Magazines about horses and ponies were stacked knee-high on the floor. She refused to throw them away.

And on her window ledge stood her pride and joy: her collection of Julip model horses and riders – Maddie and Montana, Polly and Pandora, Christie and Black Diamond – dressed in their best show gear. The two foals, Puzzle and Cloudy, grazed together riderless, hoping one day for a cosy stable yard and a monogrammed blanket each to keep them warm and dry – birthday and Christmas presents for the future.

Even the laptop Mark and Jenny had bought her for passing the Greenwich High School entrance exam was used mostly for browsing horsey sites on the internet.

Chloe wasn't at all fazed by the answer to her oft-repeated request. She'd anticipated it. It was the first stage in her negotiation strategy.

'Well can I have a gymkhana birthday party then? Please Mum? Dad?'

'And what's a gymkhana birthday party when it's at home?' Mark gave Chloe's abundant ponytail a playful yank. 'Your hair's getting more and more like Mummy's.'

'Ow! Don't *do* that, Dad!' She turned her back on him and addressed Jenny instead. 'Amy Dawson had one for her birthday. She said it was so cool.'

'And where was that, do you know?' asked Jenny.

'The same pony club as I go to with Rosie. Ashington. It only takes about half an hour. You know it. You came with us once.'

'It might be a bit expensive, darling,' said Jenny. 'I'd thought of taking you and five friends to the cinema.'

Chloe took a quick breath in and put her most earnest, adult face on. 'Well, that would be nice, Mummy, but the riding centre would be such fun. And we'd be getting fresh air and exercise instead of sitting in a stuffy cinema. Wouldn't we, Dad? And I don't think it costs all that much . . . and . . . and everyone would pay for their own ticket.'

'What do they lay on for you?'

'All the ponies obviously, Sparkle and Copper and Popeye and Gilda and all the others, and first of all you groom your pony and make it look really smart and there's a rosette for the best turned-out pony. Then you have games like apple-bobbing and egg-and-racket races, which is like egg-and-spoon but a spoon is too small to keep steady on horseback so you have a racket. And then there's party food in the barn afterwards.'

'Do they provide the food?' asked Jenny.

'You can have, like, pizzas delivered or hamburgers. Or you can ask them to do the catering and they do things like chocolate fingers and fish fingers.'

'Chocolate fingers and fish fingers? Strange combination,' commented Mark.

'Finger food, it's called, so maybe sausages would count as well.'

'Ah. I see,' Jenny laughed. 'Finger food usually means food you can pick up with your fingers – like sandwiches and crisps or cake.'

'Anything you don't need a knife and fork for, sweetheart,' added Mark.

'Well,' began Chloe thoughtfully, 'I think we'd *prefer* a pizza delivery and then come back home afterwards. We could have birthday cake here and watch some DVDs and all have a sleepover up in my room with a midnight feast. That's what I'd *like* . . . in an ideal world.' Jenny and Mark caught each other's eye, trying not to smile.

'I see,' said Mark. 'And how many friends would you want to come?'

Chloe counted on her fingers. 'Emily, Rosie, Sophie, me, Megan, Anna, Mercedes, Rona . . . eight. I think it would be eight.'

'Can they all ride?' asked Mark. 'We don't want any broken arms or legs.'

'Sort of. They all like horses. And Rosie and Sophie are like me. They *love* horses. Rosie got lots of Julip stuff for her twelfth birthday by the way. Her mum and dad gave her Toller Down Stables. It costs forty-nine pounds ninety-five. Hint, hint! The others like horses, too, but if they like they can go on a lead rein with Charlotte and Andrew. And Sparkle and Copper are really gentle. They all are, except for Merlin who can be a bit naughty if he thinks he can get away with it.'

'We'd have to take both the cars,' said Jenny. 'Five in each, including us driving.'

Chloe jumped up and down with excitement. 'Yay! And I would get first choice of pony because it's my birthday so I could have Popeye.'

'Now just hold your ponies, sweetheart,' remonstrated Mark. 'We haven't said yes yet. Mum needs to talk to the people at the centre first. They might be booked up for a start. And we'll find out how much they charge. People might not want to spend too much going to someone else's party.'

Chloe looked affronted. 'They won't mind! It's for my birthday. They're my friends. And you and Mum could drive us all to Ashington so their parents won't have to worry about transport.'

'All right, well we'll see.'

'And anyway it's a very important birthday for me. I'm going to be a teenager. I'll be a grown-up.'

'Now there's a thought,' said Jenny.

It turned out to be twenty pounds a head, and free for the birthday girl. Mark had decided to foot the bill for all the children.

'A hundred and forty pounds plus the pizzas and drinks. It's not going to break the bank and it'll give her such pleasure.'

'I just wish Mum could be here,' said Jenny. 'This time last year she was in the kitchen making hundreds of sandwiches, despite the pain she was probably in. This'll be the first birthday Chloe's had without Grandma here.'

He put his arms round her. 'She so adored Chloe. She'll be with us in spirit, I'm sure of that. Looking down on us from somewhere, smiling. Telling us off for not wrapping the presents up properly.'

'Oh God. She'd be right as well. The Toller Down thing. Where did you hide it?'

'In the wardrobe. Don't worry. I'll do it. You've got enough to do.'

It was a flawless early July day. Picture-book. Just enough streaks of wispy white cloud to draw attention to the perfection of an iridescent blue sky.

Jenny had been up until late the previous night spreading emerald-green icing over the large square chocolate cake she'd made to resemble a paddock. Miniature horses she'd borrowed from Chloe's extensive collection grazed on the sugary green grass inside chocolate Curly Wurly fencing.

When finally she put the last finishing touches to it at two o'clock in the morning, piping thirteen tiny, yellow-centred daisies on top, she realised she'd forgotten to buy birthday candles. They'd have to pick some up on the way back from the riding centre.

Eight excited little girls in assorted boots, T-shirts and colourful tracksuit bottoms tumbled out of the two cars and scampered towards the paddock where the ponies waited to be given undivided girly attention for the next hour and a half.

Jenny and Mark ambled to the office to hand over the cheque and find out where the food was to be eaten. A young woman in jodhpurs, who introduced herself as Charlotte, directed them to a creosoted barn overlooking the paddock where they set about decorating the walls with coloured Happy Birthday banners, blowing up balloons and setting out cardboard plates and cups on a long wooden trestle table.

Then, with half an hour to spare before the pizzas arrived, they leaned side by side against the fence and watched the hard-hatted party children on their party-hatted ponies cantering from one end of the paddock to the other, dismounting at one end to pick up an apple, remounting, then aiming the apple – not always successfully – into a bucket of water at the halfway mark before dismounting again at the finishing line.

By the end of the session, everyone seemed to have been the winner of something, judging by the rosettes of various colours each child had pinned on to her person by Charlotte.

With impeccable timing, just as the ponies were being stabled and petted, a boy arrived on a motorbike with a pillion load of pizza boxes.

Next on the agenda, the drive back home for birthday cake, present-giving and the rest of the evening in front of the DVD player.

'Take your boots off . . . you're putting mud all over the seats . . . oh what the heck.'

Mark at the wheel of his new pride and joy – a black Toyota Prius hybrid which ran on a combination of electric and petrol power – and Jenny following behind in the family's old blue Peugeot estate, they set off in convoy back towards Blackheath.

Fifteen minutes down the road, Jenny saw the Prius's left indicator flash and Mark swung into a service road, stopping alongside a parade of shops. Jenny pulled in behind him.

She lowered the window as he strolled towards her, smiling. His waist had expanded to a more cuddlesome shape lately, but she didn't mind that. He was relaxed and happy and that was what mattered. His hairline was beginning to recede, and there were hints of grey among the familiar wiry brown curls. She felt a stab of tenderness for him, together with a dangerously smug appreciation of how lucky she was, after seventeen years of marriage, to be married to a man she loved as much now as when they first met. Maybe more so.

'Any particular colour for the candles?'

'No – whatever they've got. I'll leave it to you.'

Pulling comical faces at the high-spirited occupants of both cars, he disappeared into a newsagent's.

Mark scanned the cramped, chaotic little shop until he found a packet of A4 envelopes. They weren't the best quality but they'd do for the parking ticket appeal he needed to send off tonight. There wasn't a great deal of choice on the birthday candle front either, so he settled for two packets of pink ones and joined the queue at the till.

An elderly man was taking an age finding the right change for a six-pack of lager and a pack of mild Cheddar cheese, peering intently down at his hand as if willing the coins to identify their value. Bored with waiting, the girl at the cash desk had drifted into a world of her own, gazing out of the window.

Mark tried not to look at the row of chocolate bars under the counter at chest height. He needed to lose at least half a stone. And there'd be cake back at the house. Beneath the sweets were ranged various local papers, journals and children's magazines. Was the latest *Pony* magazine out yet, he wondered idly?

The elderly man, having finished his transaction at last, shambled out of the shop. The rest of the queue shuffled forward a few inches. Beside Mark's elbow now was the latest edition of the *Kent Mercury*. Smiling from the front page was an out-of-focus photograph of a woman. She reminded him of someone. He didn't immediately connect the picture with the paper's headline: HEALTH VISITOR FIGHTS FOR LIFE AFTER FRENZIED KNIFE ATTACK.

It took a few more seconds for the penny to drop. And then everything ground to a halt.

'Next please.' The girl at the till was looking in his direction. The woman behind him in the queue gave him a friendly nudge.

'Your turn now.'

His turn?

Giving up on politeness, the woman tutted impatiently and reached in front of him to plonk her collection of purchases down by the till. The cashier totted them up in a flurry of electronic beeps, a twenty-pound note was handed over, some small change returned and the woman left the shop, sharing with the girl a conspicuous eye-roll to heaven.

Mark saw his own shirt-sleeved arm reach out to pick up the newspaper.

As the next customer stepped pointedly round him to be served, he stared disbelievingly at the page, trying to stop the words dancing crazily in front of his eyes.

```
Disabled mother of three Miss Sally Hart, 29,
and her health visitor Mrs Elinor Keegan, 39,
```

> were last night fighting for their lives with
> multiple stab wounds at West Kent Hospital.

The picture *was* of Elinor Keegan. He forced himself to read on.

> Mrs Keegan's husband, Daniel, raised the alarm
> when she failed to return to their home in
> Simmons Road, Fulrow Green early that evening
> and the two women were found by police officers
> when they broke into Miss Hart's flat in
> Scotfield Road. Police have named as their
> prime suspect Miss Hart's former lover Alex
> Andrews whose car was seen parked nearby
> earlier that afternoon.

At least she was still alive. He'd phone the hospital as soon as he got home.

The Mark who'd strolled into the shop looking happy and relaxed emerged looking pale and tense. Maybe he'd had an argument with someone inside, thought Jenny. Unlike him though.

As Jenny watched from the Peugeot, he took a few steps towards his car, and then stopped, turned and went back inside. Seconds later he emerged again, this time looking sheepish and clutching a copy of *Pony* magazine and a small brown paper bag. He'd evidently forgotten to pick up his purchases having paid for them.

Answering her questioning look with an attempt at a cheery wave and a wink, he climbed back behind the wheel of the Prius. Jenny relaxed. He was fine.

*

With his precious cargo of giggling girls to look after, Mark made a supreme effort to concentrate on his driving for the remaining six miles home to Blackheath. He felt numb now. Best to keep it that way, for the moment at least.

Back at the house, the kitchen filled with excited little girls, Mark left Jenny putting the candles on the paddock cake and crept upstairs with the *Kent Mercury* under his sweater.

Slumped on the down-turned toilet lid, he read the article through again. Who could have done this? So this disabled woman must have been the intended victim and Elinor Keegan had been in the wrong place at the wrong time? That seemed the most feasible explanation.

He couldn't stop staring at her picture. She looked so happy. Her eyes full of life and laughter. Maybe she'd been at a party when the photo was taken. At Christmas perhaps. There was a rosy glow around and behind her which could be firelight – or possibly fairy lights.

She didn't look much older than she had in the park that Saturday eleven years ago. He wished he could have seen her smile like that. He found himself daydreaming about the Keegans and the Elficks, sharing little celebrations, Easters, Christmases, birthdays, Mothering Sundays . . . one united, extended family. He remembered the lanky man with the ponytail, bounding down from his van with that daft puppy. Poor guy.

He dialled directory enquiries on his mobile phone and asked for West Kent Hospital.

The ward nurse sounded weary and guarded.

'I'm afraid I can't tell you anything about Mrs Keegan unless you are family.'

He just stopped himself saying 'I am family.' She might mention the call to the husband, who was bound to be there.

Instead he said, 'I understand, but I'm a close friend of the family. Can you just tell me how seriously she's been injured?'

'I can only tell you what we've released to the press. She's critical but stable. We'll know more by tomorrow morning.'

'Right. Thank you.'

What did 'critical but stable' mean?

He tried to imagine how he'd feel if it were Jenny lying in intensive care. What must Daniel Keegan be going through? And little Leonie. Would she be at her mother's bedside too? She was getting on for eleven now. He couldn't begin to imagine how devastated the little girl must be.

By painful contrast, a wave of excited girlish laughter reached his ears as the living-room door opened below.

'Mark!' Jenny's voice was calling from the foot of the stairs. 'What are you doing? We're going to light the candles.'

'Coming!'

He hid the newspaper under the wash basket, unlocked the bathroom door and ran downstairs in time to sing the birthday song to his radiantly happy daughter.

Chapter Thirteen

'You were restless last night.'

'Yes. Sorry. That wine we had last night, I think. Rioja tends to give me indigestion.'

'I did try to remind you.'

'You should have been more assertive with me.'

Jenny laughed. 'Like that would have made a difference! You were determined to down most of the bottle. I only had a glass and a half.'

'And the girls were still giggling and gossiping over their so-called midnight feast well after one in the morning, so that didn't help.'

'At least they're sleeping late this morning. We get a bit of peace for a change.'

He enjoyed Sundays usually. Slow, lazy mornings with the newspapers, a bit of idle pruning and weeding in the garden, a late, leisurely Sunday lunch . . .

Today, though, the hours stretched ahead of him; time to be passed somehow. He went through the motions of chewing the toast and marmalade Jenny had put in front of him, but gave up after half a piece. There was no point. It was like eating sawdust. He dropped the remains in the bin surreptitiously while she grazed over the *Sunday Times* colour supplement.

'I'll just stretch my legs in the garden I think. I'll take the phone out with me. I promised to ring a client.'

She looked up. 'Are you OK? You do look tired.'

'Me? No, I'll be fine. Probably the thought of all the work I've got to do this week. Got a bit of a heavy one coming up.'

'I could help you out in the shop for a couple of days if you like. I've more or less finished Maggie Bright's living room now. Just some curtain ties and a few extra cushions to buy.'

'Thanks, darling, but I'll be fine. The new assistant's turning out to be quite a reliable chap actually. Learning fast, thank the Lord. Sweet of you to offer though.'

She lifted her face to return his kiss and went back to the *Sunday Times*.

He phoned the hospital from the swing seat at the end of the garden. The news was much the same. Still 'critical but stable'.

Back in the house, he went to the computer and Googled the phrase. Wikipedia had a definition for critical: 'high risk of death without continuous intervention or life support.' It went on to say that definitions for a range of terms like, 'grave condition', 'extremely critical condition', 'critical but stable condition', 'serious but stable condition', 'satisfactory condition' and 'fair condition' varied among hospitals. He just prayed that West Kent Hospital's definition of 'stable' meant 'not expected to get any worse'.

Hang on in there, Elinor.

Elinor Keegan would have been an ideal health visitor, he was sure. Dangerous job though. He wouldn't have wanted his own wife to do it. He'd often heard about attacks on health visitors, held up at knifepoint by someone hoping to find drugs in their tote bags, or caught up in patients' domestic disputes.

At least the cops seemed to know who they were looking for. He hoped they'd caught the bastard by now.

At the kitchen table, Jenny was leafing through the news pages on the way to the crossword when the name Keegan caught her eye. It was funny how a significant name could jump out at you, even amid acres of quite dense print.

She'd never let on to Mark, but over the years she had thought about little Leonie Keegan so often. As a toddler, did she demand to have the same favourite stories read to her over and over again like Chloe had? Had she loved to pedal her tricycle like the wind up and down on the pavement outside her house? And a year or two later, had she cantered tirelessly round the garden pretending to be a glossy black mare like Black Beauty?

Perhaps she, too, had had a passion for 'My Little Pony', replaced later by a hankering for Julip model horses and all the accessories.

Six years ago, she'd pictured Leonie's first day at primary school; had she screamed blue murder those first few mornings when her mother walked away and out of the gate? How had she got on with the annual SAT exams? Did she have that talent for maths which could only have come from Mark's father? Did she wear her copper-coloured hair like Chloe did, tied back in a ponytail? It would be her twelfth birthday in five months' time. She'd be coming to the end of her first year at secondary school. Was she happy? Did she have plenty of friends?

Coming out of her daydream, Jenny ran her eyes casually over the story. DISABLED WOMAN KNIFED TO DEATH IN OWN HOME, read the headline halfway down the page.

Stabbings had got so common, they weren't big news any more. Why did they allow shops to sell these terrible knives? It was illegal to carry them and yet legal to buy them. It was crazy.

And this poor woman was wheelchair bound; struck down with motor neurone disease two years ago. How could anyone stab a woman in a wheelchair? It must have been some kind of crime of passion.

She read on. Yes, the police seemed sure the attacker was the woman's ex-boyfriend. He'd stabbed her more than twenty times, and she had died from her injuries shortly after arrival at the hospital. Even worse, her two young sons, both under five, had witnessed the stabbing. The grandmother was quoted as saying her daughter had been determined to look after the children at home as long as she could, despite the limitations of her disability. 'We are all devastated,' she said. The article went on to say that a regular carer had been helping her with the children.

Suddenly Jenny stiffened, her mug of coffee tilting, forgotten, in her hand.

```
... Elinor Keegan, was also stabbed several
times in the stomach, chest and neck.
```

Jenny managed to control her trembling enough to put the mug back on the table.

```
Police broke into the flat to find Miss Hart
and Mrs Keegan bleeding profusely from their
injuries and the children crying inconsolably.
Both women were taken to West Kent Hospital
where Miss Hart died without regaining
consciousness. Mrs Keegan's condition is said
to be critical.
```

'Do we need anything to go with the lamb for dinner? I'm going to the shop.'

At the sound of Mark's voice, Jenny sprang to her feet, jogging the table so violently that her mug tipped over, spilling coffee across the open newspaper. 'Damn!' She folded the paper quickly and scrunched it up in both hands. 'There goes the crossword.' She crossed the kitchen and stuffed the dripping pages in the bin. 'Couldn't get to grips with it anyway. I hate that setter.'

'Sorry, Jen. My fault. I made you jump. Did it spill on you?'

'No. No. It's OK. Just the paper.'

'Anything we need then?'

Jenny levered her derailed mind back on to the tracks. 'Don't think so, darling.' Yes, that sounded fairly normal. 'Oh, stock cubes. Lamb stock cubes. I think we're out.' She looked in the cupboard. Anything to keep moving, keep acting natural. She picked a little green packet off the shelf and rattled it. 'There's one left. That'll do for today but better get another one anyway.'

'OK. When are the kids being picked up?'

'I told their parents any time around twelve.' She looked at her watch. 'I'd better go and wake them up, I suppose. It's gone eleven now.'

'I'll leave you to it then. See you later.'

She checked her watch again. The kids could be left for another half an hour or so. She needed some time to marshal her thoughts.

She couldn't tell Mark. She simply couldn't. What an appalling, shocking thing to happen. He'd been so good keeping the lid on his feelings this last eleven years. But if Elinor Keegan died and he found out about it, she was sure it would come flying off again. He'd be shattered. He'd want to find out how the little girl was coping. She must be distraught, poor child. He'd want to see if he could help. She knew he would, because that was how she was feeling herself, and she wasn't the one whose emotions had verged on obsession.

The best course of action for now would be to keep tabs on the situation and when – please, when! – Elinor Keegan recovered, everything would carry on as it had before. She'd phone the hospital this afternoon and see if they'd tell her anything.

If the poor woman did die, she would have to find a way to tell Mark. It would be too important a piece of information to keep from him. She just prayed it wouldn't come to that. Elinor would pull through, surely. She must.

Chapter Fourteen

Mark waited until the digits on the clock at his bedside flipped to 05:00. At last he could call a welcome end to another long, hot, restless night.

He slipped quietly out of bed and gathered up yesterday's clothes from the back of the white-painted rattan armchair under the window. He'd get dressed in the bathroom. He didn't want to wake Jenny. She'd need to know why he was getting up so early.

Vulcan the cat opened one eye in mild surprise as Mark crept into the kitchen. This was unexpectedly early for human company. Tail vertical like a pennant, bottom in the air, the tortoiseshell stretched both forepaws out luxuriously in front of him, yawned, then see-sawed forwards to stretch the hind ones, before stepping delicately from his padded bed to launch an attack on Mark's ankles, weaving a hazardous figure-of-eight around them as his owner filled the kettle from the tap.

Mark diverted the cat's attentions with a fresh bowl of food and took his tea out to the garden.

With the pinkish glow of the just-risen summer sun glinting on the grass, and the exuberant twittering of a congregation of birds in the trees above him, the constant drone of the daytime traffic yet to begin, it was hard to believe anything could be wrong in the world.

He was loath to shatter the moment. Perhaps it had all been a nightmare. A huge mistake. Elinor Keegan was right this moment sleeping beside her husband at the house in Fulrow Green; little Leonie in her tiny front bedroom above the scarlet front door, dreaming the sweet, untroubled dreams of childhood. If only wishing could make it so.

Hunching his shoulders over his phone, he located the hospital's number.

Two hours later, Chloe and Jenny were still finishing their breakfast when he picked up his briefcase, kissed them both goodbye and left, ostensibly for work.

The traffic was always particularly heavy on a Monday morning, but at least he was going in the opposite direction to most of it, heading away from town.

'No change in Mrs Keegan's condition,' was all the duty nurse had said on the phone. Why did they have to be so damned unforthcoming? What harm could it do to be a little more informative? Perhaps at the hospital he'd be able to glean a better idea of how things were. He could try and buttonhole a passing nurse or doctor. He knew he couldn't reveal who he was or do anything practical to help, and yet he needed to be there. He couldn't have explained it, even to himself.

Maybe it was some primal instinct that impelled him to be near his own genetic daughter, at this terrible time in her life. Could he feel a pain in his chest? He put a hand under his jacket, massaging the left side of his upper chest with the heel of his hand.

*

The hospital seemed fairly quiet. Breakfast was long over, and now perhaps there was a lull before the doctors started their rounds.

Mark was only guessing. He'd been lucky enough to have spent very little time in hospitals. There'd been the visits to Jenny's poor mum dying of colon cancer, but the disease had been so aggressive, she hadn't lasted long. They'd all been grateful she hadn't had to suffer a prolonged and painful death. The suddenness had meant it was more of a shock though, especially to Jenny.

He pulled his shirtsleeve over his wrist and pushed the lift call button through the material. He'd forgotten how much he hated these places. They brought out the hypochondriac in him. He always expected to pick up some terrible contagion.

Standing in the lift next to a porter with what looked like a skip full of hospital waste on a trolley, Mark tried not to breathe in. Intensive care was on the fifth floor. He stepped out as the metal doors parted, gasping for air. Damn. He'd probably breathed evil bacteria right down to the depths of his lungs now.

It wasn't quite half past nine. A sign downstairs in the foyer had announced visiting hours from ten a.m. Would they allow visitors on an intensive care ward anyway? He hoped not. They might want to usher him to Elinor's bedside. Disastrous if the husband was there. Besides, she'd have no idea who he was and certainly wouldn't be in a fit state to be told.

All he wanted was to find out how she was. And, illogical though it seemed, just by being there, to somehow add weight to her chances of pulling through. Diffidently, Mark approached the heavy pine double doors to the ward and pushed. They were locked, of course. He pressed a switch on the right-hand door jamb. Hearing a muted buzz from just inside the ward, he waited.

Through the wire-glazed panel he saw a middle-aged nurse emerge a few yards along the corridor. He hoped she wasn't the uncooperative one who'd spoken to him on the phone earlier. She paused to tuck something into the top pocket of her uniform, frowning at the door in an effort to see who it was on the other side, then marched purposefully towards him.

Surprised by a stab of panic, it took an effort of will to stand his ground. What should he say? The ward sister turned a latch and opened the door a few inches. She was probably a little younger than he was but looked haggard, the pallor of her complexion indicating the need for a week or two's holiday in the sun.

'We don't allow visitors up here I'm afraid.'

'I've come to find out about . . . could you just tell me how Elinor Keegan is?'

'Are you press or family?'

'I'm family. Mrs Keegan is my daughter's mother.' It felt as if he were denying Jenny and Chloe, and yet it was the truth.

The nurse's demeanour took on a more sympathetic aspect. Putting the door on the latch, she stepped out from the ward to stand beside him.

'I'm sorry.' She glanced back along the corridor, then took a few steps towards a noticeboard opposite the lifts. Mark followed her. 'Mrs Keegan died an hour ago,' she told him quietly. 'She'd been doing so well, considering her injuries, but . . . I'm afraid she lost the fight. I'm really sorry.'

'Are you sure? Elinor Keegan?' She could have got it wrong. They got things wrong at hospitals all the time, didn't they? He had a fleeting absurd impulse to run into the ward through the unlocked door and see for himself.

'Her husband is with her.' The frown had returned to the

nurse's face, but more puzzled than hostile. 'You must be her . . . previous husband?'

'Oh . . . ah . . . no. We didn't . . . er, get married . . . in fact.'

Unconsciously clutching his breast again, he slumped against the noticeboard, inadvertently tearing one of the announcements from its drawing pin.

'Why don't you come to the quiet room and sit down for a moment?' Her voice was softer with solicitude now.

'Thanks.' Dazedly, he followed her to a grey painted door on the other side of the elevator lobby. She opened it and he walked obediently inside.

'I'll get someone to bring you a cup of tea.'

Mark sat down heavily on one of three grey bouclé-covered armchairs and sunk his head into his hands. He hadn't believed it would happen. He had been so sure she would pull through. 'Lost the fight'. She'd gone. She'd left Leonie with only her father; that man with the frayed jeans and rock band T-shirts and dreadful pun-covered van.

He raised his head again, vaguely taking in the sad little room he found himself in. Everything was pastel grey and blue. A framed print of a dreary, misty landscape hung on one wall. It wasn't straight. Some obscure part of his brain nagged at him to level it up.

He had to get out of here. He wrenched open the door and stumbled across the passageway to the lifts, pressing both the Down and the Up buttons. Whichever came first.

After what seemed an interminable wait, a lift arrived. Mark stepped forward and then back again to let two people out: a chaplain, in black cleric's vest and dog collar over dark trousers, and a schoolgirl . . . Chloe! No, not Chloe. Wrong school blazer. Navy blue with gold piping and a castle stitched on to the pocket. The same rust-coloured curly hair but a little shorter.

Bobbed. He must have made some kind of sound as they walked past him because the chaplain glanced over his shoulder at him with a surprised look on his face.

The lift doors were closing. Coming to his senses, Mark jammed his arm between them, forcing them to judder open again to let him through. His last sight of Leonie was standing stoically next to the chaplain at the door of the ward; neat white socks and sensible black shoes beneath the calf-length grey pleated skirt, a tissue crumpled in her small fist, waiting to be let in to see her mother for the last time.

Mark arrived home about four in the afternoon. He'd gone to the shop but couldn't face opening for business. He told Ian, his recently hired assistant, that he was feeling unwell – which was true.

'Take the day off, Ian. I'm just not up to working today.'

'Are you sure? Why don't you go home, Mr Elfick? I can hold the fort for you here.'

Mark looked at his assistant's comfortable young face. So much experience still to be written on those well-meaning but bland features.

'Go and enjoy the sunshine,' he said wearily. 'Take your girlfriend out to lunch on the river or something. Life's very short, Ian. Who knows what's round the corner. Have some fun while you've got the chance.'

'All right. Thanks, Mr Elfick. Nice idea. I'll take her to the Tate, I think. Oh, and talking of galleries, what about your appointments today? You're expected at Berkeley Square this afternoon to discuss what you want to take to that fair in New York next year.'

'Oh hell. Cliff Bradshaw and the appalling Glenda. Would you give them a call before you go and make my excuses? Tell

Cliff I'll be in touch next week to fix another meeting. Oh, and call me Mark by the way.'

He watched Ian negotiate the cobbled passageway on the way to his unexpected lunch date, attired, despite the July weather, in full three-piece suit and carefully shined black lace-up shoes. Surely a twenty-five-year-old doesn't naturally want to dress like that? He must think it's the way an antiques dealer's assistant should look. He'd have to have a word with him.

Mark turned the sign on the door to 'closed' and sat down in an Edwardian oak swivel chair under the wary gaze of a life-sized leather pig. All these ancient artefacts he'd sought and fought for. All the clever deals he'd done. None of them seemed important now. And yet there was something comforting about the resolute existence of these solid old things. Tall majestic clocks still ticked, undaunted by the tyranny of the time they told. Silver table-pieces shone, their decorative features only enhanced by the smoothing effect of two centuries of polishing. The French Art Nouveau mahogany breakfront cabinet he'd been so proud of finding in Paris faced him against the opposite wall. Stolid, immutable. An affirmation that permanence and longevity was possible . . . for some things.

There he remained with his thoughts until a chorus of clocks told him it was three o'clock. Four hours of his life had somehow disappeared.

He let himself in through the back door and his stomach lurched. On the kitchen table lay the *Kent Mercury*. Jenny must have found it under the wash basket. Damn. She'd only seen Elinor for a minute or two eleven years ago. Would she have recognised her from the picture? He almost hadn't himself.

He glanced at the happy photograph again, but only fleetingly. It was too painful. Where was Jenny?

125

More from habit than the need for a cup of coffee, he crossed to the sink and filled the kettle.

'She's died, Mark,' said a quiet voice behind him. Jenny stood pale-faced in the doorway.

He put the kettle down and turned to face her. 'Yes. I know,' he said.

Chapter Fifteen

Dan Keegan cursed. He couldn't get the gear stick into reverse. Neither by force nor by coaxing. The synchro had been threatening to go for a few weeks now. He put his foot back on the clutch and tried pushing the stick forwards. It wouldn't go into first either. He'd have to get home somehow using second instead. If he could get out of this parking space, that was.

He'd have to buy another van; find the money for it somehow. He usually liked to sell his vans before they sold out on him. This one had beaten him to it, it seemed. Now he would be late home again.

In the three months since Elinor died, he had been working longer hours than ever. It was Sod's Law. Half his regulars seemed to have had some emergency or other. He couldn't let them down. He couldn't afford to.

He'd always valued the independence of working for himself. When he'd done his apprenticeship, he'd hated being told what to do, what time to start, when to finish, when to take a lunch break . . . he couldn't wait to get out on his own. Now, for the first time he regretted being a one-man band. He had only himself to rely on.

If it weren't for Leonie he wouldn't have cared. He could go and live like a hermit somewhere. Back to Kerry, maybe, where he'd been born and spent the first fifteen years of his life, before his parents split up; where his sister still lived.

But his responsibility now was to his daughter. She had seven years of secondary school ahead of her. And maybe university or college after that. She was a bright kid. He couldn't let her miss out on things because Dad didn't have enough money.

Today had begun on the outskirts of Maidstone with an airlock in a central heating system which looked as though it dated back to Biblical times. Two hours of wrestling with the bleed nuts on nine rusting old radiators had been followed by a call to Sevenoaks to deal with a clapped-out boiler pump, then to a blocked macerator in Orpington. He had managed to carve himself a ten-minute break for a ham and cheese baguette in the van, before spending the afternoon in the dingy attic of a large detached house in Borough Green installing a new shower cabinet for a pinch-faced woman in her sixties who didn't even offer him a cup of tea.

Finally, just as he'd been preparing to go home, the Maidstone client from the morning had called Dan's mobile to say the airlock had come back and he'd schlepped the twelve miles back there to spend four more hours draining the system of several gallons of black gunk before repressurising it.

It was well past seven. And now the damn van had turned against him. It was all too much. He could have cried; something he wasn't used to doing. Until recently.

At first, after Ellie was killed, he had held himself together. He'd had to, for Leonie. The kid was trying so hard to keep her own emotions together, probably for Dan's sake. He couldn't fall apart. It wasn't until nine weeks after the funeral that he had finally allowed the tears to flow.

It had been a Friday evening. The end of a long week. Another long week. He and Leonie had been sitting side-by-side on the sofa in front of the TV, Boot the dog lying on the rug at their feet, trays on their laps, forking the rather good spaghetti Bolognese Leonie had made into their mouths.

The eleven year old had taken on her mother's enthusiasm for cooking and, like Elinor, had learned to make meals that could be kept warm in the oven if, as was too often the case, he came home late from work.

This particular evening, he arrived back a little before eight and went upstairs as usual to shed his working denims and shower off the pungent mixed aroma of metal and drains he usually brought home with him.

Seeing him return to the living room, scrubbed and relaxed now in his favourite baggy karate trousers and ancient white sweatshirt (wearing anything white was a luxury he couldn't, for obvious reasons, indulge himself in during his working day), his damp hair slicked back behind his ears, Leonie got up from her homework to put the pasta on to boil.

'I got two DVDs out of the school library,' she announced from the kitchen. 'They've just got some new ones in. I got *Wallace and Grommit* and *March of the Penguins*.'

'Right. Well we'll watch one while we eat your delicious spag bol then.'

'I had a fight with Sonia James to get *March of the Penguins*,' Leonie had continued, as Dan stood in the doorway watching her. 'I was first in the queue and Sonia pushed in and tried to grab it. But then Miss Barnforth said Sonia should let me have it first because my mummy had died and she should be nice to me.'

'Oh.' Miss Barnforth didn't sound the soul of tact exactly.

'I said to her it's nothing to do with my mummy. It's just about being fair, that's all. And Miss Barnforth just gave me this sickly smile and patted me on the head. It made me cross, Dad, because it was like Sonia had to *let* me have the DVD because she should feel sorry for me. But I was there first anyway.'

'And Sonia's not your friend in any case, so what happened to Mummy is none of her business, is it?'

'So then I said OK *she* could have it and I'd have it after her, but she wouldn't take it then.'

He swallowed. If only he could protect her. Write the script for her life for the next few weeks and months until the pain had stopped being quite so close to the surface. But there was nothing he could do. She was out there on her own, as he was. In fact she seemed to have coped with everything with more composure and self-possession than he had. She'd handled all the publicity, the children in the playground nudging and whispering; the people who said either too much or nothing at all. She was made of sterling stuff that was for sure. The genes – whoever they belonged to – certainly seemed to be good ones.

But nurture was as significant as nature, and Elinor had been the most wonderful mother. Leonie had picked up so many of her characteristics: strong minded – to the point of stubborn at times – principled, dependable, warm-hearted, but also fantastic company. A great sense of humour and an uncomplaining, easygoing nature.

He'd never been totally happy with Ellie doing that job. The local papers were often reporting stories of attacks on health visitors in some of the rougher areas they had to visit, particularly after dark. But it was typical of Ellie to make light of all that. She'd loved her job; counted most of her clients as personal friends and would have done just about anything for them.

The visit to Sally Hart had been a favour. It hadn't been one of Ellie's scheduled days but the woman had asked her to drop by her flat to witness some legal documents or something. If only Ellie had been just a bit less damned obliging for once . . . made Sally wait until the next time she was due to work there.

He and Leonie had supported each other through the funeral, with the help of a few close friends. And his sister Bernadette and her little boy, Fergal, had come over from Ireland for a couple of weeks to cook and clean for them, comfort them and generally keep everything together. School holidays were about to begin for the summer and Leonie couldn't be left on her own all day.

After two weeks at home, he'd started working again. He couldn't afford to lose clients.

Then, at the end of September, just as he and Leonie had begun forging a new routine for themselves without Ellie, the court case had brought the whole thing back on to the front pages again.

The guy had pleaded guilty but insane, which made the whole process more long-drawn-out than it should have been. And of course there were two charges of murder; the stabbing to death of the fiancé could be said to be a crime of passion . . . But Elinor had just been in the way, basically.

If she'd only turned up an hour earlier or an hour later, it might have been the three of them sitting on the sofa this Friday evening, eating spaghetti Bolognese and watching a DVD.

To Dan's ineffable relief, the Andrews character had been found guilty of both murders and sentenced to fifteen years on each count. The lawyers had warned him that Andrews might appeal against the length of the sentence by pressing his plea of insanity, but Dan had put that out of his mind. What mattered was that the guy had been convicted and was safely shut away in a Category B jail. Justice had been done. His and Leonie's loss acknowledged at least.

The strange thing was, he couldn't bring himself to hate the man. Ellie's murder had been so random, so impersonal. He

blamed Fate, in a way, more than he blamed Andrews. He wished
he believed in God. He could have blamed Him then.

Gradually all the fuss around the court hearing had subsided
too, and everyone around them was getting on with their lives as
if nothing had happened. Even Bernadette had stopped calling
every two days, reducing her contact to an average of once a
fortnight. He and Leonie would have to pick up the pieces of
their lives as best they could, in their own way and in their own
time.

Watching his little girl bustling around the kitchen now, Boot
on the cruise for scraps, doing his best to trip her up, he wanted
more than anything to sweep her up in his arms, tucking her
chubby little legs around his waist like he used to. But the mood
wasn't right. He wouldn't want her to think he was feeling sorry
for her. She'd just been saying how she hated that. All he'd found
to say was something like:

'So now you've been made to feel you should be grateful for
special treatment which you didn't ask for and don't want.'

'Yes. Like I'm teacher's pet or something. Oh well.' Leonie
shrugged. 'Daddy, can you strain the pasketti?' She'd called it that
since she was little and it had been the family's way of
pronouncing the word ever since. Like 'remang' for meringue.

She opened the fridge and took out a can of lager for him
and a Sprite for herself while he stirred the pasta into the sauce
she'd made and dished it up rather clumsily on to their two
plates.

'Right. All set.' Followed by a disconsolate Boot, nothing
edible having landed on the kitchen floor, Dan carried the tray
into the sitting room. 'What's it to be then? *Wallace and Grommit*
or *March of the Penguins*?'

'You can choose, Dad. You've had a hard day.'

'Hey . . . you fought for them, you choose.'

'I know, we'll dip for it.' She put the two DVD cases side by side on the coffee table and pointed a biro-stained little index finger at each in turn. 'Ickle ockle, chockle bockle, ickle ockle out. Hooray! *March of the Penguins* is the winner!'

Smiling, he settled his tray on his lap and watched Leonie crossing the room to load the DVD. She felt responsible for him, he could tell.

He wished he could find a way to make her see that she should be putting herself before him. At a time when she should be having the most carefree time of her life, she seemed to be more of a parent than he was. She shouldn't be trying to take the place of her mother.

Every Saturday morning she would write out a shopping list and then the two of them would take the van into the town centre and push a trolley round Sainsbury's together. When they'd ticked off everything on the list, they'd park the trolley by the cafeteria and have a cappuccino and chocolate chip muffin each before paying the bill and heading for home.

Yes, he'd have fallen apart without her. There was no doubt about that. She sat back down on the sofa next to him.

'I'm sorry you're on your own so much, Leo.'

'That's OK, Dad. I don't mind really.'

'Are you quite sure you're OK? Because I could always turn jobs down after five or six o'clock.'

'No, Daddy, honest. I've got lots of stuff to do. Anyway, we need the money, don't we? Specially if you're going to take me to Disneyland Paris for my birthday like you promised.' He put an arm round her and squeezed her shoulders.

'You're just the best girl a dad could want. You know that, don't you?'

'And you're the best dad, so we're quits.' She wriggled out of his grasp. 'Come on then. Press "play".'

He pointed the remote control at the DVD player and flipped through the opening preamble.

'Lots of people in my class saw this in the cinema last year. It's supposed to be really cool.'

'Well it would be, wouldn't it? It's the Arctic.'

'Very funny. Actually it's the *Antarctic* Daddy.' She nudged him with a sharp little elbow in the ribs. He retaliated by pinch-tickling her just above her right knee.

'Careful,' she squeaked. 'Stop it! I'm spilling my drink.'

Dan wasn't halfway through his spaghetti before he was wishing *Wallace and Grommit* had won the 'ickle ockle' dip.

Having expected a pretty straightforward wildlife docu-drama about penguins, he was unprepared for the emotional hammer blow he was about to be dealt.

It was a film to give anyone a lump in the throat under the best of circumstances, but for Dan the resonances were almost unbearable from the start. Such hardship in the pursuit of producing one baby.

The two of them sat enthralled, watching the story of hundreds of Emperor penguins processing doggedly across seventy miles of shifting icy wastes to reach their breeding ground. There, each couple would produce a single egg.

When the time came for each mother to trudge back the seventy miles to the sea to feed herself and bring food back for the coming baby, the egg had to be transferred to the father's care, and passing the egg from her feet to his without letting it come into contact with the ice was a perilous business. When one couple bungled the procedure, and the precious egg they'd been through hell to produce rolled across the snow to a pathetic, freezing death, Dan felt his whole chest constrict with the sadness of it. Putting his tray to one side, he pulled his legs up, tucking his bare feet underneath him. Snuggling against him, riveted to the screen, Leonie let her thumb creep into her mouth.

Not a moment too soon, the mothers returned to the breeding ground, bellies full, just as the chicks were hatching. But some fathers and chicks waited in vain. There was no mother returning. Either the savage cold or the maw of a predator had claimed her life.

Leonie tucked her arm into Dan's and leaned her cheek against his shoulder, both their faces damp.

'Shall we watch the rest of this some other time, Dad?'

Dan cleared his throat. 'If you want to, angel. It's up to you.'

'I don't mind. You say.' Back on the screen the chicks were hatching. 'Oh, they're so cute. Look, Dad.'

He suspected her concern was more for him than herself, although he couldn't be sure. Certainly, he was having a titanic struggle with his emotions.

On the day of the funeral he'd been too busy to dwell much on his own feelings. His main concern, apart from watching out for Leonie, had been to make sure the humanist service went without a hitch: worrying about the poems he'd chosen for Ellie's closest friend and her brother to read, steeling himself for the performance of the short piece he'd chosen to play on his saxophone, terrified that his fingers would tremble too much to be able to play at all; not to mention repeating endless instructions on the mobile phone to various friends and family members who'd got themselves lost trying to find the crematorium.

He'd had to hold himself together for Leonie's sake. He couldn't subject her to the sight of her father howling like a baby. He'd had to seem strong.

Since then, the deluge of grief he'd been expecting to swallow him up had somehow failed to happen. He had just felt numb.

He'd worried that maybe something was wrong with him. If he couldn't weep for her loss, perhaps he hadn't loved Ellie as dearly as he'd thought.

But there, out of nowhere, sitting on the sofa in front of this DVD with the remains of Leonie's spaghetti Bolognese on his lap, it had happened. The dam broke. A searing pain had surged through his body, grasping at his heart, constricting his lungs, cramping his larynx, jabbing at the backs of his eyes, twisting inside his very eardrums.

Enough of his capacity for rational thought had stayed with him to give him the strength to hold on; to wait until Leonie had gone to bed before he allowed himself finally to let go of the pent-up grief he hadn't until now known how to express.

Later that night, as Leonie slept, he'd lain in his bed heaving painful, racking sobs into his pillow. But as he did so, he became aware of another feeling: a bass note deep down amidst the anguish. It was a sense of relief. He *could* feel. He *could* grieve. He had loved Ellie so much. He would always love her. And he would endure this and live on without her to take care of their daughter.

Chapter Sixteen

'Give me death or divorce any day!' Bangles clanking on her wrists, Annabel was grappling ineffectually with the black bin-liner she'd just torn off the roll Jenny had brought with her. 'Nothing could be as stressful as this. What on earth made me think it was a good idea to move?'

Jenny removed the bag from her friend's hands, adroitly separated the edges between moistened index finger and thumb and handed it back. 'You've landed a job to die for in Dorset, that's why.'

'I must have been mad. How are we going to have all this lot packed up by tomorrow morning?'

'Well, you've been here a long time,' said Jenny, looking around the huge, familiar cluttered living room that had always looked like a cross between an artist's garret and a Turkish nightclub. 'You've collected a lot of . . . um . . . stuff.'

'I thought it could all go to the charity shop, but now that it comes to it, I can't part with anything. Look at all these books.' She gestured at the recesses either side of the chimneybreast, filled from floor to ceiling with shelves, sagging now beneath the weight of several hundred books of all shapes and sizes. Paperback fiction, hardback books on wildlife and historical journeys, biographies of old Hollywood stars, huge glossy volumes on art and artists. 'I'll probably never open any of them again but they're my friends. They're the story of my life. My context.'

'All right, keep them for now, then. See how you feel when you're unpacking them the other end.'

'And I can't give my records to Oxfam either.' She stooped to open the double doors of the long oriental-style cabinet under the window, pulling out a fistful of albums at random. 'I haven't even got a record player now, but the memories . . . Wow, look, Jenny, Prince. Remember?' Wafting her arms above her head, she wiggled her jeans-clad hips from side to side.

'"Purple rain, pu-urple ra-in."'

Jenny laughed. If it hadn't been for the white streaks that had started appearing in her friend's unruly dark hair over the last year or so, she could have been seventeen again.

Annabel shuffled through the records she was holding.

'*Thriller*. He may be a weirdo, Michael Jackson, but he's such an entertainer. Oh and Queen, look! Brian, I love you still!' She kissed Brian May's white-suited image on the front cover, and then hugged the dog-eared album tight to her chest, causing her breasts to bulge above the strappy vest she was wearing. 'Do you remember that night at Wembley Stadium?'

Jenny's face lit up. 'Oh God! That was just the best concert I've ever been to.'

'1986.'

'I'll never forget Freddie Mercury, just kind of materialising out of the smoke, or dry ice or whatever it was, brandishing the microphone over his head . . . The sound literally *hit* you. Every bone in my whole body was vibrating. It was like being swallowed whole!'

'And thousands and thousands of people, all hot and sweaty,

all singing "We Will Rock You" and waving and swaying. Like one big animal. We were right up near the front. How did we manage that?'

'I think we booked early. We queued for hours to get the tickets, I remember.'

'And the next day was Saturday and we went out together and both bought this album at Our Price.'

'I don't think I've got my copy any more. I had a purge a couple of years ago and replaced all our vinyl with CDs. All the ones worth replacing, anyway. I flogged our records on eBay in a job lot. Mark wouldn't speak to me for a week. Apparently I chucked out some valuable old singles.'

'Didn't he get a say in it?'

'You know what Mark's like. If I'd waited for him to make a decision, they'd be cluttering up our living room to this day. Anyway, I was busy getting my design business off the ground and I needed the space. I was trying to go minimalist at the time. Not that I ever managed it.'

'And how *is* Mark?' ventured Annabel.

'He's doing OK. The murder hit him pretty hard. It hit us both pretty hard, to be honest.'

'That poor little kid.'

'Mark saw Leonie, you know. At the hospital.'

'Really? You never told me!'

'He said it was such a shock. She walked out of the lift in her school uniform, right in front of him. She's got the same hair, he said. A bit shorter, but just like Chloe's.'

'Did Mark speak to Leonie?'

'No. She was with the hospital chaplain. They walked past him on the way to the ward. Heartbreaking.'

Annabel lowered herself on to one of the giant Persian floor cushions that strewed her living-room floor.

'My God. Can you imagine? Your mother stabbed to death like that? Just because she was in the wrong place at the wrong time. So . . . senseless.'

'It's weird, Annabel, but it's brought out this surge of such strong maternal feeling towards her. I so much want to go and give her a huge hug, you know, take her in my arms and stroke her forehead; tell her she's got another mother if she should need one; that I love her. And I do feel I love her. There's this almost physical pulling.' She pressed her hand against her chest. 'I've tried to imagine what it would have been like for Chloe if it had been me that was murdered. But it's impossible of course. And how he must feel too. The father.'

'At least the guy who did it is banged up now. You must be glad to have got some . . . what the hell did people say before someone invented the word "closure"? I can't think of another way of putting it. You know what I mean, anyway.'

'Yes, except that it isn't closure, is it? Not for little Leonie. She's right on the threshold of adolescence. So much ahead of her to deal with without a mother to, you know, be there for her; see her through it. It's too painful to think about.' Jenny scrambled to her feet. 'We'd better get on.'

She picked up a pile of records and put them in the bottom of one of the removal company's cardboard cartons. 'There. We've started. You fill that with the rest of your records and I'll start on the books.'

Chapter Seventeen

It felt just like it had eleven years ago. He was older, possibly a little wiser and had a more expensive car, but the route was almost exactly the same.

The emotions were certainly the same. Excitement mixed with apprehension, self-justification mixed with guilt.

The motivation was the same too. He wanted, he *needed*, to know that his daughter was all right. She'd lost her mother in the most brutal way imaginable. How was she coping? If he could just get a glimpse of her, he'd get an idea. He'd be able to tell just by seeing her, he was sure. His instincts would tell him.

There was always the possibility that the Keegans had moved house. He'd cross that bridge when he came to it. He could ask whoever lived there now for a forwarding address.

It was beginning to get dark as he guided the Prius into Simmons Road. The clocks would be going forward the weekend after next and that would be it. Winter again. Already, a light was on behind the frosted glass strip in number 115's red-painted front door. Another glowed in the window of the little bedroom above it.

The once carefully tended shrubs and perennials in the tiny front garden were looking neglected. The privet hedge bulged untidily over the brick wall and behind it, vying for growing space, peered a couple of gangly evergreens in dire need of pruning. The front gate was stuck in the open position, embedded amongst the shrubbery.

Mark looked at his watch. It was nearly half past six. Leonie would have been home from school for about two hours.

There was no sign of the plumber's van. Until he saw that, he couldn't be certain the Keegans still lived there. He opened his briefcase on the passenger seat next to him and took out a Sudoku puzzle book from a zip section in the front.

It was a little after a quarter past eight when some sixth sense made him wake from an uncomfortable doze. A dark blue van was pulling up outside the house. Gone was the battered old green and black one with its homespun artwork. Apart from a yard-long horizontal score above the wheel arch, this one was rather smart. Enclosed in a pale-blue droplet-shaped decal on the side were the simple words DeeKay Plumbing Services and a mobile phone number.

As the driver's door slid back, Mark shifted down instinctively in his seat, but he needn't have worried. The man who was climbing out looked in a world of his own; recognisably the same person who'd bounced out of his old Transit eleven years ago – tall, still slim and athletic-looking – but the spring in the step had gone. So had the ponytail, although the chunky light brown hair around his collar was probably still long enough to tie back.

The dog had aged too: flecks of grey around the muzzle and distinctly more sedate than the flopsy pup of eleven years earlier.

Dan Keegan locked his van and trudged down the side of the house, presumably to let himself in through the kitchen door. He looked exhausted.

*

The ground floor of the house was in darkness when Mark got back to Wordsworth Grove; only Vulcan there to greet him, patiently waiting on the front doorstep to be let in. Jenny was in bed, propped up on pillows, glasses on the end of her nose, reading a book by the light of her bedside lamp.

'You're in bed early. It's not even ten o'clock.' He'd been looking forward to sharing a drink of something in the kitchen with Jenny. And come to think of it, he hadn't eaten anything either. Oh well, he needed to lose a few pounds.

A cool 'Hello Mark' was the only reply he got. He'd have to get into bed with her if he wanted to talk. He walked across the room to give her a companionable kiss. She tilted her face slightly to receive it, eyes still fixed on her book.

'Chloe's still up,' he said. 'I can see the light on under her door.'

'Mm. She's got her geography project to finish.'

'Oh God. The organic farming thing. I promised to help her with that.'

'Don't worry. She's managing without you. I went through the notes with her myself after supper.'

He popped his head round his daughter's door.

'Hi, Squirrel.'

She didn't look up. 'Hi, Dad.'

Chloe was kneeling on the floor in her pyjamas and dressing gown, tapping away on her laptop keyboard, using her bed as a desk. He picked his way over books, papers and open tins of coloured pencils to peer at her computer screen.

'You writing up that farm trip?'

'Yup.'

'Sorry I wasn't home earlier to help.'

'S' all right.'

'Ah. Online messenger. Who's this you're talking to? *"Monkey See, Monkey Do. Monkey No See, Monkey Step In Doo."* What kind of name is that?'

'Oh, that's Jess.'

'And who's calling themselves *"Nobody's Perfect, But I'm So Close It Scares Me!"*?'

'Mind your own beeswax, Dad.'

'Someone with an ego.' He smiled. It was pointless, obviously, to ask why these kids didn't use their real names. Chloe minimised the messaging screen to stop him reading any more. 'Are you still using MySpace? I hear Facebook's all the rage now? And something called Peebo?'

'Bebo. Look, Dad. I'm trying to work on my farm project.'

'Sure you are.'

'I am! Jess was just asking me what I'm writing about natural predators.'

'Predators? On a farm?'

'They have to attract good insects to eat the bad insects and larvae and stuff.'

'Oh I see. Instead of pesticides.'

The message alert jangled.

'But I can't get this done if I keep getting interrupted.'

'Well go off line then.'

She frowned irritably. 'I mean by you.'

'And is that the most comfortable way of working?' he continued, pushing his luck. 'Why don't you use your desk?'

'Not enough space. You're really holding me up, Dad. I've got to give this in tomorrow morning.'

'You've left it a bit last minute, haven't you? You did the trip about ten days ago.'

'Dad, if you haven't got anything helpful to say, can you please leave me in peace to get this finished.'

For a moment he considered telling her not to be so rude, but reflected that she hadn't in fact been quite rude enough to warrant chastisement. 'OK then, I'll say goodnight. Mum and I are having an early night.' He kissed the top of her head. 'Just don't stay up too late. Better to get some sleep in the bank now and wake up early in the morning to finish.'

'Dad!'

'OK, I'm gone! 'Night.'

'Night, Dad. Love you.'

'Love you too.'

Chapter Eighteen

'I knew you were up to no good. I *sensed* it.'

Not yet fully undressed, Mark wriggled into bed beside his wife to keep warm. Jenny didn't like central heating in the bedroom. 'She's a latchkey kid, quite evidently, Jen.'

'Don't even speak to me. I don't want to know.'

'I'm really sorry. I should have told you what I was doing.'

'You shouldn't have gone there! It's . . . picking the scab off the wound. Just as we're trying to get a perspective on things.'

'It was a bit of a spur of the moment thing really.'

'Oh sure. You drive the best part of thirty miles to sit outside someone's house on the spur of the moment!'

'Come on, Jenny. Quit the moral high ground. You're curious too. You know you are.'

'Yes, of course I am. I think about that little girl all the time. Really. All the time. But *I'm* trying to do the right thing. We're not *entitled* to involve ourselves in her life. It only makes things more painful anyway.'

'But she's our flesh and blood. She's woven into our very instincts. It would be unnatural *not* to care. *Not* to be concerned about her welfare.'

'Keep your voice down,' hissed Jenny. 'Chloe will hear us.'

'All we're doing is setting our minds at rest. Trying to. Surely that's understandable.'

'No! You're supposed to be a grown-up. You're supposed to be able to control your thoughts and actions.'

'Well, aren't you just the paragon of virtue . . .' Mark flung back the bedclothes and strode towards the door. 'I'm going to clean my teeth.'

In the bathroom, he looked angrily at his face in the mirror, noticing for the first time the deepening lines either side of his nose and mouth. Perhaps he and Jenny would never be able to discuss Leonie calmly and rationally. It seemed they were destined to battle on with their own feelings as best as they could. Negotiating the same ocean in separate ships.

'So did you actually see her?' demanded Jenny as he climbed back into bed beside her.

'No. I didn't. I got there about half past four and she must have got back from school already. The lights were on, so she was definitely there.'

'But you saw the father?'

'Keegan. Yes, I saw him. It was nearly half past eight by the time he rolled up. It's not right leaving her by herself like that when she must be grieving so much for her mother.'

'It's no use thinking about it.' Jenny switched off the bedside lamp, throwing herself on to her side away from Mark. 'It's just too upsetting. Get some sleep.'

'Well I don't think we should give in without a fight.'

Jenny was silent.

'She must be feeling very alone right now.' He knew she hadn't gone to sleep. He could sense her body, rigid in the darkness beside him. 'I mean it's crazy that we can't just simply let her know we're here. Let her know she's got family she didn't know she had . . . and a sister. How exciting would that be!'

Jenny snapped the lamp back on and turned over to face Mark, propping her head on her elbow. 'Darling, you're being ridiculously naïve. Don't think I haven't had thoughts like that myself. Of course I have. But . . . look. Think of it this way; if we didn't know about Leonie's existence, we'd be happily getting on with our lives. And she'd be coping with hers, as she is now.'

'But that's a pointless thing to say, since we *do* know she exists.'

'Mark – it's no use talking like this. We have to keep out of it. That's what we agreed, back in that clinic with baby Chloe sleeping in my arms. Surrender all ties. That's the legal situation. What the law of the land says. It's bloody painful, but we don't have a choice.'

'Well in my opinion the "law of the land" is a blunt instrument. Where's the humanity? In the old tribal days, before we had these intransigent "laws of the land", common sense prevailed. If a child's mother or father died, the rest of the tribe quite naturally took over the parental role. It probably still happens that way in some parts of the world. Now that makes sense. That's humane.'

Jenny put her hand out to stroke Mark's cheek. 'You've got a big heart and you want the best for everyone. I know that. But you're leaving me behind. Can't you see? We're in danger of losing each other.'

'Just because I don't want to take the shit life dishes out sometimes? Because I want to try and shape destiny for once, instead of the other way round?'

'We used to be a good team, you and I.' Jenny sounded tearful. 'Now you're off on this crusade, which you seem to think belongs exclusively to you.'

'We're *still* a team, Jen. Come on, I love you and I need you. I want you by my side on this crusade, as you call it. I don't think I can do it without you.'

'So stop wandering off without me, then. I feel just as grief-stricken in all this as you do. It would be nice if you recognised that. It's called sharing.'

'I know. OK. You're right and I'm wrong. It's all crazy wishful thinking. Let's just forget it for now and go to sleep.'

'If we're going to survive this, Mark, you and me, as a partnership, we're going to have to keep talking. Keep telling each other what we're feeling. And maybe we can talk our way through the pain; all the different stages. Things will get better, gradually. Because gradually things will get better for Leonie, as she comes to terms with her loss and her life moves on. And maybe Daniel Keegan will meet a new woman. Provide a family unit again. Who knows?'

'Oh. God. I hadn't thought of that. A stepmother. Something else to worry about.'

'Listen, Mark, there'll always be something to worry about. There always is with a child. Especially a girl. Schoolwork, boyfriends, staying out late, drugs, alcohol . . . Everything we worry about for Chloe. We just can't go there. Chloe's our daughter. She's the one we have to concentrate on.'

'Make love to me.'

'Oh Mark. That's your answer to everything, isn't it?'

'I wish it was.' He pulled her towards him. 'I so wish it was.'

Chapter Nineteen

Mark pushed his way up the escalator. This was really annoying. He had so much to do today. He'd made the mistake of mentioning an appointment with a client in Cobham and Jenny had jumped at the chance to shove a shopping list into his hand.

'You'll be going past Bluewater then. Brilliant!'

'Well, yes, but I . . . I'm going to be really busy.' He hated shopping precincts. Mooching women with big arses banging their shopping bags into his legs.

'Don't be ridiculous. It's hardly out of your way at all. It'll take you half an hour at the most. Saves me taking a whole morning out of *my* life. *I'm* busy too at the moment, in case you hadn't noticed. I've got that house in Wimbledon to finish before the family moves in on Saturday week.'

'I thought you'd already finished that.'

'The inside's just about done, but they want me to do the garden now. I told you.'

'Oh yes. Right.'

'And Chloe's old winter blouses are too small for her now.'

'She's going to have big boobs. Like her mother.'

'At least they make decent-sized bras these days. At her age I was squeezing into horrible white broderie anglaise things two cup sizes too small and four inches too big round the back.'

He looked appalled. 'I don't have to buy bras as well, do I?'

'No. Fool. Just two school shirts. Thirty-four chest. She's only got short-sleeved ones left. Actually make it three.' She had snatched the list back, slammed it on the hall table and scratched vigorous alterations on it with one of Chloe's coloured pencils. 'And why not get her a couple of new sweaters while you're there. Get thirty-six chest for those. She likes them baggy.' More scribbling. 'And a purse belt.' She pushed it back at him. 'There you are. It's all on the list. Just ask the assistant to get them for you. Look helpless. You're good at that.'

'Oh, thank you.'

'You're a star.' She kissed him. 'I'm off to the garden centre. Think yourself lucky I don't make you come with me to lug four huge bags of compost into the car. That's what blokes are for, after all. Lifting heavy weights.'

He'd smiled. 'You'll just have to try looking helpless yourself then, won't you?'

Reaching the first floor, he peered irritably at the Store Directory. He'd got twenty minutes at the most.

He absolutely must be in Cobham by eleven thirty. These new clients were a young French couple. High fliers. He'd met them just once before when they'd called at his shop, and they'd struck him as rather meticulous types; not strong on humour. Perhaps it had just been the language barrier, but he didn't want to risk upsetting them this early in the relationship.

He cursed himself for not having come up with a decent-sounding excuse the moment he'd heard Jenny utter that word 'Bluewater'. For not having headed her off at the pass.

But here he was in John Lewis's at ten thirty in the morning surrounded by 'Back to School' signs. He'd hoped the school uniform department would be deserted on a Tuesday morning, but a lot of other parents seemed to be buying their school uniforms rather late too.

He stopped near one of the cash tills and stood looking around him in a bemused, lost sort of way. The only two assistants he could see were too busy to notice him. He'd just have to search these things out for himself. Look for brown and yellow.

He wandered aimlessly around the labyrinth of aisles. Chloe had always complained about the dreadful colours school uniforms were. And she certainly had a point. They were all bottle green, dark blue, brown or maroon. Jenny had pointed out sensibly that dark colours didn't show dirt and stains so much as bright pastel ones. To which Chloe had muttered a mutinous 'gross' and cast her eyes skywards.

Something jolted him back to the here and now. Something had jabbed at his subconscious. What was it? He turned and walked back the way he'd come, past an aisle of dreary grey flannel skirts and trousers.

A woman, probably in her early thirties, spiky-haired and fake-tanned, ludicrously dressed in a red hooded anorak, calf-length yellow and black patterned leggings and a pair of clumpy silver trainers, was holding two blue blazers against herself, trying to gauge the sizes. The lapels and hems were piped in yellow. The badge on the pocket was yellow too. A stylised castle or turret with four crenellations. Leonie Keegan's school blazer!

Trying his best to look nonchalant, he managed to walk on past the woman and found himself approaching a rack of familiar brown garments. Chloe's uniform. What was it Jenny had asked him to get? His brain was too busy controlling his emotions to remember.

Reluctant to take his eyes off the woman in the anorak, he

153

groped in the inside pocket of his jacket for the crumpled list and shook it out. Right. Sweaters size thirty-six. Two. He rifled through the rack, laying the items over his arm. Long-sleeved shirts size thirty-four. Three. What else? Purse belt. Where were those? Must be a different section.

Across the store, the spiky-haired woman had put one of the blazers back on the rail and was walking in the direction of the till, clutching the smaller size on its hanger like a trophy. Mark fell in behind her in the queue.

'Not easy, this uniform business, is it?'

She turned to look at him, glanced behind her to see if he was addressing someone else, then having confirmed she was the object of his attention, replied,

'Yeah. Well. You want them to last, don't you, but then if you get them too big they won't wear them at all.' She hitched the strap of her silver handbag higher on her shoulder. 'I got her a perfectly decent second-hand one to start with but she turned her nose up. Why does it have to matter so much?'

He smiled his frank, boyish smile. 'The trouble is, it *does* matter to them at that age and there's nothing we can do or say to change their minds.'

Evidently unimpressed by this piece of analysis, she turned back towards the cash desk. He cast around for something else to say to keep the conversation going.

'Busy today, aren't they?' he ventured.

'I don't know why they don't put more staff on.' She addressed this in the direction of the woman at the till rather than Mark. 'It's just crazy not to increase the staffing levels at the start of the new school year,' she continued loudly. 'There's nobody around to help when you're trying to make a decision. And then you have to queue for half an hour for the privilege of paying.'

Mark's anxiety level rose. She seemed about to 'go off on one' as Chloe would have put it. He adopted the affable, well-modulated tone that usually served him well in tricky social situations. 'If my daughter had her way, there'd be no such thing as school uniform at all.'

'Oh, sure. Tell me about it. My Sonia would be kitting herself out at Top Shop given half a chance. And she'd be wanting something new every week as well. I'd be broke by the end of the first term.'

'At least your daughter's uniform is a reasonable colour.' He pointed to the sweaters and shirts he was holding. 'My daughter's is brown and mustard yellow. She hates it.'

'My Sonia wouldn't *go* to a school with a brown uniform.'

The till was pretty close now. He didn't have much more time. 'Where is your daughter's school?'

'Sevenoaks.'

'Oh yes? Which one?'

'Hawkshill Park. Where's your daughter?'

'Oh, we're in Blackheath. She's at Greenwich High School.'

'Oh. Posh.'

'Well, not really *posh*.'

'It's a public school isn't it?'

'Yes.'

'So. It's posh.'

She turned her back on him and he found himself looking down into her anorak hood. He waited quietly while she paid for 'my Sonia's' blazer.

Snatching the green and white striped carrier bag off the counter, she marched towards the down escalator without a backward glance.

The woman at the cash desk was looking at him askance.

'I think it was something I said.' He smiled ruefully.

Chapter Twenty

'Hello, is this Mrs Jennifer Elfick?'

'Yes?'

'Good evening, Mrs Elfick. My name is David Ackland. Custody sergeant, Sevenoaks police.'

'Police?'

'Don't worry, madam, nothing to be too concerned about. Your husband Mark is with us at the moment and he has requested us to put in a call to you. We'd like you to come here to the station if you would.'

'Mark?' Jenny sank down on to the sofa. 'What's happened?'

'We're keeping him here at the station while we ask him some questions following an incident an hour or so ago.'

'Oh my God. Has there been an accident?'

'No, madam, there hasn't been an accident. I'm sure he will explain things when you see him.'

'But is he all right? He's not hurt?'

'No, Mrs Elfick, your husband is in one piece. He's absolutely fine.'

'Has anyone else been hurt?'

'No, no one has been hurt.'

'So . . . what's this incident then? It's something to do with the car, is it?'

'I'm sorry to seem uncooperative, Mrs Elfick, but I can't tell you anything on the telephone.'

'I don't understand. Why can't my husband talk to me himself?'

'Best you get the whole story when you arrive at the station, Mrs Elfick.'

'But . . . if he's not hurt and you're not letting him go, you must think he's done something wrong. Please tell me what's happened.'

'As I say, madam . . .' He tailed off, evidently reluctant to keep repeating himself.

'I've got to pick my daughter up . . .' Her voice was cracking now. What had Mark done? Surely it couldn't be too serious. A motoring offence . . . But they wouldn't be holding him in custody for that, would they? 'I'll see if I can get a friend to look after her.'

'There's no urgent hurry, Mrs Elfick, if you want to make the necessary arrangements for your daughter first.'

'All right, so how do I find the police station?'

The grandfather clock in the alcove beside the fireplace showed twenty minutes past five. The traffic leaving London would be at its worst.

'Head for Sevenoaks town centre. Once you get to the High Street, heading south, follow the signs to the shopping centre and we're a short way down on the left. You can't miss it. And there's plenty of parking.'

'OK, right. I'll get there as soon as I can.'

Ahead of her at the reception desk, a couple with a buggy looked little older than Chloe. Sixteen at most. The girl, wearing pale pink baggy tracksuit trousers and hoop earrings, her hair scraped back into a skimpy ponytail, had had her mobile phone snatched, it seemed. The pasty-faced boy with her, tattooed on both arms from wrist to elbow was, presumably, her partner. He was in the midst of what had already been a lengthy account of the incident, judging by the world-weary demeanour of the silver-haired man behind the desk.

'. . . so then we're coming out of Costa's yeh, and Celeste's mum rings, right . . . And Celeste is like talking to her, yeh, and this geezer just comes up from nowhere and grabs the phone straight out 'er bleedin hand? In't that right, darl?'

'I only had it a munf.' The girl yanked the sleeve of her tracksuit over her wrist and brushed it across her nose.

The clerk's eyes met Jenny's for a split second; a flicker of something shared.

Beneath his line of sight, in its high-tech buggy, the couple's child had been frowning pensively at the chocolate biscuit it had been licking. Now, slowly, purposefully, it stretched out a chubby arm, opened its fingers and let the soggy remains fall on to the floor.

'All right love, if you'd just like to fill this in at the other end of the counter there.' The desk clerk pushed a form across the counter towards Celeste. 'We need full name, address, description of the stolen goods, precise time and place the incident occurred, then we can get you your crime reference number.' He looked across at Jenny. 'Yes, madam?'

Jenny raised her voice enough to reach him across the child and buggy. 'I think you're expecting me.'

'What was the name?'

'Jennifer Elfick. My husband . . .' She paused. She couldn't decide how to continue with the sentence. He came to her rescue.

'Ah, yes, Mrs Elfick.' He indicated four plastic chairs along the wall. 'Take a seat over there for a moment please.'

She wandered towards the chairs but remained standing, searching in her handbag for nothing in particular.

A uniformed constable pushed open a wire-glazed door beside the counter.

'Mrs Elfick?'

'Yes.'

'I'm PC Driscoll.' Should she shake hands? No. It wasn't that kind of situation. 'Come with me.'

Jenny followed him back through the door and a few yards along a narrow corridor, he stopped and ushered her into a bare lilac-painted room, furnished with three mauve-upholstered wooden chairs.

'Please sit down, Mrs Elfick.'

Jenny perched stiffly on the edge of one of the three chairs. PC Driscoll positioned one of the remaining two facing her, a couple of feet away.

'Is my husband all right?'

'He's fine. Don't worry.'

'Where is he? Can I see him?'

'We've still got him in the custody suite for the moment.'

'The custody suite!'

'You'll be able to see him in a while. I'd just like a word or two with you first if I may.'

'I see. Should I contact a lawyer?' In dramas, people in this kind of situation would say, 'I demand to see my solicitor.' As if you had someone on personal standby, twenty-four seven, for all eventualities. Perhaps some people did.

'There won't be any need for that.' Driscoll appeared to be smirking at some private joke. 'Nobody has been charged with anything at this point in time and this is just an informal conversation.' He opened a notebook in a black plastic cover.

'Having said that, a few formalities briefly if you'll bear with

160

me. First can you confirm for me that you are Mrs Jennifer Elfick, wife of Mr Mark Christopher Elfick?'

'Yes, that's right.'

'And your address?' The door opened and a young woman officer with short dark hair walked into the room and perched herself on the chair next to Driscoll.

'This is PC Fairweather. She and I apprehended your husband this afternoon.'

'Hello.' Jenny tried to picture the unimaginable; Mark being arrested by these two. Had they handcuffed him? How humiliating. What the hell had he done?

'Sorry, Mrs Elfick.' Driscoll's attention returned to his notebook. 'We were confirming your address?'

'Forty-seven Wordsworth Grove, Blackheath, London SE3.'

He scribbled something. 'Right. Now. Mrs Elfick,' Driscoll continued. 'To put you in the picture, this afternoon a little after sixteen hundred hours, a Mrs Enid Barnforth, the deputy head teacher at Hawkshill Park Grammar School in Sevenoaks, reported a man for causing a serious breach of the peace outside her school.'

'When you say "a man", you mean my husband, do you?'

'Indeed I do mean your husband, Mrs Elfick. Mrs Barnforth told us he was watching the children through the fence as they left school for the day and taking pictures on his mobile phone. When the parent of one of the girls at the school, a Mrs Virginia James, approached him to ask what he was doing, he became violent and abusive.'

'But that doesn't sound like Mark at all.'

Fairweather spoke up. 'This parent tells us in her statement that she has good reason to know that your husband has no connection with the school.'

'That's right, he doesn't,' asserted Jenny.

'She described his behaviour as sinister and frightening,' continued Fairweather. 'Those are the words she used.'

'We had no alternative but to bring him in under the Public Order Act for harassment and causing a breach of the peace,' added Driscoll.

'Look.' Jenny searched the faces in front of her, but it was impossible to decide which was the more sympathetic of the two. 'I'm finding it hard to believe this is happening. There'll be a perfectly understandable explanation.'

'Might he have known any of the children at the school?' asked Fairweather.

'It's highly unlikely. Unless he was with a client who happened to be meeting their child . . . But, no, I can't imagine he'd be doing that.' She racked her brains. What had he said he was doing today? She hadn't asked him. 'What was the school again?'

'Hawkshill Park. It's a girls' grammar school. Not far from here.'

'I've never heard of it. Ah. Oh God.' Jenny felt hot blood rising to her neck and face and then just as quickly draining away. 'It might be . . .'

'Yes?'

'Did he tell you he was looking for one particular child?'

'That's pretty much what he said, yes.'

'Would it have been Leonie Keegan?'

'That's the one, yes,' affirmed Driscoll.

'I think I know what he was doing.'

Driscoll waited, raising an encouraging eyebrow.

'We've got time if you have.'

'Can we get you a drink?'

Perhaps Fairweather wasn't so hostile after all.

'A glass of water would be good. Thanks.'

Propping the door open with her sensible-shoed foot, Fairweather called down the corridor. 'Bob! Some water in the family room please.'

Driscoll waited for Fairweather to resume her seat next to him. 'Right, Mrs Elfick. You've got our undivided attention.'

'Our daughter Chloe was born after IVF.'

Driscoll leaned back in his chair, folding his arms. 'Yes we know about that. And this schoolgirl he was . . . showing an interest in . . . is the result of an embryo donation by you and your husband.'

'That's right, yes.'

The clerk from the front desk took a step into the room holding a white plastic cup. Fairweather stood to take it from him, passed it over to Jenny and sat down again, feet and knees pressed neatly together.

'So, my husband must have told you . . . Her mother was killed. Murdered.'

'Yes. We know about the murder.' He could have sounded a little less dispassionate about it, thought Jenny.

'The chief super at the station here was in charge of the investigation,' added Fairweather.

Jenny looked at her appealingly. 'Obviously we were very upset. You can understand that, can't you? It was such a terrible, terrible thing to happen to a child. And Leonie is our . . .' She attempted a sip of water from the flimsy plastic cup, but her hand was shaking too much. She gave up trying and put it down on the floor beside her. 'Listen.' She fought to keep her voice steady. 'Mark and I are Leonie's *genetic* parents. We've been incredibly concerned about her. How else would we feel? It's basic force of nature. We tried so hard not to think about it But . . .'

'But you did think about it.'

'Well, yes. Of course.' She'd run out of road. 'He didn't tell me he'd found out what school she was going to.'

Fairweather crossed her legs with a swish of black Lycra. 'What do you think your husband's intentions were?' she enquired.

'I don't think he'd have approached her. He just wanted to see her. That was it, I'm sure.'

'Doesn't it strike you as inappropriate behaviour though, Mrs Elfick?' Driscoll weighed in. 'Hanging around outside her school. Outside her house as well, I gather.'

'I suppose I can understand how you might see it that way. Maybe he shouldn't have done it. He definitely shouldn't have done it. But it depends what you mean by inappropriate. She's his daughter. He cares. Deeply.'

'But it worries you that he didn't tell you?'

'I'm not happy about that. No.'

'What', Fairweather folded her arms across her bust, 'do you think your daughter Chloe would make of her father's behaviour?'

'Oh God. Does she have to know?'

'I suppose that depends on any consequences there might be.'

'I can't believe this is happening.' Jenny put her head in her hands. The officers exchanged glances. She pulled herself together. 'Where's Mark? What are you going to do with him?'

'Well, the next step is one or two routine checks with Social Services; on our patch and in Greenwich,' said Driscoll.

'What sort of checks?'

'Well, he's not listed on the Sex Offenders Register, but we still need to make sure he hasn't been reported before for hanging around schools or making approaches to children.'

'He hasn't! Of course he hasn't. Oh God, this is awful. You're making him sound like a paedophile.'

'I'm sure you have every confidence in him.' Driscoll stretched his stocky legs out in front of him, inadvertently kicking Jenny's handbag with his chunky black lace-up shoes.

She bent to move her bag further under her chair and picked up the cup of water. This time she managed to keep her hand steady enough to gulp down some of its contents. A terrible thought occurred to her. 'You don't have to tell Mr Keegan about this, do you?'

'That'll be up to the Social Services.' He seemed to be addressing the ceiling now. Jenny turned to the policewoman for some eye contact.

'So you're reporting him to Social Services?'

'They'll be getting a full report, yes, via our Child Protection Unit. That's normal procedure.'

'And what will they do?'

'It all depends on how they choose to assess the situation,' said Fairweather, somewhat wearily, Jenny thought. 'It's not our remit here.'

'But will they approach Daniel Keegan?'

'It's possible. Probable actually. What they do, and how soon they do it, will depend partly on their workload I expect.'

'But he has no idea we even exist!' Jenny looked wildly from Driscoll to Fairweather and back to Driscoll again. 'It would be a total bombshell. For him and Leonie. You can't do that to them.'

'I think our Child Protection Unit might take the view that your husband has demonstrated a certain, shall we say, preoccupation with this child over a period of a decade or more, and therefore might think it advisable to inform her father about it.'

'Because,' added Driscoll, 'let's face it; he's been to some trouble to keep track of this family. The reasons for it I can understand to some extent after what you've both told us. But nevertheless, he's gone to great lengths to find out where they live, then to find out what school the girl goes to. How do we know he won't want to take things the next logical step further and make actual contact with the child? And then if Mr Keegan found out the police actually had your husband in custody but we didn't take any preventive action, he'd be entitled to make a formal complaint. It'd be seen as a dereliction of duty on our part. We are accountable. Us and Social Services. You can understand that, I'm sure.'

'But there won't *be* a future offence, for goodness' sake! Mark has never spoken to the father or the child in nearly twelve years. He's not likely to now. And if I thought there was the slightest sign of him doing that I would make sure it didn't happen. I promise.'

'Mrs Elfick.' Clearly, as far as Driscoll was concerned, the conversation was at an end. He hauled himself to his feet. 'If you'd like to wait in here for the time being . . .'

Taking her cue, Fairweather stood too and began to follow him towards the door. Jenny almost ran after her.

'Look. Please. Mark wouldn't ever do anything to hurt or upset Leonie in any way. He's a kind-hearted, gentle person. He cares about Leonie. You're talking about a man I simply don't recognise.'

Fairweather's answer was forestalled by Driscoll from the corridor, lowering his voice in a perhaps deliberately unsuccessful attempt to sound sympathetic.

'Don't take this the wrong way, Mrs Elfick, but that's what they all say. "Not *my* husband, not *my* son . . ."'

Stumped for a reply she sank down on her chair again. How could Mark have been so stupid? Fairweather was closing the door behind her. 'Excuse me,' called Jenny. 'When can I see my husband?'

Fairweather stuck her head back round the door. 'I'll go and find out the state of play for you. It shouldn't be long now. Best if you wait here. It's a bit busy out front.'

'I need to make a phone call. The people looking after my daughter will need to know what's happening.'

'I'll bring you a phone.'

'It's OK, I can use my mobile, but I need to know how long you think . . . when shall I say I might be back?'

'I should think you'll be out of here by . . .' she glanced up at the digital clock on the wall, 'half past nine. Ten maybe.'

Chapter Twenty-One

'Jen, I'm so, so sorry.'

He wanted her to put her arms round him. Make everything better. But he couldn't move. She'd push him away, he was sure. Her distaste for him was palpable. He felt physically ill. She said nothing, glanced at him quickly, then looked away again.

'Please Jenny. In all the years we've been together, I've never seen you look at me like that. As if you despise me. This is worse than anything. Worse than those five hours in that cell.' But of course he couldn't blame her. He did feel despicable. As if the words 'child molester' had been inscribed on his forehead. 'Jenny, please. I feel I've lost you somewhere. Please come back to me.'

Jenny made a poor attempt at a smile. 'I'm done in. I'm going to have a bath.'

The two of them had arrived home shortly after ten o'clock, first having reunited Mark with his car, still parked where he'd left it near the school, six hours and half, a lifetime, ago.

Even the car felt violated. There was a parking ticket on the windscreen and the police had left the glove box hanging open after they'd searched it. What for, he couldn't imagine. Images of child pornography? He shuddered.

They'd driven back towards London in their separate cars with their separate thoughts. Mark had arrived at the darkened house first, Jenny having made the short detour to collect Chloe from her school friend's house.

In the car, Chloe had been more interested in regaling Jenny with the TV programmes her friend was allowed to watch – two hours of *Friends* and *Will and Grace* on E4 apparently – than finding out how her parents had spent the evening.

Back home, she had disappeared obediently off to bed with a nonchalant peck on the cheek for each of them. And then there was no longer any reason to prevent Mark and Jenny from confronting what had happened.

'We need to talk,' Mark had said quietly.

'Damn right we do. Except that I don't feel like talking to you ever again. I felt so humiliated in that police station. Cheap and dirty.'

He understood only too well her need for a bath. More than anything, that's what he wanted too.

Very often they'd chat to each other in the bathroom of an evening, one sitting on the closed toilet lid while the other lay in the bath, swapping stories about the day they'd had, making routine plans, discussing points from the day's news, sometimes even getting into the bath together.

Tonight he waited in the bedroom, perched uneasily on the end of the bed until she'd emerged, towel-turbaned and wrapped in her bathrobe.

Finally he could closet himself in the bathroom to lie miserably in the warm soapy water, trying to cleanse away the sense of humiliation and shame that clung to him like stale perfume.

He found Jenny downstairs with two large glasses of brandy.

'Better?' she asked.

'A bit, yes. What about you?'

'A bit.'

'Jenny, you do believe me, don't you? I wouldn't ever, *ever* think of molesting a child.'

'Of course you wouldn't. I know that. It was just . . . being subjected to those questions, and knowing you were there in the cells somewhere. It all felt so earth-shatteringly . . . serious. I've never even been inside a police station before.'

'I have. A couple of times – after that burglary at the shop a couple of years ago, remember? But not down where the cells are. It's a totally different thing being hauled in as a criminal. Being fingerprinted, having everything confiscated. And the handcuffs. That was the worst thing. Outside the school.' Unconsciously, he clutched his breast at the memory. 'And sitting there in the cells, I began to believe I really had done something terrible. I kept having to tell myself, "Look, you haven't done anything wrong. You haven't done any harm to anyone. Don't let them get to you."'

'What the hell *were* you doing, though, Mark?'

'Look, Jen, can we go outside and talk in the garden? I just feel a desperate need for fresh air and open skies. And we don't want Chloe to hear us talking either.'

'It's a bit cold.'

'It's not that cold tonight. Put my jacket over your bathrobe.'

Clutching their brandy glasses, they wandered outside. Somewhere in one of the trees near the garden fence a lone blackbird still sang. A soft fragrance came and went with a light breeze.

'It's strange,' mused Mark. 'I never notice the smell of that plant in the daytime. It's only at night when I come out to look for Vulcan. I don't even know which plant it is.'

'It's called scented mignonette,' said Jenny bleakly. She didn't mention that the woman who owned the house she'd been working on in Wimbledon had made her cross that plant off her suggestions list only yesterday. 'Why?' Jenny had protested. 'It's gorgeous. I've got one in my garden.'

'That plant is a heartbreaker, darling,' she'd said. 'It'll bloom for a year or two and then, quite suddenly, for no reason you can think of, it will die on you. Put a viburnum in instead. They don't let you down.'

The swing seat creaked gently under their weight. They sat in silence for a while, listening to the blackbird, cupping their brandy glasses in their hands in a vain attempt to warm the chilly liquor they contained.

'It was that bloody woman in John Lewis.'

'What was?'

'I saw her clock me. Spiteful cow.'

'For pity's sake, Mark. I'm too tired for complicated conundrums.'

'She was in the school uniform department when I went to Bluewater. I saw her buying a school blazer like the one Leonie was wearing at the hospital when . . . that day her mother died.'

'So . . . you asked her what school it was?'

'Well yes. I chatted to her a bit in the queue. Then of course when she saw me outside the school, she recognised me. She knew I had nothing to do with Hawkshill Park.'

'Maybe she thought you were following her. Or that you were after her daughter.'

'I doubt it. I just think she's an olive short of a pizza frankly. She was so rude, Jen. I had my mobile phone in my hand. I'd just been speaking to Ian back at the shop. I admit it had occurred to me to take a photo of Leonie if I saw her. I thought I could show you. Anyway, this woman comes rushing up to me saying "You're the man in Bluewater, aren't you? What are you doing here?"'

'So I said something feeble like, "Oh I'm just waiting for my friend's daughter." And she said, "Like hell you are. What's her name then?" I didn't want to mention Leonie for obvious reasons so I made up a name – Emily O'Brien – and she said "OK, what year is she in?" and I kept busking it and said, "Year nine." And she said, "Well you're a liar. I've never heard of an Emily O'Brien in year nine and I'm on the parents' committee." And then she had the nerve to try to snatch my phone. We were grappling with each other like kids fighting over a toy. I managed to shake her off and she nearly fell over. Then she was really furious. Everyone was staring at us. It was so embarrassing. She screamed at me, "What is your name? I demand you give me your name." I said something a bit smart-Alec like, "My name belongs to me and I certainly wouldn't give it to *you*." Then there was a whole lot more argy-bargy and eventually I just yelled at her to bugger off and mind her own business. At that point she stormed off saying she was going to "report me to the deputy head". I laughed. Well, she sounded so childish. It didn't cross my mind that she'd call the police. I carried on looking out for Leonie, hoping I hadn't missed her in all the kerfuffle. And the next thing I know, two cops have arrived and she's talking to them and pointing me out. I never did get to see Leonie, incidentally, thanks to the vicious hag.'

'The two cops who arrested you gave me the impression you'd been pretty vicious yourself,' said Jenny. 'I couldn't believe it.'

'Well, I was pretty stressed out when they came up to me. I'd just had this really upsetting shout-up and all I wanted was to be left in peace to get a discreet look at Leonie.'

'So what did you do?'

'I just vigorously protested my innocence, that's all. I hadn't done anything wrong, Jen. There was no reason for the police to come on all heavy and arrest me. So I admit I wasn't exactly co-operative to start with.' His voice broke. 'I hadn't done anything wrong.'

He was clutching at his heart again. Softening, Jenny put her arm round his shoulders and waited, gently rubbing his back, while he struggled with his composure.

'They started off by asking me what did I think I was doing outside a school I had no connection with. And of course I couldn't give them any simple answers. Then they accused me of assaulting that woman. As if! I've never hit a woman in my life. She told them I was a pervert apparently. Said I'd been spying on the children and taking sneaky pictures. Suddenly it dawned on me they were actually arresting me. They put handcuffs on me. Like a criminal.'

'Well, you know what you've done now, don't you? The police have to refer the whole incident to their Child Protection Unit and the Social Services.'

'Yes I know. And they've got my DNA on record for the rest of time too. Not a great feeling.'

'I don't think you've taken on board the full implications.'

'Um . . . I'm not sure what you mean.'

'They'll probably report this whole business to Keegan.'

'Oh.' Mark was silent for a moment. 'Perhaps that wouldn't be such a bad thing.'

'Mark, it'll be a complete bolt from the blue. How do you think he's going to react? And how do you think Leonie will take it? She's had enough to cope with.'

'He wouldn't have to tell Leonie, would he?'

'How do I know? The social workers might want her to be warned about this man following her about, don't you think?' She drained her brandy glass. 'The police didn't seem to know exactly what they'll do. Outside their remit apparently.'

'You know, I can't help feeling it might be better for all of us in the long run to know the truth and recognise each other's existence. Everything out in the open.'

'Well you're an idiot! We don't want some faceless social worker breaking incredibly sensitive news like this to Leonie. There she is, still coming to terms with Elinor's terrible murder and then she's told that the mother she's grieving for wasn't her biological mother after all? The shock. It doesn't bear thinking about.'

'Can't we talk to the social workers?' asked Mark desperately. 'Appeal to them? Shouldn't we have a say in what they do? It's our lives after all.'

'I don't think that's an option. No. And what about Chloe? Have you thought about the effect of all this on her?'

Mark was massaging his heart again. 'But Chloe doesn't need to know about any of this, surely?'

In the moonlight, Jenny could see tears glistening in his eyes. She took his hand away from his breast and placed it in her lap, stroking it gently. 'Maybe we needn't worry. It's just . . . well . . . if they do go and tell him you've been spying on him for eleven years – and spying on his child – he's liable to be pretty angry. We don't know what he'll do. We should be prepared.'

'It's not spying. Don't use that word. I don't see it as spying.'

'What then?' she countered. 'Observing? Watching? Monitoring?'

'Keeping track of. In a totally benign way.'

'It comes to the same thing.'

'Oh Jenny, surely we can wait and see what, if anything, happens next?'

'We should try to work out how we'd explain things to Chloe though, just in case. A contingency plan at least.'

'I s'pose,' said Mark reluctantly.

Jenny looked at her wrist, but she'd taken her watch off for the bath. 'Look, we're going to have to sleep on this now. I can't think straight any more, Mark.'

'I'm sorry, Jen. I'm so sorry for everything.'

'I'm sorry too. And we might all end up being even sorrier. I know you meant well but . . . who knows how much damage has been done.'

Chapter Twenty-Two

Annabel was late as usual. Jenny hadn't minded waiting.

She ordered a glass of champagne, flirting mildly with the maître d' who always seemed genuinely pleased to see her and Annabel. This Chelsea restaurant had been a favourite of theirs for years. Diffused autumn sunlight shone gently through the vast skylight above her. Glasses gleamed against crisp white tablecloths: the promise of good food and wine.

Jenny felt her brow relax and her shoulder blades soften. This was how her life ought to be: calm and uncomplicated. Pleasurable. Fun, even.

'Darling girl!' Jenny found herself enveloped warmly in fragrant, lavender-coloured linen. 'I've kept you waiting; I'm sorry, but wait till you hear why. Etienne!' She embraced the maître d' almost as enthusiastically. 'Two more glasses of champagne please, darling. We're celebrating.'

She settled herself opposite Jenny. 'I'm rich!' she announced to most of the restaurant. 'I've just delivered my five paintings and two sculptures to this contemporary women artists exhibition in Draycott Gardens and while we were setting them up, some VIP or other was in there getting a sneak preview. I reckon he's an old rock star. He looked like a cross between Roger

Daltrey and Sacha Distel. Designer jeans. Blond hair turning grey?' She looked questioningly at Jenny who laughed and shook her head.

'Not enough to go on I'm afraid.'

'Anyway, whoever he was, he went off in cahoots with the gallery owner and apparently he is going to buy, not only one of my flower paintings – the biggest one with the poppies; I don't think you've seen it have you? – but my bronze giraffe as well. He just fell in love with it. He kept stroking its neck. That's two and a half grand before the exhibition's even opened! How about that?'

'Hey Annabel, that's wonderful.' A waitress brought two more glasses of champagne and Jenny raised hers to chime against Annabel's. 'Congratulations. They're getting to be your trademark now aren't they, those giraffes of yours.'

'I'm getting quicker and quicker at them too. I must say I'm doing much better work in my new place. Much more space and much more light.'

'I'm so pleased. And there's money in them thar giraffes, obviously,' Jenny laughed. 'Here's to sticking your neck out! It's such a tonic to see you.'

'You too, darling. That's the one bad thing about going to live in Dorset. The teaching's great, my studio's great, but I miss you terribly. Now tell me about you. I got the distinct impression on the phone that all is not well. Let's order and then I want to know everything.'

'. . . So we've just got to cross our fingers and hope it all blows over.' With all the talking, Jenny hadn't made much progress with her linguine alle vongole. In fact it looked much the same as it had when first it had been put in front of her. She loaded her fork with a hefty mouthful. 'I'll never get through this lot.' She grimaced. 'And I hate leaving food. Middle-class upbringing.'

'So when are you going to tell her? Chloe I mean.' Annabel picked up a lamb cutlet bone in her fingers and nibbled delicately at what meat was left on it.

'We're hoping we won't have to tell her anything.'

'Why not?'

'Because it'll just cause a whole lot of pain and aggravation for no purpose.'

'But she has a right to know, doesn't she? What if she finds out somehow? I reckon you should, you know. Explain about the donated embryos. She knows she was conceived with help, doesn't she?'

'Yes. We told her as soon as she was old enough to understand.'

'"Dotty in a Dish" you called her, I remember. Daft pair!' Annabel smiled affectionately. 'But you've never let her know that she might have brothers or sisters in the world?'

'We didn't get into all that, no.' Jenny gave up on her pasta, compressing it to one side of the plate to make it look as though she'd eaten more than she had. 'Far too complicated, technically and emotionally. The counsellor didn't recommend it either. She said it would just give rise to questions in Chloe's mind that could never be answered.'

Annabel picked the last cutlet bone off her plate and examined it thoughtfully.

'So you're determined not to tell her she's got a sister?'

'Not unless we have to.'

'You might get away with it I suppose.'

'It just depends if we think the Social Services are going to stick their noses in.'

'And if they do?'

'Then we'll cross that bridge when we come to it.'

'But Jen, by then the bridge might well have been blown to pieces and you'll find yourself having to swim for your life in the current.'

The waitress arrived to reclaim their plates and put a dessert menu in front of each of them.

'Shall we do what we usually do and share a pud?'

'Yes. You choose. Something chocolatey with two spoons.'

Jenny studied the menu. 'Looks like it'll just have to be the chocolate parfait with clotted cream ice cream then.'

Annabel groaned. 'Not clotted cream ice cream! Oh well, what the heck. Who wants to be a spindly old maid anyway? And let's have a glass of dessert wine to go with it. Neither of us has got to work this afternoon and we're celebrating, remember.'

'I know, but Mark's working at home today, catching up with paperwork or something. What's he going to think when I come bowling home totally tiddly?'

'Oh for Christ's sake, darling. You worry too much these days. Far too concerned about other people's welfare. What about you? You've had a tough time over the last few years. You're such a great person. You *deserve* to be happy.'

Jenny blinked causing, to her own surprise, two hot tears to run down her face and on to the tablecloth. 'Now look what you've done,' she tried to laugh, blotting under her eyes with her napkin. 'You'll make me ruin my make-up.'

'Anyway, I don't think Mark's in any position to play the moral righteousness card right now, do you?'

'You're right. Let's go for it. I'll get a cab home.'

'I'm not letting you change the subject though.'

Jenny sniffed, refolding her napkin on her lap. 'That's better. Give me a hard time. I can manage that. It's sympathy I can't cope with.'

'I'm not intending to give you a hard time, honestly, darling, but don't you think Chloe has a right to know the full story? Don't you feel perhaps you owe her that?'

'I prefer to think I owe her peace of mind.'

'Jenny, don't be swayed by what Mark says. He's like most men; he's an emotional coward, bless him. You shouldn't keep secrets from the people you love most.'

'That's fine to say but I just don't want to risk her reaction. Not just now anyway. She's thirteen. The worst, most puritanical age, especially for a girl.'

'You think it's going to be easier later? I'd have thought the longer you leave it, the longer she can accuse you of hiding the truth.'

'I suppose so. Maybe I've been an emotional coward myself. I think it's just always felt more like my story – mine and Mark's – than Chloe's.'

'Let's say you do decide to tell her now. How do you think she might react?'

'I don't know, Annabel. She's my own daughter and yet I just can't think myself into her head on this one. She might be angry that we've kept this secret from her all her life. She might be jealous of this other daughter . . . On the other hand it might be that she just couldn't care less. She might even be delighted. She used to say she wished she had a sister to play with. One thing I won't do at this stage is tell her about Mark's arrest. She'd be horrified.'

'All the same, better she hears the truth from you than from someone else. If those social workers go round to Keegan, who knows what he might do. Listen, dearest Jenny. I don't want to come on all moralistic. But I'm your best friend. I'm also Chloe's godmother and I don't want to see either of you hurt. I just believe that if we don't confront the truth in our lives it has a nasty habit of creeping up behind us and biting us on the bum. And that's all I'm going to say on the subject. For now. Ooh look. Goody. Here comes chocolate.'

The cab U-turned, manoeuvering around a dark blue trades-man's van at the kerb, and rattled off down the road. Foraging fruitlessly in her handbag for her door key Jenny walked somewhat unsteadily up to the front door and rang the bell.

Mark's face as the door opened looked pale and strained.

'Sorry I'm a bit late home.' Jenny stumbled over the doorstep and fell against Mark's chest giggling. 'Oh dear. I'm no good at drinking at lunchtime these days.'

'Jenny, we've got a visitor.' He spoke so quietly, Jenny hardly heard him.

'We had champagne. Annabel's sold half her new stuff already . . .'

'Daniel Keegan is here.'

Jenny looked blank. 'Who's . . . ?' Then the smile froze on her face. The van outside. 'Oh. Oh God.'

She felt like an open sports car that had been bowling merrily along sun-dappled country lanes and had rounded a bend straight into a yawning black hole.

'He's had a visit from the social workers.' Mark led the way into the living room. Standing with his back to the fireplace, too agitated to sit down, was a tall, slim man in his early forties, wearing jeans and a brown and cream striped T-shirt. At a subconscious level, she took in a face that, though deeply lined, had a youthful, alive look about it; brown eyes which looked used to smiling, but were hot with anger now; wavy, collar-length brown hair.

At the sight of Jenny entering the room behind Mark, Dan Keegan's expression changed to one of astonishment. He took a breath to say something but words seemed to fail him. The three of them stood looking at each other for a moment, dumb-founded.

'This is my wife, Jenny,' Mark managed finally. 'Um, Jenny, this is Daniel Keegan.'

'Hello,' said Jenny hoarsely. She cleared her throat and tried her voice again. 'Please. Sit down. If you two don't need to, I certainly do.' She sat down heavily on the sofa, politely indicating the armchair to Daniel.

He sat reluctantly, perching on the edge of the cushion, ready to jump up at a moment's notice for fight or flight.

Jenny turned to Mark. 'Have you offered our guest a cup of tea?' she looked enquiringly at Daniel. 'Or coffee? Wine?' Receiving no reply, she looked anxiously back at Mark. 'Have we got any beer?'

'I don't need anything just now thanks.'

Jenny almost jumped. He had a wonderful voice. Deep and musical. It seemed to unlock something inside her. She found herself wanting to cry. To curl up on the floor at his feet like a baby and just sob and sob . . . until the deep, dark well of tears in her soul was finally empty.

Instead, a calm, practical voice she recognised as her own, was saying, 'Actually, it's quite a relief to meet you after all these years.'

'I wish I could say the same. You'll forgive me if I say that you are the last people I ever hoped to meet.'

Jenny traced the weave on her pashmina with her index finger. Mark was twisting at his wedding ring. Daniel Keegan looked warily from one to the other.

Mark glanced up at Jenny. 'I've promised Mr Keegan we'll never go near his house or Leonie's school ever again.'

'I've lost my wife. I'm not going to lose my daughter as well.' The rich voice was jagged with emotion.

'We wouldn't want that to happen,' said Jenny quietly. 'Of course we wouldn't.'

'That damned doctor.' He stood up and paced across the room to the French windows, his back turned to them, looking out on to the garden. 'He's OK, of course, at his South African ranch; living the life of Riley no doubt.'

'Did you contact him then?'

'He's retired. They wouldn't give me his address. What's the use anyway? It's all far too late. My only concern now is to protect Leonie. She's been through enough.'

'We've been concerned for her too,' said Jenny gently. 'Ever since we read about your wife's terrible death.' She stood up and walked over to stand beside him at the window. 'We've thought about both of you a lot.'

'I don't need your concern. It's no use to me. Quite the opposite. What I need is for you to leave me and my daughter alone. Leave us in peace.'

'I think you're forgetting something here.' Mark joined the two of them at the window now. 'However difficult it is for you to accept, we are Leonie's biological parents. We care about her. It's only natural. You've always known we exist. And we've always known *you* exist. Isn't it just plain stupid to bury our heads in the sand and pretend otherwise? Shouldn't we all behave like mature adults and accept each other into our lives? And what about Leonie? She's got a sister.'

'Mark . . .'

'Isn't it just a bit selfish of you not to let her know that?'

Daniel Keegan shot out a strong, freckled arm and seized Mark by the collar, turning him round, pushing him up against the French windows. Jenny could see the door handles gouging into the small of her husband's back.

'Please . . . don't . . .' Jenny clawed at Daniel's shoulder, pulling at his T-shirt, but he was oblivious to her in the white heat of his rage, his face just centimetres from Mark's.

'You smug bastard. Leonie has lost her mother. Elinor bore her and gave birth to her. Twelve hours of difficult labour. I cut the umbilical cord. We have brought her up, nurtured her, loved her . . . She's *my* daughter. *I* am her father. Not you. You don't count. You've never had anything to do with her. I will not have you coming along and telling her her mother wasn't her real mother. I'll kill you first. I mean it!'

'It's all right, we do understand . . .' began Jenny gently.

Mark had gone white.

'I'm her father too!' He was struggling for breath. 'What about my feelings?'

'What's going on? Dad! Leave my daddy alone!'

Flinging her schoolbag to the floor, Chloe launched herself across the room and set about pounding Daniel's back with her small fists. He dropped his hold on Mark's collar and turned to face her.

'My God,' he murmured.

Jenny grasped Chloe and put her arms round her. 'It's all right, Chloe darling. Just a bit of an argument.'

Daniel straightened his T-shirt and brushed ineffectually at a lock of hair that kept falling over his eyes. 'I'm sorry.' He was addressing Chloe. 'I'd better go.'

'I'll show you out!' Mark couldn't disguise the tremor in his voice. The two men left the room.

Chloe was trembling. 'Who's that horrible man? Why was he hurting Daddy?'

'Sit down, sweetheart.' Jenny guided her daughter towards the kitchen. 'When Daddy comes back we'll tell you what that was about.'

*

185

A couple of paces from the front gate Daniel hesitated, turning to look back at Mark, who stood watching him from the doorway.

'I'm sorry your daughter had to witness that. I promised myself I wouldn't lose my temper.'

'I'm sorry she had to see it too,' said Mark quietly. 'I've got some explaining to do now.'

Vulcan appeared from nowhere and leaned, purring, against Daniel's legs, expecting to be stroked.

'All the same, I hope I've made myself understood. Leonie is all I have now. I won't have you turning up laying some kind of claim on her, not now of all times.'

'Yes, but I'm not . . .' There was so much more Mark wanted to say, but it would all have to go unspoken. He had to go in and talk to Chloe.

'I don't want to hear "yes but". I meant what I said, Elfick. If I ever see hide or hair of you anywhere near me or my daughter I'll be on to the cops like a shot. And after what happened last week I don't imagine they'll be treating you with a great deal of sympathy. You have been warned.'

Daniel turned and strode towards his van. A disgruntled Vulcan stalked into the hall before the front door slammed shut.

'You remember we told you about how you were born? How you were our little miracle because it had been so difficult for us to make baby-seeds?'

'I know all about the reproductive process, Daddy. You don't have to use baby-language. Anyway what's that got to do with you and that man fighting in our living room?'

Sitting next to his daughter on the sofa, Mark put his arm around her shoulders in the old bedtime story-telling pose.

Jenny was sitting on the carpet in front of them, legs tucked up underneath her, trying not to look too intense. 'Just be patient, sweetheart. Daddy's going to get round to that in a minute,' she said quietly.

Chloe fidgeted irritably under her father's arm. 'You're both scaring me. Just tell me.'

'All right, well, we told you we had some baby-seeds left over after we made you. Sorry, embryos I mean.'

'That was ages ago. I'm thirteen now.'

'Yes, it was, but it's important. Listen. So we decided to give our spare embryos to the doctor so that he could give them to couples who wanted to have a baby but couldn't.'

'Because they couldn't make their own embryos.' Chloe picked up the TV remote control and began idly polishing the buttons with the cuff of her school jumper. Mark took it gently out of her hands and put it back down on the coffee table.

'Exactly. Mummy couldn't have any more babies so we couldn't use them anyway . . . So we donated them to make some other mums and dads as happy as we were when we had you.' Mark ran his hands through his hair. 'Oh dear, this is quite some mountain to climb.'

'You're doing fine.' Jenny rubbed his forearm. 'Keep going.'

He looked back at Chloe, 'And then . . .' He took one of her hands and began stroking it. Chloe pulled it away and put her thumb into her mouth.

'Don't do that, sweetheart.' It was Jenny's turn to take hold of her hand. 'You really should have grown out of that by now. You'll end up with braces on your teeth.'

'And then,' Mark was anxious that Chloe shouldn't lose the thread of what he was saying. 'We found out that one of our embryos had been given to a mummy and daddy in Kent and it had grown into a baby.'

'So . . . was that man the baby's daddy?'

187

'That's right. Yes he was. He's the baby's daddy.'

'Of course the baby isn't a baby any more,' added Jenny.

'How old is it then?'

'It's a girl. She's eleven now.'

'Oh.'

Mark continued. 'We're not really supposed to know anything about her, actually – who she is, or where she lives, or anything, but then . . .'

'What's she called?'

'Leonie.'

'Leonie what?'

'Er . . . well . . . Keegan. Her name's Leonie Keegan.'

'And why—'

'Everything was fine,' Jenny interjected quickly. 'We knew about the Keegan family but everyone was getting on with their lives. Then, nearly three months ago, we found out that Leonie's mummy had died. She was killed. It was in the newspaper. Really awful. And that's when we – Daddy and I – got very worried about Leonie, because she must have been feeling so devastated. You see, she's sort of our daughter too, because she was our embryo in the first place.'

'Before you gave her to the people in Kent.'

'Yes.' Mark took over the baton again. 'So that means the little girl is, biologically speaking, your sister.'

Chloe's grey-green eyes clouded. 'Not my real sister though.'

'Well, yes. She *is* your sister. I expect it's a bit of a strange idea to get used to at first,' said Jenny gently.

'But quite exciting . . . maybe . . . to think you've got a younger sister?' faltered Mark. 'A nice surprise.'

Chloe's face flushed. 'When I came in you were shouting at him, "I'm her father." But that man is her dad. Not you. You're *my* dad. Is that why he was so cross?'

188

'Well, yes. Sort of.'

'I don't blame him. And what about you, Mum? Do you think of her as your daughter?'

'Well . . . it's hard to explain. Obviously we don't think of her in the same way as we do about you. Nothing like it. We've never spoken to her; never even met her. She doesn't know we exist.'

'But you want her to know we exist.'

'Not necessarily.' Jenny looked at Mark for help but he'd buried his head in his hands.

'Why do you want another daughter? You've got me.' Her eyes were filling with tears. 'Anyway, you gave her away. You can't give something away and then take it back.'

'We're not trying to take her back,' interposed Mark. 'It's not . . .'

'Why do you have to spoil everything? We were perfectly happy and now you want . . . this other girl. Someone we don't even know.' She ran out of the room, banging the door behind her.

'Oh God,' breathed Mark.

They heard her footsteps thumping up the stairs and the muffled slam of her bedroom door.

Chapter Twenty-Three

Leonie could hear the music halfway down the street. Def Leppard. Her dad's favourite band. She smiled and quickened her step.

Daniel was lying full length on the sofa staring at the ceiling. She crossed the room and turned the volume down, making him start. He hadn't heard her come in. He turned his head to see his daughter standing in front of the stereo looking at him reproachfully; hands on hips, head on one side. She looked so like a child imitating an adult, Daniel had to smile.

'Really, Daddy. That was so loud. What will the neighbours say?'

'Oh, they won't mind. Why would they? That's good music that.' Laboriously, he rearranged himself into an upright sitting position.

'Are you all right, Daddy?'

'Yes fine, angel, thank you.'

'Why are you home so early then?'

'I had a bit of a headache so I took the afternoon off.'

'Have you taken some paracetamol?'

'No. I didn't think of it. Not a bad idea though.' He began to get to his feet.

'Stay there, I'll get them for you.' She ran off into the kitchen.

It was true, his head was pounding. And he couldn't shake off a searing feeling of shame. Not for his feelings – they were legitimate enough – just for losing control of his temper, particularly the girl seeing him like that.

Still, it felt good to have made his position clear and hopefully to have put paid to any chance of that Elfick guy snooping around ever again. He was still furious every time he thought about that.

But his visit to Wordsworth Grove had given rise to a whole new and unexpected set of feelings. He had seen Leonie's genetic parents. And her sister. The two children looked so like each other. And like the mother too. The pale, flawless skin and auburn curls; the clear, sea-coloured eyes; soft, sensitive lips and those dimples which gave the whole face an almost mischievous expression.

It had been a shock.

Suddenly he felt an outsider. For the first time in his life he wondered whether he was, after all, fully entitled to call himself Leonie's father.

How ridiculous. Of course he was. He'd brought her up, hadn't he? Eleven years. And yet what could he offer her? He could earn reasonable money, but only if he worked long hours.

Perhaps Leo would be better off with a two-parent family who felt a strong bond with her, who had more money than he did. And a sister for company.

He must stop this. It felt like a betrayal of Elinor to even entertain these thoughts. But it was true. Oh Elinor, why couldn't you be here? I need you so much. Why did you have to go and see that woman that afternoon?

He felt a stab of anger towards her. He'd told her that job was dangerous. Why couldn't she have carried on as a doctor's receptionist, instead of insisting on training as a health visitor? But then she wouldn't have been the wonderful, unselfish, adorable woman he'd loved so much.

'Elinor, Elinor. Help me here. Tell me what to do.' he moaned into his hands.

'What, Daddy?'

Leonie was back with a glass of water and two tablets in her outstretched hand.

Dan shook his head and tried to smile. He couldn't trust himself to speak. He took the glass of water, picked the tablets out of her hand and swallowed them.

'Why are you sad, Daddy?'

'It's just that I miss Mummy so much sometimes. You do too, don't you? I know you do.'

'Yes. But Miss Conway at school, she's my favourite teacher, she says that Mummy is still with us but we just can't see her. She is looking after us from heaven. I talk to her all the time.'

'So do I, Leo. All the time.' He bent forward and buried his face in his hands again. He couldn't bear Leonie seeing him like this. She rubbed the small of his back with her little hands.

'Your T-shirt's got a rip in it, Daddy. Mummy would have mended that.' She sighed. 'I can't do sewing. I could try though.'

He sat up, took a deep breath and pulled Leonie on to his knee. 'Forget about that. It's not important. Give me a hug and tell me where you'd like me to take you for supper tonight.'

'You mean go out?'

'Absolutely. Yes.'

'Are you sure? I was going to do us fish fingers and oven chips tonight.'

'You do too much around this house with all your schoolwork to fit in and everything. Let's both take the evening off. Where do you fancy? Pizza Express? Teetoes?'

193

'I can't take all the evening off, Dad. We did an experiment at school today to show about what happens when we heat metals and I've got to write it into my science book.'

'Oh that takes me back. Bimetallic strips and thermostats and all that, is it?'

'We didn't do the last thing you said. Just the bimetallic strip with copper and iron and we heated it up with a Bunsen burner and it bent over because copper expands more than iron.'

'Good stuff. OK, so you get going on that now and we'll go out in . . . let's say . . . an hour and a half. Six o'clock. How's that?'

'Wicked.' She jumped off his lap. 'Can I use the computer first?'

'Sure, of course you can. I'm going upstairs for a nice long bath.'

'Are you feeling better now?'

He smiled and ruffled her hair. 'You always make me feel better, angel.'

'Good.'

Chapter Twenty-Four

'Chloe. Supper's ready.'

Jenny heard Chloe's bedroom door open.

'I'm not hungry.'

'Come on. It's chicken pancakes.'

'I'll eat it in my room. I've got loads of homework to do.'

'You will not eat it in your room. You'll come down and take a proper meal break.'

'I don't want to speak to you. Either of you.'

'OK. That's your prerogative, but you'd better come and eat now or it'll go cold.'

'Is she coming down?' whispered Mark back in the kitchen.

'I hope so. The next step would be going up and physically dragging her down and I don't think that's an advisable option right at this moment.'

'She's too big for that now anyway,' mused Mark. 'When did that happen?'

'About five years ago.' Jenny smiled wryly.

The floorboards creaked upstairs. Jenny and Mark exchanged glances.

'Let her call the shots, remember,' hissed Jenny. 'Just don't blow it.'

Chloe marched in and sat down in front of her plate without looking up.

'You might find it needs extra salt,' said Jenny. 'I'm trying to use less of it in my cooking these days.'

'I bought a cookery book myself the other day,' said Mark.

'Really?' Jenny was genuinely surprised. Even Chloe looked up at him. 'You haven't taken an interest in cooking since . . . for about fourteen years.'

'Well I think it's time I took it up again,' said Mark. 'Properly. All the best chefs are men anyway.'

'That's just hype,' snorted Jenny.

'Seriously though. You're earning quite well lately, darling, and I've been thinking, maybe I should start spending a little less time at work and a bit more at home. Being useful.'

'I wouldn't worry,' murmured Chloe mutinously. 'By the time you've learned to cook anything decent I'll have left home.'

'You don't leave school for another five years,' Jenny pointed out. 'And you'll still be based at home even if you go to university.'

'I'll be doing a gap year,' said Chloe loftily. 'Probably in South America.'

'Right. Well. Sounds um . . . interesting.'

'Better work hard and pass all your exams first time then.' Mark realised the comment might irritate her before he'd got halfway through the sentence. He was right.

Chloe slammed her knife and fork down on her plate.

'Why didn't you tell me?' she shouted.

'We weren't supposed to know. That was why. We were trying to pretend to ourselves we didn't know.'

'How often have you seen her?'

Jenny looked at Mark.

'I've seen her twice,' he said. 'Both times incredibly briefly.

Once when she was a baby. And once after her mummy died.'

'Does she still live in Kent?'

'Yes, that's right.'

'Whereabouts in Kent?'

'Near Sevenoaks.'

'Quite near my pony club.'

'Yes. Not far from there.'

Chloe picked up her knife and fork again and pushed the remains of her pancake about thoughtfully on her plate. Mark and Jenny continued eating in expectant silence.

'Does she look like me?'

'From a very quick glimpse of her, I think she does, yes.'

'And she doesn't know about me? About any of us?'

'No. Well, not unless her dad tells her about us, but I don't think he will.'

Another heavy silence.

'Do you wish she could be your proper daughter? The same as me? Living here?'

'No! Of course we don't. We don't even know her,' exclaimed Jenny.

'What about you, Daddy? You'd like her to live with us, wouldn't you?'

'For goodness' sake! Of course not. All I'd like us to be able to do is to think of her as a kind of cousin, maybe. You know, think of her as part of our family.'

'But that man – her dad – why was he so angry? Does he think you want her to live with us?'

Mark was stumped for an answer to that one. 'I don't know what he thinks really.'

Jenny tried to come to the rescue. 'I think he's in shock. He's only just found out about us. It can't be easy to come to terms with.'

'Yes, and having a sister is a really, really important thing. It's a mega thing. I always wanted a sister. And you both knew I actually did have one. But you didn't tell me about it.'

'It wasn't such a simple—' Jenny began.

'Why would you think it didn't matter to me if it mattered so much to you? That's why I don't think I'm ever going to forgive you.'

'We deserve you being cross with us,' said Mark. 'Especially me.' He cast a guilty glance at Jenny. 'It's been mostly me that wanted to make contact.'

'Well thank you, Daddy. It's nice to know that Mummy and me aren't enough for you.'

'Oh God, it's not like that at all, Squirrel. Of course it's not. You mean the world to me, you and Mummy. I just thought we'd all like to get to know each other a bit. Families are so important. You know what they say about blood being thicker than water. And little Leonie doesn't have a mummy any more.'

'Perhaps you'd rather have her than me.'

'Now you're being ridiculous. You know you are.'

Chloe pushed her plate away and stood up. 'I'm going upstairs to do my homework.'

'At least she didn't slam the door this time,' commented Jenny as they heard their daughter's footsteps receding up the stairs.

Mark stood up to tackle the used saucepans at the sink. 'Do you think we've mollified her a bit at least?'

Jenny unclipped her hair and let it fall around her face, rumpling it with her fingers. She leaned back in her chair, 'I think there'll be more flak to come, but at least she knows the truth now. Or most of it.'

'She can't really think Leonie could ever take her place in the family, surely?'

'I think she was just saying that. Testing us maybe. I think what really upset her was that we'd kept it all a secret from her.'

'You know I think she could forgive us if she came to enjoy having a sister.'

'That's not going to happen, though, is it? Keegan has told you never to darken his door ever again. He wants nothing to do with us and that's that.'

'It's so frustrating. Surely there must be a way of making Keegan see sense. We could be such a support for him.'

'Listen, darling. I know it's hard for you to accept, but he's never going to see it that way and we have to respect that. I've had to collect you from the police once; I don't want to end up visiting you in jail. Or hospital. That wouldn't help anyone.'

He shrugged. 'It's just so difficult when all my instincts are screaming at me to be and feel one thing and everybody on the planet is telling me I'm in the wrong.'

'I've been thinking, Mark. Do you remember Yvonne? We had those sessions with her when we were deciding what to do with the embryos?'

Mark turned the saucepan upside down to drain beside the sink and rejoined her at the table, wiping his hands on the tea cloth. 'You think I need professional help then.'

'She might help you talk things through; get things clearer in your mind. She's a wise old bird. I remember how useful she was to me around the time you first found out about Leonie.'

'She might have retired by now.'

'I'd be surprised. She'd be in her mid-fifties now I should think. I've still got her old number. Try ringing it and see if she's still there.'

'I'll think about it.'

'I'll phone her for you if you like.'

'I'm quite capable of making my own appointment, thank you, darling.'

'Well I think you should.'

'Oh all right. You think I should. You've made your point.'

'And how about planning a little holiday for the three of us? Get on the internet next week while I'm down in Dorset with Annabel and find us some winter sunshine for half-term. The Caribbean. Or Morocco maybe. That's not so far. And maybe it'll help us get back on track with Chloe.'

Chloe opened her school rucksack and turned it upside down on to the floor. Sorting through the contents with her foot, she bent at last to pick up a geography text book. The French was supposed to be handed in first but she didn't feel in the mood.

She'd start with the climate change project. Geography was her favourite subject. She sat down at her desk and opened her laptop computer.

As usual, before she did anything else, she signed into her messenger service. Who was online at the moment? *Lil Miss Angel Dust.* Chloe tutted to herself. Katie Nelson. She was always on. A bit sad really. Desperate to talk to anyone. *IFoundNemo* was on too. He was usually online about this time.

She'd met him in a chatroom about horses. He'd told her his real name was Clyde and he had a live-in job as a groom at a stable yard up near a place called Filey somewhere on the Yorkshire coast. She wasn't sure how old he was. He looked late twenties. But she was fascinated. What a brilliant job to have. She'd got to know the names of all the horses he looked after: Badger, Wobble, Silver Mist . . . He sent her pictures of them. Badger was her current desktop background.

There was a pling. *Po-po Catty Petal* was signing in. That was Emma. Wait till she heard about this new sister her parents had suddenly announced. And Dad getting nearly beaten up. She began tapping on her keyboard.

Two more plings in quick succession and *Livininabox* and *DinoManiac* were there too. Great!

Chloe called up the climatology web reference she'd been given at school, promptly minimised the window and settled down to an hour or so of online friend-juggling.

Chapter Twenty-Five

Yvonne Allitsen had hardly changed in the thirteen years since Mark had sat beside Jenny at the Greenwich fertility clinic, knowing their last three embryos were languishing, frozen in limbo, somewhere in the basement beneath them.

He remembered she'd had two teenage children. Maybe they'd grown up and had children of their own by now. He wanted to ask her about them, but he wasn't here to talk about Yvonne's family life. He only wished he were. The clock on the little table was ticking. He had forty-five minutes to try to make sense of his tangled emotions.

She sat opposite him, neat and compact; her bobbed fair hair a dustier colour now, but her eyes as darting and watchful as he remembered them.

'So, Mark,' she began. 'You've been coming up against it a bit lately.'

'That's one way of putting it. You got my letter then.'

'I did. Thank you. You've been through a painful time.'

He had to make an effort to talk around what felt like a small rock at the back of his throat. 'I'm in the wrong whichever way I turn.'

'Does your wife think you're in the wrong too?'

'She has the same feelings as I do in many ways but . . . she's always been a more practical person. She's very concerned about Leonie's welfare too, of course. We can't help it.'

'But does she think you're in the wrong?'

'She thinks I handled things badly. And she's right; I did. Particularly with that incident at the school. I was stupid. And yet, I needed to see Leonie. I had to. I'd do the same again, but obviously I'd try not to lose my rag with the police and end up in the cells.'

'And what about your daughter, Chloe?'

'She's angry with me. And that hurts. Chloe's the most important thing in my life. She comes first. Before anything else. Even Jenny to be honest.'

'Why do you think she's angry?'

'I think it was a shock, mainly. And I think she feels Jenny and I were deceitful. But if I had told Chloe she had a sister, it wouldn't have ended there. She'd have wanted to know everything about her . . . who she was, where she lived . . . it would have got out of hand. She would have romanticised the whole thing, I'm sure. She was always saying she wished she had a sister. But we weren't supposed to know. That was the bottom line.'

'Playing devil's advocate here, do you think perhaps Chloe had a right to know she had a sister, no matter how difficult it made things for the adults involved?'

'Maybe. I just don't know any more. Because *I* knew, why does that automatically means *she* should have known? What I can't get to grips with is, when you're supposed to tell people what you know and when you're not. To keep a secret or not to keep a secret, that is the question.'

'Mm,' Yvonne murmured. 'It's *knowing* that has been at the root of your problems here right from the start, isn't it?'

'So I'm damned for keeping quiet. Then I'm damned for trying to bring things into the open. I don't know right from wrong any more.'

'Is Daniel Keegan keeping things quiet do you think, or has he told his daughter where she comes from?'

'I'm pretty sure he hasn't told her. He was desperate to make me promise I would never make contact again. He said he's already lost his wife and he's not going to lose his daughter. He's in pain, poor guy. I can see that. And I do feel bad about it.'

'So he thinks you want to take his daughter away from him?'

'I don't know what the social workers said to him, but when he came to our house I hope I made it clear we had just been worried about her, that's all, after Elinor Keegan's murder.'

'From his point of view though, he has a daughter on the brink of teenage and her mother has been cruelly taken away. Not only is he coping with his grief – and with Leonie's – but he has no one now to share the enormous responsibility of bringing her up. He has to be both mother and father now and he's probably not sure he's up to it. He almost certainly feels threatened by you.'

'That's exactly why I thought it would be good for him to know we care and that we'd like to offer any help or support we can. I just want him to treat us as family. Because we *are* family.'

'Perhaps he feels that's a choice he should make, rather than you.'

'You asked me just now if I didn't think Chloe had a right to know about her sister, even if it made things difficult for the adults. Doesn't the same apply to Leonie?'

'The problem is, Mark, the law doesn't acknowledge that right for an embryo-donated child. Not until he or she is eighteen.

Then they can find out their origins for themselves. If they want to.'

'But what if they don't know there's anything *to* find out?'

Yvonne inclined her head in her birdlike way.

'It's true. A lot of them don't . . . and I grant you that things may have to change in that direction. In these days of genetic progress and stem cell research, the amount of information that goes with a child's genetic roots is increasing, so withholding it has more implications.'

'So if, for example, it turns out that there's some medical problem in a child's genetic family which he or she could have inherited – or indeed if they have a wonderfully clean bill of health and life expectancy – shouldn't they be told about it? It's not just sentimentality. It's practical. People should know who they are.'

'Mark, higher minds than mine make the rules in the material world. My job is to help people find their way through the maze of their private, psychological one.'

'I think it's crazy. We're constantly reading about the Child Support Agency trying to trace fathers and get them to face up to their responsibilities; and here am I, a father who would have every excuse to turn his back, wanting so much to do the right thing.'

'Yes, I can see that and I admire you for it.'

'Well thanks, but where does that get me? We're in a world where scientists can do wonderful things. Miracles. They can take a barren couple, plant someone else's embryo in the woman's womb and make it grow. But then what? It's not for the scientists to address the "then what" . . . which is that the real parents of that miracle embryo are just supposed to quietly take a hike. The generous benefactors are now just an unwanted complication, an inconvenience. I know where my daughter is. I know who she is.

I know she's suffered this terrible, traumatic thing with her mother's murder and yet I'm told: how dare you concern yourself with your own child.'

'The law is quite clear though, Mark. You sign away your rights at the moment of donation.'

'That's a cop-out, Yvonne. What about *her* rights? The law is fine for facts. But human beings are more complex than a string of facts and dates. And I think the law is plain wrong if it means children can be created and then have their origins kept secret from them. Nobody has thought this through yet. The law is useless, and forgive me, Yvonne, but counsellors are useless too.'

Wearily, Yvonne put her clipboard face down on the low table in front of her. 'For what it's worth, Mark – and I've worked in this field for many years now – I do think it should be a more open process. I've come to believe that there's too much secrecy surrounding embryo donation. Everyone should know about the existence of everyone else from the start. A kind of extended family set-up. The secrecy is the problem in my opinion. By definition, somebody always knows a secret . . . and there's the weak spot. There's the spawning ground for betrayal, recrimination, deceit, manipulation and yet more secrets.'

'Surely someone has to take a stand against the system then?' Mark leaned forward eagerly in his chair. 'These scientific advances are all so new, the law is bound to lag behind. It's through people like me and Jenny and Daniel and . . . well, sadly not Elinor now . . . but it's only through people like us and our painful experiences that the law is going to come round to understanding . . . to evolving.' He slumped back, arms hanging at his sides. 'I think the best thing I can do now is open the whole thing right out. I can't retreat into the shadows. It's wrong. We all need to behave like adults – acknowledge each other and learn to accept each other. Don't you agree?'

Sue Cook

'Mark, you have to consider the agreements you entered into all those years ago. I'm not here to tell you what to do. My purpose is to try to help you through the thought processes; see things more clearly. What I will say is, keep your channels of communication open with Jenny and with Chloe. Your relationship with them is the most precious thing you have. Don't jeopardise that with secrets.'

'But I am not the Devil personified?'

Yvonne smiled. 'You're a good person. Just like the rest of us, you're trying to muddle through as best you can. That's the most any of us can do. Keep hold of that good heart of yours, that's the best advice I can give you.'

Chloe: hi ems wots happenin?
Em: Not much. You?
Chloe: Same. Mums staying with my godmother for the weekend. Dads in the kitchen cooking something fishy. The whole house stinks.
Em: ollie c looked at me today
Chloe: wow
Em: in a meaningful way
Chloe: thought you'd gone off him
Em: no
Chloe: you said hes got short legs
Em: still fit tho . . .
Chloe: i'm staying at yours tomo remember
Em: yeah I'll get mum to make your fave pasta sauce with bacon
Chloe: yum
Em: bring dvds I'm bored of all mine
Chloe: new harry potter or little miss sunshine?
Em: bring way more than that . . . we got 2 days of fun

Force of Nature

Chloe: i just found out i've got a sister

Em: what?

Em: you sure?

Chloe: yeah, think so

Em: how come

Chloe: complicated . . . after I was born mum and dad donated embryos to some other couple so that means the other couples baby is my sister

Em: cool. what's she like?

Chloe: dunno. haven't met her

Em: how old?

Chloe: about 12

Em: year 8 kid

Chloe: yep

Em: could find her on bebo or myspace

Chloe: yeah maybe

Em: lets look now

Chloe: nah

Em: wots her name i'll look if u like

Chloe: cant be arsed

E: oh go on

C: sometime when I feel like it

Em: maybe when youre at mine then. can't wait for tomo.

Em: my mum will pick us up after school

Chloe: cool see u tomo lol

Em: don't forget dvds

Em: bye hun xxxx

Chloe: ☺ xxxx

Em: ♥

Chapter Twenty-Six

On her knees on the cracked tiled floor of Annabel's kitchen, Jenny plunged both hands deep into an enormous sack full of moist, dark multipurpose potting compost. The sink and draining boards were strewn with a tangle of uprooted plants. Outside, rain was lashing the garden from a heavy grey sky.

'It's like Armageddon,' said Jenny as a sudden gust of wind threw a volley of hail against the kitchen window. 'Someone round here must have upset the gods.'

As if on cue, there was a growl of distant thunder.

'We just got these inside in time,' said Annabel. 'Poor things would have been battered to death.'

'Hand me those busy lizzies, would you?'

Obediently Annabel scooped an armful of plants out of the sink and knelt beside her friend.

'Here we are darlings . . . Jenny's going to put you to bed, all nice and cosy for the winter.' Jenny began teasing out the mesh of roots, separating them into individual plants and laying them out in a row beside the pot she'd just filled with compost.

'Thanks for doing this, Jen,' said Annabel. 'Much as I love bedding plants, I'd never get round to all the palaver of bringing them all in and then planting them all out again next year. It's so much easier to buy a whole lot of new ones every spring. All this seems too much like hard work to me.'

Jenny trailed a clump of bare roots into the pot, and began heaping the dark earth around them, pressing and patting them firmly into place, letting the flowers poke their heads jauntily over the edge on their stems. 'It's no hardship just bringing them in over the winter to protect them from the frost. It's a labour of love really. I've got plants I've had for years; they keep on dividing and growing and dividing again. They're like old friends.'

Annabel stood back admiringly, wiping her hands on the baggy denim overalls she usually wore to paint and sculpt in. 'You're a real chip off the old block, aren't you? Just like your mum.'

'Oh, Mum was a magician. A green witch.' Jenny smiled, reaching out a loamy paw for the glass of Sauvignon blanc on the soil-strewn floor beside her. 'You could take her the deadest looking dried-up old stalk and go back in a month and find it sprouting green shoots all over the place.'

'Do you remember how she used to embarrass us when she took us out for walks as kids? She always had a pair of scissors in her bag and she'd whip them out whenever she saw an interesting plant in a park or someone's front garden and snip off a cutting or two which she'd pop into a rolled-up plastic carrier bag she always kept in her pocket. "A bit of judicious pruning will only do them good," she used to say.'

Jenny laughed. 'We used to walk on ahead and pretend we had nothing to do with her.'

'She was good fun, your mum.' Handing Jenny a clutch of brilliant red geraniums to work on, Annabel knelt on the floor beside her friend and looked sideways at her under her eyelashes. 'You must miss her.'

'I do. A lot. Especially at times like now, with all this business with Leonie. I'm quite worried about Chloe. She's not her usual happy-go-lucky self lately and I don't know whether something particular is bugging her or if it's just part of growing up . . . becoming a teenager. Mum would have got her to talk, if anyone could.'

'She's not a happy bunny then, our Chloe?'

'No she's not. She's a pain in the neck, to be honest. Secretive, sulky, monosyllabic . . . She spends hours in front of her computer in her room talking to friends on Googlechat or whatever it's called. If Mark or I put our heads round the door she quickly minimises the screen and tells us we should knock before we come in.'

'That's all standard teenager stuff, surely?'

'I suppose it is, but it's hard to tell what's normal teenage stuff and what's a direct result of finding out she's had a full-blooded sister all these years.'

'What gets her goat? The fact that you didn't tell her?'

'I think that's mainly it. She feels we deceived her. I must admit it's quite a bombshell to drop on a kid.'

'Quite. Has she shown any interest in following up on this sister? Getting in touch with her?'

'No sign that I've seen. In any case, we told her that Leonie's father wants no further contact between our two families, and she seemed to accept that quite readily.'

'Not surprising, after seeing the man trying to give her dad a thumping. But you'd think she'd show some curiosity about Leonie.'

'She did at first. She wanted to know how old she was and if they looked alike and so on. Then a couple of days ago she asked what school she goes to, but beyond that she hasn't wanted to discuss it.'

Annabel handed over another clutch of plantlets. 'What about the murder? I'm surprised she hasn't wanted to know about that.'

'Oh yes. She certainly wanted to know about that. She was horrified, like we were. She was in floods of tears . . . and very sorry for Leonie. A couple of times lately she's told me she's dreamed that I had been murdered. It hit her quite hard. That must be another reason for her being a bit subdued at the moment.'

'For sure, yes.' Annabel reached down a clean pot to be filled with compost. 'I was wondering . . . Another reason . . . Do you think she's jealous at all? You always told Chloe she was special because of the way she was born. Now she knows there was another special "Dotty in a Dish". She might be feeling that she's lost, you know, her specialness in your lives.'

'Oh dear, I do hope not. Both of us take any chance we get to tell her she's the most important thing in the world and how much we love her. Almost too often at the moment.' She patted the last of the geranium stems into the soil. 'Oh well, I guess we'll all weather the storm. Eventually.' She scrambled to her feet. 'Right, there we are, all your babies safe in their winter beds.' She grabbed hold of the worktop, wincing. 'Ow, my legs have gone to sleep.'

'Getting old,' laughed Annabel, struggling to get off her knees herself. 'Now for a top-up on the old Sauvignon blanc by way of reward.'

'Where do you keep your brush and dustpan?'

'Under the sink. Where am I going to put all these pots now?'

'Why don't we line them up in front of the French windows? I'll do that while you start dinner. All this indoor gardening has given me an appetite.'

Annabel took a chopping board from a hook on the kitchen

wall. 'Do you think Chloe worries that there might come a time when Leonie does become part of your lives and she'll have to share you?'

Braving the rain for a moment, Jenny opened the kitchen door and slung the contents of the dustpan outside. 'No, really Annabel. We've made it absolutely clear to Chloe that all Mark wanted – we wanted – was simply to let Leonie know that she had family she hadn't been aware of before, who would be there for her if she ever needed us. That's all. There's never been any suggestion of us moving in on her life in any way, or her moving in on ours.'

'Well, the sight of Mark and Keegan fighting in her living room that afternoon must have been awful for her, poor baby. Seeing *any* men fighting is scary, let alone your own dad.'

'Yes, it was I think. I really wish she hadn't had to witness that.'

'And they were fighting over Leonie ... which probably doesn't make Chloe feel too good.'

'Oh God ... I wish I knew what's really going on in her little head. As I said, I so wish Mum were here. Mark and I are suffering from damaged credibility at the moment.'

'Well *I'm* always here, Jen, if she ever needs someone outside the family to talk to. I'm so fond of Chloe. I think she's fond of me too.'

'Oh, she is. There's no doubt about that. Thanks.'

'Tell her to come down and spend a few days with her good old Auntie Annabel. We're only five minutes' drive away from the seaside, tell her.'

'I will. She'd like that, I'm sure. You might have to order up some better weather though.'

Annabel reached up, took an onion from a basket on top of the fridge and began attacking it with a knife on the chopping board.

Suddenly, mid-chop, she stopped. 'Jenny. I've just thought of something else.'

'What?'

'I don't know, maybe I shouldn't say anything. It's not my business.' She started to chop again, but less energetically.

'Come on, Bels, we're old friends. There's nothing we shouldn't be able to say to each other.'

Annabel put down the knife and wiped her eyes with the back of her hand. 'Well, it's just that your mum died of colon cancer, didn't she?'

'That's right. Why?'

Annabel blew her nose on some kitchen paper and took a sip of wine. 'And you have to have regular screening now because it's a hereditary disease, right?'

'Yup. I have to be screened every two years. And once a year after I've turned fifty.'

'And so Chloe will have to get regular screening one day too?'

'Yes, she will, I'm afraid. From the age of twenty.'

'So what about Leonie then? She's got the same genetic make-up as Chloe, so she should be screened, too, when she gets older.'

'I suppose you're right. Yes.'

'But she won't know, will she?'

'No,' said Jenny slowly, 'I suppose she won't. They asked us so many medical questions before the embryos went up for adoption. I remember there being concerns because of Mark's father's heart problems, so the Keegans will have known about that; but obviously we had no idea Mum was going to get colon cancer.'

'So don't you think Leonie should be warned? To take the proper preventative steps later on? If her father isn't telling her where she really comes from, she'll never know, will she?'

'Oh God, Annabel. I hadn't thought of that.'

The two of them were silent for a moment or two while the implications sank in.

'But there's nothing I can do, is there?' said Jenny at last. 'Our hands are tied.'

'I suppose you could tell Keegan about it sometime.' Annabel threw the pieces of chopped onion into a pan of smoking oil on the hob.

'Dear Mr Keegan,' pronounced Jenny over the sound of sizzling, 'I know you said we shouldn't contact you ever again but I thought you might like to know that Leonie's grandmother died of colorectal cancer. Yours sincerely, Mr and Mrs Embryo Parents.'

'Well, daft as that sounds, maybe you will have to do something exactly like that. I don't want to be overdramatic – overdramatic? *Moi?* – but it could be the difference between life and death for the kid one day. Anyway, let's change the subject for now. Penne alla Bella ready in half an hour.'

Jenny gazed at the browning onions, lost in thought.

'Oi. Dilly Dreamboat. Chop a carrot or something. There's nothing you can do right now. I didn't mean to cast a damper on things. Tell me what you're doing for your birthday next weekend.'

'Oh, who *gives* a damn. Nothing I expect. Trying not to think about it. Worrying about Mark and Chloe as usual I expect . . . And Leonie. You're right, Bels. We can't just turn our backs on her. But that is exactly what we're expected to do. The police made Mark feel like a criminal for wanting to take an interest in her. So did her father.'

'I can't think of a way round it. You keep hearing these days the phrase "the child's interests are paramount", the little mantra of the so-called professionals. But so often they're not, are they? It's still the adults deciding what they *think* the child's interests are.'

Sue Cook

'"The child's interests are paramount,"' repeated Jenny. 'The question is, where do Leonie's best interests lie? Jogging along happily with Daniel Keegan, the man she knows as Dad . . . who *is* Dad as far as she is concerned? Or turn her world upside down to inform her of her true genetic heritage – which may or may not turn out to be of any relevance to her future welfare?'

Annabel rummaged in a cupboard for an enormous lid to put on the pan of now gently simmering meat sauce. Straightening up, she gave Jenny a long sympathetic look. 'You've had a bit of a hard row to hoe this last fifteen years, haven't you?'

'Annabel, just don't. Don't start sympathising or I'll turn to a blubbering lump of mush. Put the lid on it. Literally.'

Annabel smiled, put the lid on the pan and bent to check the size of the flame on the gas ring.

'Darling Jen. I don't want to be sentimental. But for ages now you've been trying to hold everything together; trying to keep tabs on Mark, protecting Chloe. It must be like—'

'I'll tell you what it's like, Bels. It's like I hardly exist any more, not as a person in my own right. It's like Mark, Chloe and I are in this little boat out on the ocean . . . and it keeps springing leaks . . . and I'm running round the hull desperately plugging up the holes. No sooner have I mended one, than another one springs up and I rush over and plug that, and then there's another one and another one and I can't sit down for a single moment or we'll start sinking.'

'Perhaps it's time you rowed ashore, darling. You need a break. You've been needing one for a while now.'

'I can't just let things drift though. You've made me realise that, Annabel. There's a decision to be made here, for the sake of that little girl at least.'

'*Two* little girls actually,' said Annabel. 'Plus three adults.'

218

'The child's interests are paramount,' mused Jenny. 'Sounds so simple, doesn't it?'

'And right this moment *our* interests are paramount. Pour us another glass of wine, for goodness' sake.'

Chapter Twenty-Seven

It was a few minutes past one in the morning when Mark put the Prius into electric mode and coasted silently round the corner in Simmons Road, coming to a stop at the kerbside forty yards or so down the road from number 115.

His heart began pumping harder in his chest. Keep cool. Keep calm. He groped clumsily under the passenger seat in search of the eBay purchase that had arrived the day before yesterday. If his plan worked, it would be seven pounds thirty-five well spent. He flattened it against his chest and zipped his jacket up over it.

Pushing the car door to, rather than slamming it shut, he padded round to the boot, opened it and took out a black ten-litre fuel can. He lowered the lid but again did not slam it shut. Must avoid attracting attention at all costs.

He glanced up and down the street, praying no one was watching him from one of the windows. He must look so bloody furtive. He could almost hear the presenter's voice on that television crime programme.

'At around ten past midnight, a witness remembers seeing a man, probably in his late forties, wearing a dark-coloured, pull-on fleecy hat and bulky denim jacket and carrying what was almost certainly a petrol can, approaching Daniel Keegan's Transit van.'

He felt a bit of a veteran now though. Nothing would be quite as much of a shock to the system as that first brush with the police. And he hadn't been breaking the law then. This time he was. He could hear the swish of his own blood in his ears as his heart pumped it round his body. It reminded him of the time he went snorkelling in Greece. He hadn't enjoyed it. The sounds in his head of his physical self, the very engine room of his being, labouring away to keep him alive, made him feel panicky.

Quietly, he positioned the ten-litre can on the pavement beside the van. The first hurdle was the filler cap. If it was locked, that would be the end of it. The filler door creaked open on its hinge. Please don't anyone hear. No keyhole. Brilliant.

He waited. No lights went on. No curtains seemed to be twitching. So far so good. Mark twisted the cap off. It opened easily. Now for the tricky bit.

Reaching into his jacket, he could smell the rancid sweat of fear in his armpits. He pulled out the siphon pump; a length of hosepipe with a copper nozzle inserted into one end. A metal ball jangled inside it. The business end. Following the instructions that had arrived with the package, he fed it down into the van's tank and began wiggling it up and down.

A trickle of diesel ran into his container on the pavement and then stopped. He wiggled the hose some more, resulting in another trickle which, once again, dried up the moment he stopped jiggling the nozzle in the gas tank. Dammit. When he'd practised with a bucket at the kitchen sink that afternoon, he'd got it flowing beautifully.

He couldn't stay here all night. Nothing for it. He'd have to suck the other end and risk a mouthful of fuel. Gingerly he put the open end of the pipe, already tasting of diesel, into his mouth and sucked. He managed to let only about a teaspoonful of the disgusting stuff into his mouth.

Managing not to gag, he spat as quietly as he could into the gutter. It was worth it though. The fluid rushed from the hosepipe – drenching his shoes and trouser hems before he could get the end back into the container. He cursed under his breath. Thank heavens Jenny was in Dorset with Annabel. She'd certainly have wanted to know why he was creeping back to the house at two in the morning reeking of diesel.

He just hoped Keegan hadn't filled up recently. He'd been here a good fifteen minutes as it was. Any excess would have to go down the nearest drain. Diesel was fairly innocuous stuff. He hoped it was, anyway. The marble rattled gently in its copper sleeve as the fuel coursed into the can.

Chapter Twenty-Eight

Mark was wide awake the instant the radio alarm came on. Maybe a split second before. Had his heart been beating this fast all night?

05:24.

He'd had a little over three hours' sleep. He'd be tired later perhaps. Right now he was high as the proverbial kite on adrenalin.

Ten minutes later, chewing furiously on some gum from a packet Chloe had left on the table in the hall, he was once again at the wheel of the Prius heading south.

Heart FM woke Dan at five minutes to eight as usual. 'Spirits in a Material World'. He got out of bed and boogied to the window to open the curtains.

Grey sky again. This Police number took him back. His old band, the Fingerprints, used to play their own, slightly slower version of it. Must be a good fifteen years ago now. Before he and Elinor had discussed starting a family and decided he'd better train up for a job that would keep him closer to home and bring in a more predictable income.

Humming along with the melody line, he dragged his jeans

off the back of the bedroom chair and held them up near the window for inspection. A bit grubby. The hot-water cylinder cupboard he'd spent most of yesterday afternoon working in could have done with a good hoovering. But these jeans had seen worse in their time. A lot worse.

Elinor had always washed and tumble-dried his working clothes every night as a matter of course. He'd go downstairs in his boxers in the morning to take them off the kitchen airer, stiff and clean and smelling of soap powder. Even when she was working late, she never forgot.

Holding the jeans by the waistband, he gave them one hard flip to shake any surface dust off. These would live to fight another day.

Dan and Leonie ate breakfast in the kitchen these days, perched on stools at the work surface.

Elinor had always set the table in the dining room. It would be the last thing she did before she came to bed. Clean, crisp tablecloth, placemats, knives, forks, cereal spoons, butter in a butter dish, sugar in a sugar bowl, milk in a milk jug . . . all the right crockery and two, sometimes three, packets of cereal to choose from.

These days, Dan and Leonie always had the same thing. Dan had cornflakes and black coffee, Leonie had Honey Nut Cheerios and apple juice. All the paraphernalia on the table wasn't necessary. It had been nice when Elinor was there to do it but now, when it came down to it, it was unnecessarily time-consuming.

Sometimes at the weekend, Leonie would decide to fry a couple of rashers of bacon and an egg for them both with some toast.

She had appointed herself head of Sunday breakfast occasionally when her mum was alive. Dan smiled to himself.

She'd appear in their bedroom doorway, a little figure aged seven or eight, one tea towel knotted around her waist, another folded over her arm, waiter style, the dog in attendance, wagging his tail.

She'd have a menu written out in coloured pencils, with everything she could think of that anyone might want for breakfast. There were kippers on offer and 'smoaked haddack', every 'sireal' Kelloggs ever manufactured, every 'friut juce' she could think of, plus bacon and every method of cooking an egg.

Dan and Elinor would sit up in bed pretending to um and er over the menu, eventually plumping for something they knew was available in the fridge and that she could manage to produce without cutting or burning herself.

'You wouldn't have any orange juice by any chance?' Dan would say.

'Of course we've got orange juice. Look where it says,' Leonie would lisp, leaning over them to point at the menu with her index finger.

'Oh good, then I'll have orange juice please.'

'OK,' writing it down on her little notepad, 'that's one orange juice. What about the lady?'

'Well now let me see.' Elinor would glance from the menu to the ceiling and back again as if racked by indecision. 'I think I'll have, no I won't, I'll have . . . oh, why not treat myself just this once . . . I'll have apple juice, please. And one slice of toast with apricot jam please. Have you got apricot jam?'

'Yes we have, madam. And sir?'

'I'll have the cornflakes with milk on the side, please waitress.'

'Tea, coffee?'

'No thank you,' they'd say quickly, mindful of possible disaster coming back up the stairs with the tray. 'Just juice today.'

Sometimes happy memories hurt more than unhappy ones.

*

'Earth to Daddy.' Leonie's arm had disappeared past the elbow into the packet of Cheerios, trying to scrabble the remains from the bottom of the packet into her bowl. 'I said we need to go shopping on Saturday. We need more cereal, soap . . . lots of things. I'll make a list.'

'You're an angel, my angel. I couldn't do without you.' Was that emotional blackmail, he wondered, because he'd been feeling threatened, scared she might be taken away from him? He found himself questioning his motives so often lately. He really must try not to do it.

'I'll rinse the dishes now, Leo. My first client's not till nine, and only down at Sevenoaks, so I've got fifteen more minutes than you've got to be out of here.'

She made a face. 'French grammar this morning. Wanna swap, Dad?'

'Sure. You won't mind spending half the morning with your hand down Mrs Wilkinson's toilet will you?'

'Oh gross. On second thoughts, I think French grammar could be very fun. See you, Dad.' She stood on tiptoe to kiss him on the cheek. He bent at the knees to make it easier.

'See you later, darlin'.'

'Don't forget to shave!'

Ker-slam.

The house seemed to shrink the moment she left it. The silence, the stillness, were almost unbearable. Boot felt it too. The dog stood looking at the door she'd just gone through, head on one side, ears up, willing her to come back through it again. After fifteen seconds or so he gave up hope, turned and trudged back into the kitchen where Dan was running the cereal bowls under the tap and up-ending them on the drainer to dry.

He shaved quickly by feel over the kitchen sink. Elinor would have been horrified. So would Leonie. He dragged his old

228

grey, sticker-covered toolbox out from the cupboard under the stairs.

'Right then, Booty boy. There are lavatories out there to be dynamited, boilers to hit with spanners, washing machines to kick back into life. It's a tough job, but someone's got to do it.' Boot wagged his tail and waited for Dan to open the back door. 'Into the fray we go, my old mate.'

The two of them emerged from the side of the house. Dan opened the driver's door, letting Boot bound in ahead of him to take his place bolt upright and expectant on the passenger seat.

Putting the toolbox on the driveshaft cover between the two of them, he climbed in himself, leaving the door hanging open, and inserted the ignition key. The engine coughed into life and he slammed the door. First gear, and the van set off up the street, managed about five yards, stumbled and then stopped.

'Come on. I'm the one with the job to do, all you've gotta do is get me there. Not too much to ask, is it?' He turned the ignition off and on again. A splutter, but no life beyond that. He tried again. Not even a splutter this time. 'For God's sake!'

He checked the fuel gauge.

'It's bloody empty!'

True, he hadn't filled it up since last Wednesday, and he hadn't checked it when he parked it outside the house yesterday, but he hadn't done that much mileage, had he? He should have had a couple of gallons in there at least. How could he be so stupid? All this business with the Elficks must be getting to him even more than he'd realised. Hadn't he had enough to cope with? Would life ever again get back to seeming normal and straightforward and – dare he even think the word – happy? Perhaps it wouldn't. Well, perhaps it would, but it would take some time.

Anyway, this wasn't the end of the world. He had a five-gallon can in the back. It was the can he'd transferred from the old van and he hadn't had to use it for a good ten years. Maybe more. Diesel didn't go off did it? No, of course not.

'Stay there, Booty pal. Just a slight technical hitch. We'll be on the road in no time. Just gotta fill her up.'

The sound of someone gently clearing his throat behind him made him jump, losing his connection between the nozzle of the can and the filler hole. He leapt back just in time to stop diesel spilling all over his feet.

'Oops. I'm sorry,' said a voice.

Looking up in irritation, Dan's face drained of its colour. 'You!'

'Yes, I'm really sorry. I know what you said, but . . . look, Daniel, I . . . I need to talk to you.'

'How dare you come here! This is my home!'

'You came to mine.'

'Get lost will you, Elfick. I've got a job to get to.'

Hearing the voices, Boot jumped down from the van and came round to see what was going on.

The two men stood looking at each other. A stand-off.

'Just give me five minutes,' Mark pleaded. He hoped Keegan wouldn't notice the effort he was having to put in to not trembling.

A neighbour, walking by with a Jack Russell, slowed down to eyeball them curiously. Boot nosed his way up to her terrier's rear end to get better acquainted.

Dan glared at the woman. The last thing he needed was a scene out here in the street. He screwed the cap back on the now-empty can, slung it in the back of the van and slammed the door shut. 'Five minutes,' he snapped over his shoulder. 'No more.'

Dan strode back towards his house, leaving Mark to follow uncertainly in his wake, Boot trotting purposefully past him to resume his rightful place at his master's side.

Dan back-kicked the kitchen door shut behind them. Mark found himself standing in a small, old-fashioned kitchen: pale blue, melamine-veneered cupboards, a couple of stools with vinyl padded seats, a drainer full of dishes and cutlery, a fridge humming sporadically in the corner.

Above their heads on an indoor line were pegged a few items of clothing, including, Mark registered with a sharp shock of recognition, a pair of purple pyjamas covered in leaping cats and kittens – identical to the ones Jenny had bought for Chloe from Miss Selfridge last Christmas.

Dan was leaning back against the fridge, arms folded, looking at him with what looked like a mixture of suspicion and intense dislike. Not an auspicious combination.

'I know what I promised the other day, but I just had to see you,' Mark blurted. He'd thought of a few good opening lines on the drive over. What the hell were they?

Dan's expression changed, now a blend of anger and near-admiration. 'Did you siphon the diesel out of my van?'

'I was going to give it back to you. I've got it in my car.'

'You devious bastard.'

'I couldn't think of another way of getting you to listen to me.'

'Why would I want to listen to anything a sly . . . scheming . . . sneaky . . . pillock like you would have to say?'

'All right, yes, I have been scheming. And yes, I suppose I've been sneaky too. But I've had no alternative.'

'Oh. Forced into it, were you?'

'Come on, Daniel, just for one moment can you just try to see things from someone else's point of view. I didn't want to be handed the information about Leonie all those years ago, but I was.'

'You made considerable efforts to find out who and where we were. Don't bother pretending otherwise. The social workers told me.'

'That's right. I did. I'm her biological father. How could I just shrug and turn my back, pretend I have no connection with my own flesh and blood? I wish I *could*, but I can't. I just have this basic human . . . drive to make sure she's OK in the world. You can understand that, can't you?'

'Well, let me reassure you then. Leonie is OK thank you. Absolutely A-OK. Couldn't be more OK. So there you are. Now you can feck off out of it and we can all get on with our lives.'

'Daniel, you keep looking backwards all the time, thinking if only this hadn't happened. But it *has* happened. And now we have to find a way forward.'

'No we don't. We don't *have* to do anything. All I want . . .' A mobile phone trilled. Dan fished in his jeans pocket . . . 'is for you to leave us alone.'

He studied the number display for a moment before answering it. 'DeeKay.' A pause. Mark could hear the chirrup of an insistent female voice on the other end. 'Well I'm sorry about that, Mrs Wilkinson, but I'm afraid the world doesn't revolve around you and your lavatory. I'll be there as soon as I can but if that's not good enough for you, be my guest and call another plumber.' He clacked the phone shut and dropped it back into his pocket. 'I don't know why I'm having to say this to you again. The last thing Leonie needs right now is a bunch of strangers coming along telling her that she's supposed to feel some sort of tie to them. You are no use to us, Elfick. Far from it. Get that into your arrogant head, why don't you?'

'*I'm* arrogant!' Mark could feel his knees beginning to go weak again, but with indignation now. 'All right. I know you've been through a hell of a tough time. I won't insult you by saying I understand how you feel, but I am at least trying to.'

Dan snorted. 'I actually don't give a flying—'

Mark held up a hand. 'Just hear me out. You owe me that at least.' He took a deep breath. Daniel was silent. Good sign. 'This hasn't exactly been a picnic for my wife and me either. We didn't just give up those embryos without a second thought. It took a lot of agonising, but eventually, even though we realised it meant we could have a child or children elsewhere in the world that we'd never know about, we decided to give them the chance of life. You wouldn't have Leonie if it weren't for us. Doesn't that deserve some consideration, some measure of respect?'

'Sure. I know that. And we were grateful. It was the answer to our prayers. But, hell, we're talking years ago. And let's face it, you fathered an embryo. Something that wouldn't have got beyond a dish if it hadn't been for us. *I've* fathered a *daughter*. For the past eleven, nearly twelve, years I've fathered a living child. From *birth*. From the time she started growing in my wife's womb in fact.'

'Daniel, it took *both* of us – me and you – to get that little life beyond a dish. That's the bloody point!'

'The *point*—' Dan's face was as close to Mark's as it had been back in Blackheath when he had pressed his spine pressed against the French windows. Mark stood his ground and hoped he wouldn't get spit in his eye again. 'The point, my friend,' Dan continued, 'is that you weren't supposed to contact us. That was the *deal*. That's the *law*. And you,' he jabbed a finger into Mark's chest, 'have broken the law. *None* of this is my fault.'

'Oh right. The law. Of course. It's all so simple, isn't it?' Mark shuffled sideways to gain himself a little more space. 'Listen, stuff happens. Things don't work out all nice and neat according to some rigid pre-arranged plan. Human feelings don't tend to follow laws – why would they? Even if they made perfect sense, which, actually, I don't think they do in our situation.'

'Oh, fine. So let's all do what the bloody hell we choose when we choose and sod the consequences.' Dan flicked a lock of hair out of his eyes. 'What are you? Some middle-class, anarchist throwback from the sixties? You make me sick.'

'Daniel, what are you so frightened of? You honestly think I'd try to take Leonie away from you, don't you? Do me a favour.'

'I don't need to be frightened of anything, buddy. *You're* in the wrong here, not me. And that's the top and bottom of it.'

'You can't seem to get past that, can you? We're *both* victims of circumstance here. Look. There's no point trading insults. Whatever we think of each other, it's Chloe and Leonie we should be thinking about.' He glanced up at the kitten pyjamas pegged on the line. 'Two little girls who are sisters . . .'

'Your point being?'

'Just think of the fun they could have together. They could have so much to offer each other . . .'

'Leonie has plenty of friends. She doesn't need—'

'Friends are one thing, but being an only child can still be lonely. I was one myself.'

'Don't you come here telling me my child is lonely. What do you know?'

'Well, Chloe has always said she wishes she had a sister. I remember when she was three or four, she went through a phase of setting an extra place at the tea table for "her little sister" along with her favourite toy pony and teddy.'

Dan forgot himself for a moment with the memory jolt. 'That's what Leonie used to do, exactly. She had toy ponies too. Still has as a matter of fact.'

Mark gave a short chuckle. 'Chloe's always been pony mad . . . almost before she could talk.'

Dan's expression softened a little. 'Leonie too. Anything to do with horses.'

'She was always on at us to buy her a pony,' Mark continued, encouraged. 'Obviously it was impossible. Almost impossible. It would have needed a paddock and feeding and exercise . . . She still gets on at us about it though.'

Dan's face set hard again 'Leonie would no more dream of asking for her own pony than fly to the moon. We don't live in that kind of world. Which is why, Elfick, this whole conversation is pointless. We're from different bloody planets.'

'Sure. I'd agree with you there. All the same,' Mark took a deep breath, 'after what Leonie's had to go through, don't you reckon she'd be chuffed to think she has other family? You could think of Jenny and me as a kind of auntie and uncle. And the two girls . . . both nuts about horses . . . only eighteen months apart . . . I bet they've got loads in common.'

'You know diddly squat about me and Leonie.' Dan turned his back on Mark, resting his forehead against the fridge door. 'I am doing the best I can,' he was plainly struggling to stop his voice breaking, 'in the only way I can. You are not bloody helping.'

Mark waited uncertainly.

'Right.' Dan remained with his back to Mark. 'You've said your piece. Now please go.'

'All right. I will. I just have to say one more thing. You don't care about me or my family, you've made that abundantly clear. But what about Leonie? Don't you think she deserves the chance to make her own mind up? You love Leonie very much, that's obvious. But your relationship with her harbours a . . . a fundamental deceit. And that's wrong.' He took a step towards the back door, opened it, then turned. 'She has a *right* to know the truth, you know.'

Leaving the door open, he walked down the side passage towards the street. Would there be running footsteps behind him? Would he turn to see a fist heading for his face? Or would a voice call 'OK, come back. You're right. Let's sit down and work something out'?

Silence.

It was beginning to rain as he fumbled in his jeans pocket for his car key.

Fifty yards along the road, the adrenalin had ebbed away; Mark's foot turned to jelly on the accelerator pedal. At the end of Simmons Road he turned left.

Priory Gardens had been given a smart new sign and he was pretty sure the fence had been replaced, but apart from that, the little park looked much the same.

He parked in the very same bay he'd used ten years before; the day he'd tailed Elinor here – and Jenny had tailed him. He turned the engine off and sat listening to the raindrops pounding on the car roof.

Two decent ordinary blokes, that's all they were, each wanting nothing more than to be the best dads they could possibly be to the daughters they loved. Shouldn't that make things easy? Shouldn't that make everything right? Why then were both their hearts breaking? He put his head down on the steering wheel and wept.

Chapter Twenty-Nine

'Don't you think she deserves the chance to make her own mind up?'
That infernal man's voice kept sneaking into his head. *'She has a*
right *to know the truth, you know.'*

Damn him. Elfick was right. He knew that. He wasn't stupid.
But how, in practice, could he possibly drop a bombshell like
that on Leonie only eleven weeks after her mother's death?

If he could have seen into the future all those years back; that
this man Mark Elfick would suddenly emerge from the
woodwork, then he and Ellie would have told Leonie the truth
from the start. It wasn't that they hadn't wanted to tell her; it was
just that it had seemed too complicated to explain to a small
child and somehow it just never happened.

The reality was that it had been all too easy to forget that
another couple had been involved in Leonie's arrival into the
world. It might have been different if they'd gone through the
years of treatment the Elficks had undergone, but it had been
plainer sailing for Dan and Ellie. Leonie had grown in Ellie's
womb and had been born in the normal way. She just felt like
their own genetic daughter.

Of course they'd both wondered sometimes . . . where Leonie
got her aptitude for mathematics; her total lack of interest in

singing or playing an instrument when he and Ellie had loved music so much – Ellie had had the voice of an angel – and the profusion of curly hair was a characteristic neither he nor Ellie could find in their ancestry.

Would Leonie get round to wondering about these things herself one day? She'd showed no sign of it so far. And now, if she were to find out that he and Ellie were not her genetic parents, how would she react? Anger that she'd been deceived? Acceptance? Understanding, even? Or just plain indifference?

One thing was for sure: if she was going to learn the truth, he should be the one who explained things; but it had to be in his own time and in his own way. And he simply couldn't tell Leonie now. Not until she'd had more time to get over Ellie's death.

Trouble was, it didn't look like Elfick was just going to go away.

Oh Ellie, come back.

There was one solution: how would the child feel about living near his sister in Ireland? Bernadette wouldn't object. Far from it. She loved her niece like a daughter. She'd also remarked that Leonie should have a female influence in her life.

'It won't be easy for you bringing her up by yourself,' she'd warned. 'Teenage daughters can be complicated creatures.'

'I know that. I had one for a sister,' he'd retorted.

'Seriously though, you've got periods, boys, fashion-mania . . . all to come. I'll buy you a parenting book for Christmas.'

'Look. Thanks. There's no need to rub it in. I'll manage,' he'd replied stiffly. Bernadette had a heart of gold but she'd never been the soul of tact.

Dan's thoughts ended as they so often did lately, mired in a slough of futile regrets and resentments. None of this was supposed to have happened. Elinor being so cruelly taken from him, and now the Elficks to deal with. Coping with all this alone was just so bloody hard.

'Come on. Can't do any harm to look her up.'

'You're not to tell anyone else.' Chloe cast her eyes around her friend's bedroom in a vain hunt for something to divert her attention. She was wishing she'd kept her mouth shut now.

'How do you spell Leonie? There can't be too many of those around.'

'Promise me, Emma!'

'Look. I'm your friend aren't I? We'll try Bebo first and then MySpace . . . Leonie Keegan . . . Hmm . . . Wow, there's loads of Leonies. What does she look like?'

'Mum and Dad said she looks quite a lot like me.'

'None of these are her, are they?'

Chloe pulled her chair reluctantly closer to her friend's and peered at the screen. Emma scrolled down through photos of posturing girls of various shapes and ages. 'Definitely none of those no. Forget it, Em. Let's watch a DVD.'

'What's her school?'

'I can't remember,' Chloe lied.

'Yes you can. You said your dad told you.'

'Somewhere in Sevenoaks. Something-or-other Park.'

'Think, Chloe. Come on. Oh, hang on. Never mind. I think I've found her. She's on Bebo. Leonie Keegan. This has got to be her. She calls herself *The Lion Princess*, would you believe. She's got forty-seven friends.'

'Oh my God. My heart's gone all funny. *"Lion Princess"* . . . This is weird.'

'Hey, she does look like you, Chlo. Geekier, but really like you. It's the hair.' She scrutinised the screen. 'The hair and the big, greeny-grey eyes.'

'Let's have a quick look at her profile then. I hope it's not too embarrassing.' Did she want to like this girl or hate her? Chloe wasn't sure.

'OK,' said Emma, reading from the screen.

♥Heya I'm leonie but everyone calls me lionhead because of my curly hair, ive tried straitners and even my mums iron once but nuffin makes any difference so guess ill be living on the wild side for the rest of time hehe♥

♥Things i love♥
horses, my dog, horses, banoffee pie, horses, long baths, horses, people who aren't two faced, horses, going out for pizzas with my dad, oh and horses

'Another horse lover then, Chlo-Chlo. Must be in the blood.'

Was the little prickle she felt pleasure or jealousy? Again, Chloe couldn't decide. Was she being doubled? Or halved?

'Let's see what films she likes,' Emma continued.

♥Films♥
wallace and grommit, little miss sunshine, march of the penguins, shrek, all the harry potters of course

'Hmm. Not particularly original,' commented Emma. 'What about music?'

♥Music♥
I'm not really musical. My dad is. He plays the saxophone. He used to do gigs and stuff but now he mostly just sings in the bathroom. I like Eric Clapton, Coldplay, Keane and lots of other stuff.

Chloe studied Leonie's electric-pink Bebo page disapprovingly. 'Hasn't she heard of anyone cool like the Kaiser Chiefs or Razorlight or GoodBooks?'

'Let's look at her pictures.'

'I don't know. This feels like spying a bit, doesn't it?'

'We do it with other people. What's different about doing it with Leonie Keegan? She's supposed to be your long-lost *sister* for God's sake.'

'Yes I suppose so.'

'Her pictures are nearly all horses. *Portraits* of horses. You've got lots of horses on yours but at least you've got people with most of them.'

'She's only about eleven though,' said Chloe defensively. I shouldn't have involved Emma, she thought. I should have done this by myself. 'Are we going to watch this DVD or not? I'm bored with this now.'

Emma was browsing through more of Leonie's photos. ' "Me, Dad and my dog Boot in my garden",' she read. 'He looks nice, her dad. Kind of smiley and sad at the same time.'

'That's not what he looked like when *I* saw him.' Grabbing the mouse from her friend's hand, Chloe clicked on 'Sign out'.

Chapter Thirty

A lone pigeon, club-footed, scavenged fruitlessly for edible litter. Waterloo station seemed to be better swept now that they'd refurbished it. Mark stood waiting by the barrier on platform eleven. Jenny's train was late.

She'd said she'd get the Tube or a taxi home but he had insisted on coming to meet her. He wanted to tell her about his meeting with Daniel Keegan. She was going to be pretty pissed off with him going back to Fulrow Green yet again without consulting her. He planned to suggest a glass of wine and a snack in a wine bar before they collected Chloe from Emma's house.

In a public place, he was hoping Jenny wouldn't feel able to give full vent to her anger when he told her what he'd done.

Jenny banged her glass of vodka and tonic down on the restaurant table.

'You did *what*? Do you *want* to go to jail? Are you *trying* to bring shame and humiliation on us all? Particularly your daughter who'll have to go to school and face all the nudges and whispers from her schoolmates if the story gets into the press? I go away for two days – just *two* days. *Every* time you take matters into your own hands you end up in trouble. Keegan isn't a rational man at the moment. We've seen that for ourselves. I'm amazed he didn't report you to the police. This time they'd have charged you for sure.'

'Can I speak now?'

'I give up. I really do.'

Mark glanced uncomfortably round the tapas restaurant they'd happened on a couple of hundred yards from the station. Expanses of glass, stone flooring and shiny-surfaced wooden chairs and tables fortunately conspired to make the acoustics so bad that customers would be finding it hard to make out what the person sitting with them was saying, let alone people at any of the neighbouring tables.

'It was when I saw Yvonne while you were away – it made me realise, talking things through with her – if *I* don't sort this situation out, nobody will. You won't. Keegan won't. It has to be me.'

'Why can't you just face facts?' She stopped. A sullen-faced waiter in a crumpled white shirt with a button missing and red satin bow tie was wordlessly offloading little brown earthenware dishes on to their table from a lacquerware tray: tortilla, fried calamares, chorizo and patatas bravas. He shambled away. Jenny continued. 'The situation is not sortable, Mark. Keegan doesn't want us in his life. Face it.'

'I needed to have one last try. See if I could connect. I'm sorry but I'm not ready to just lie down and accept defeat. I simply want to cut the crap and apply some straightforward common sense.'

'Which of course is defined by creeping around in the middle of the night siphoning off somebody's petrol and then ambushing him on his way to work, risking getting beaten up or arrested or both.'

'Neither of which actually happened.'

244

'More through luck than judgement.'

'I wanted him to know I had no intention of trying to take his daughter away from him. And to ask him whether he didn't think Leonie should be given the chance to make up her own mind about acknowledging our presence in the world . . . especially Chloe's. The two girls could have such a lot to offer each other. That's all I said really.'

'And he showed you the door of course.'

'He did hear me out first though. To his credit. Basically he just wants everything to go away. But of course it can't. What's happened has happened.'

'So what did you achieve, do you think?'

'I don't know yet. Maybe, just maybe, he'll get round to telling Leonie. I know it sounds self-righteous, but he's not being honest and straightforward with her, is he? Now that he's met you and me and Chloe, he really ought to tell her the truth. How do you think Leonie will react a few years down the line if she finds out he's been keeping us a secret from her?'

'This isn't just about Daniel Keegan, is it, Mark? Be honest. It's about you too, you and *your* needs.'

'All right, maybe it is in some ways. I'm human. I have feelings. Genuine, caring feelings. I'm not ashamed of them and I can't deny them. Nor can you, Jenny.' Mark picked up a cocktail stick and began carving the piece of tortilla on his plate into ragged bits with it. Neither of them had so far touched the food in front of them. 'I love you and Chloe. So much. You know that. And, ever since I've known about Leonie I've had feelings for her too. Isn't that natural? It's not just some shallow egotistical indulgence. I can't bloody help it. I would stand back if I thought it was the best thing for Leonie. I would, truly. But I think she would be better served by knowing the truth. She *should* know the truth. It's her right, dammit. And then once she knows, it's up to her what she wants to do with the information. She might be pleased as punch to discover she has close blood relatives who care about her. Or she might want nothing to do with us. That's her call. Absolutely. Is that so selfish? Is it? God help me, I don't know any more.'

'Oh Mark. I don't know either. I think I've been trying so hard to keep you on the straight and narrow that I haven't allowed myself to work out my own feelings. I care about her too. I feel the same pull. But from what I saw of Daniel Keegan's attitude the other day, I reckon the more you pester him, the more intransigent he'll get.' Jenny studied Mark's face. He looked like she felt. Exhausted. Grey. 'Somehow we've got to stop this,' she said. 'We're driving ourselves crazy.'

'Do you want any of this?' Mark spooned a blob of cubed potatoes and a few morsels of chorizo on to Jenny's plate.

'I'd rather have another drink I think.'

Mark raised an arm in the direction of the waiter who looked pointedly through him before turning and disappearing through the swing door into the kitchen.

'Miserable bugger.'

'Daniel Keegan has been through an appalling six months. He's frightened. And he's coping with all this alone. He needs time and space. We can give him that, surely?'

'Of course we can. Yes, yes. You're right.' He closed his eyes, took a long, deep breath, let it slowly out and opened his eyes again, looking sadly into Jenny's. 'Let's go home.'

Chapter Thirty-One

'Bernadette! Phone call.'

'Who is it?'

'Your brother.'

Bernadette took the handset with stained, rubber-gloved fingers.

'Dan. How are you doing?'

'Been better, Bernie. Have you got a minute?'

Bernadette glanced across the salon at the thirty-something woman leafing sourly through *OK* magazine, tinfoil spikes haloing her head. 'I'm doing some highlights.' She looked at her watch and lowered her voice. 'OK, I've got about five minutes before I stick her under the tap.'

'Bernadette. I need your help.'

'What's wrong?'

'I need you to find me somewhere to live.'

'What do you mean? Here?'

'Yes. Killarney. Near you. Like you suggested before.'

'Dan! That's brilliant. I thought you were determined to stay in Kent.'

'I've changed my mind. You said Leonie needs a woman in her life. You were right, Bernie. I can't . . .' She heard a choking sound at the other end of the line.

'Dan? What's the matter?'

'Got a bit of a cold, that's all.' His voice sounded muffled. 'Wait a mo.' She heard him blow his nose.

'So have you sold your house then?' she asked when he came back on the line.

'No, no. This is early days. I'll not put it on the market till I've seen what's around in Killarney.'

'And what about your work?'

'Didn't you say your Declan could put some work my way?'

'Yeah he could, I'm sure. He's got plenty going on right now, working on three different houses at the same time.'

'Typical builder!' Dan laughed.

'So what sort of price are we looking at?'

'Two-fifty thousand tops. I don't want a big mortgage any more. I want to spend less time working and more with Leonie. And I want to play in a band again.'

'You should be able to find a nice little three-bedroom place easy for two-fifty. What does Leo think though?' Across the salon, the junior was sweeping hair from the floor in slow motion. 'Callum . . .' Bernadette caught his eye, jerking her head in her client's direction. With exaggerated care, the boy propped his broom against one of the dryers and sashayed over to stand behind the woman, becoming straight away sidetracked by the article the client was reading, bending over her shoulder to get a closer look. 'I've got to go now, Dan; I've got to smack a junior round the head. I'll wander round a few agents at lunchtime and call you later.'

'So.' said Jenny. 'What shall we do this weekend?'

'As little as possible.' Mark flopped on to the sofa, draping his legs over one of its arms. 'Watch the athletics on TV. And at some point I've got to drive over to Midhurst. One of my clients wants me to buy back a William IV dining table I sold him three years ago.'

'Rosie's mum's picking me up in a minute.' Chloe pulled a banana off the bunch in the fruit bowl and stuffed it into her rucksack along with her fleece jacket. 'They've got a new pony at the stables. Have we got any cartons of juice? If not can I have five pounds to buy some stuff on the way?'

'. . . doesn't go with the rest of their furniture apparently. I said to him, why not buy some more William IV pieces then? I've got a couple of lovely carvers . . .'

'She's called Snowflake. She's an Appaloosa. Her last owners didn't look after her properly. She had lice and redworm and everything when they got her. How can people be so selfish and cruel?'

'And what about you, Jenny?' said Jenny. 'What would you like to do? Me? Oh, don't worry about me; I'll just do some washing and ironing, and then when I've done that I'll wash the car, and then I'll cut the lawn before I go out and buy something for Sunday lunch tomorrow because if I don't nobody else will, and then maybe, just maybe, if I'm really self-indulgent, I might sit down and drink a toast to myself to say Happy Birthday.'

Chloe and Mark widened their eyes at each other.

'Oh. God. Jenny. I forgot.'

'Well, not to worry. Why should you remember something as trivial as my birthday? You just carry on doing what you were going to do.'

'*I* hadn't forgotten, Mum. I was going to get you something on the way home. That's why I wanted the fiver.'

'Why don't we go out for dinner tonight? I'll book a table. Where do you fancy?'

'Oh that'll make it all right, won't it? Steak and chips and a bottle of Merlot. I don't want to go out for bloody dinner. I want you to take the trouble to find out what I *do* want.'

'All right, what do you want to do?'

'Do you really want to know?'

Chloe hoisted her rucksack on to one shoulder. 'I'll go and wait outside.'

'Oh no you won't,' exclaimed Jenny.

'Hang on a moment, Chloe,' said Mark.

'But Rosie will be here any minute now.'

'Tell her you're not going,' said Jenny firmly. 'You can go and see Snowdrop or whatever her name is some other time.'

'But Mum. That's not fair!'

'Maybe not. Life isn't always fair. Get used to it.'

Mark looked at Jenny in astonishment. This was so out of character. He didn't know what to say. She had seemed depressed and prickly ever since he confessed to his last visit to Keegan. Perhaps it was simply the inescapable fact of another birthday. That must be it. Next year she'd be fifty. A real milestone. Not that she looked it. He swung his legs off the sofa and got up to put his arms round her. 'My darling Jenny. I'm really sorry I forgot your birthday. It must be because you never seem to age. The older you get, the more beautiful you look. And you don't usually set much store by your birthday anyway.'

'Come off it, Mark. You haven't the first clue how I feel about my birthday. You take me completely for granted. Nothing I do or say counts for anything. I feel like I'm virtually invisible most of the time.'

'That's not—'

'Do you know something? I'm sick and tired of trying to make everything all right all the time for everyone else. For once, just once in my life, I'm going to put myself first. OK? I'm going to do what *I* want to do. And what's more you – both of you – are going to go along with it.'

'We don't take you for granted. Do we?'

'I need a bit of cherishing. A bit of spoiling. Just for once.'

'You do. You do! Absolutely. And that's exactly what you're going to get. You deserve it, my darling. Starting from now. Isn't that right, Chloe?'

Chloe dumped her rucksack on the floor and flounced out of the room.

'Where are you going?' Mark called after her.

'To tell Rosie I'm not coming because my mother's thrown a humongous wobbly.'

Jenny shrugged hopelessly and sat down on the sofa Mark had just vacated. 'Sorry. I shouldn't have lost my rag. I just feel a bit overwrought.'

'No, you're right to be angry. I don't mean to take you for granted, but maybe I do. I suppose I always think of you as the dependable, practical one of the two of us. You are always so . . . unshakeable . . . so solid.'

'Well, I'm just as full of insecurities and worries as you are, Mark. You must know that. It's this business with Leonie. It's really getting to me.'

Mark walked round behind her and put his hands on her shoulders. 'I know. It's been a tense time for both of us.'

She covered his hands with hers and squeezed them. 'I feel ashamed of myself now. Perhaps we'd better tell Chloe she can go to the stables after all.'

'No. You wanted a family day for your birthday and that's what you're going to have. If I were a fairy godfather, how would you wish to spend your day? One wish.'

'You'll laugh.'

'Try me.'

'I want to go to Gorilla Kingdom at Regent's Park.'

'Really?'

'I've always adored gorillas and I've wanted to go ever since it opened back in the spring. I mentioned it to you a couple of times but you didn't seem to register.'

'Right. In that case, that's where we'll go. It's a good day for it too. Nice clear sky.'

Chloe clumped back into the room holding a few envelopes which she thrust into Jenny's hand. 'Post. Birthday cards for you mostly. Maybe that'll put you in a better mood.'

'Oh. Thanks.'

'You two finished arguing now?'

'We weren't arguing,' protested Mark.

'Sure. Didn't sound like it.'

'I'm sorry I shouted, darling.' Jenny tousled her hair in unconscious despair. 'I was hurt that you both forgot my birthday, that's all. It was childish of me.'

'I didn't forget,' grumbled Chloe. 'I told you, I was going to get you something later. I think you just wanted an excuse to shout at us.'

'That's a bit unfair. Why do you say that?'

'Because you're grumpy all the time. Both of you are. Things haven't been the same in this house since that man came round and you were forced into telling me about . . . you know . . . Leonie.'

'I don't know why you should think that,' said Mark. 'Everything's the same as ever. What do you think has changed?'

'Do you want to talk a bit more about the situation with Leonie?' Jenny enquired uneasily.

'Only if you've got any more to tell me?'

'I'm afraid not.' Mark shot Jenny a warning look. He didn't want Chloe knowing about the petrol siphoning.

'I don't think you are telling me the truth. What you really want is— oh never mind.'

'No, go on darling, explain what you mean,' Jenny persisted gently.

'What you really want is to get to know Leonie. And you're upset because you can't. And you're miserable and snappy with *me* because of *her*. So it's not fair.'

'Oh Chloe,' exclaimed Mark. 'I'm sorry, I really am. Things are going to change now, sweetheart, I promise. We *were* hoping we might all get to know Leonie, I admit, but . . . it ain't going to happen. We're not allowed to and that's that.'

'We'd be breaking the law if we did actually so we absolutely mustn't,' Jenny interjected. 'We just have to put it all behind us now and forget about it.'

Mark pulled gently at one of his daughter's corkscrew curls, watching it spring back into position in her ponytail. 'Sweetheart, we love you to bits. The last thing either of us wants is for you to be unhappy.'

'Well,' mumbled Chloe, only slightly mollified, 'all I can say is, it's just not much fun here any more, that's all.'

'Life does get a little bit less fun in some ways as you get older,' tried Jenny. 'Now you're in year ten you'll have more responsibilities: more homework to do, more decisions to make about what subjects you want to specialise in and all that kind of thing. That's the way life goes. It's called growing up.'

'Great.'

'Anyway,' said Mark brightly, 'it's Saturday so we can forget all about school for now. Mum's had this great idea. We're going to the zoo.'

'The *zoo*? I'm giving up seeing Snowflake to go to the zoo! What do you think I am, a little kid?'

'Mum wants to see the new gorilla enclosure at Regent's Park as part of her birthday treat. And so that is exactly what we are going to do.'

Em: where you been all day?
Chloe: zoo. don't ask
Em: zoo? Who with?
Chloe: its my mum's birthday today. she decided she HAD to see the gorillas
Em: oh cool
Chloe: my mum and dad being really weird
Em: what sort of weird
Chloe: snappy and grumpy . . . whispering to each other in the kitchen when they think I can't hear
Em: snappy with you?
Chloe: each other as well, everyone
Em: why
Chloe: gotta be about this other girl I think
Em: the sister?
Chloe: yeah
Em: so what you gonna do about it
Chloe: just let them get over it i spose
Em: what if they don't?
Chloe: i'll come and live with you ☺
Em: were they weird at the zoo
Chloe: no . . . happiest they've been for days. Dad bought her cuddly gorilla
Em: aaah

A pling announced *IFoundNemo* signing in. Clyde. Chloe smiled.

Chloe: hang on
Chloe: brb

Clyde was someone she could confide in. There were some things she didn't want her school friends knowing about, making lame comments.

They'd gone into a total omigod-fest over Leonie. Omigod you've got a sister! Omigod how did you find out? Omigod does she look like you? Omigod will she come and live with you?

Clyde never, ever, said omigod. Clyde was older and wiser than Emma and Rosie and the others. And there was something liberating about knowing that she'd never meet up with him face to face, nor, more to the point, would her parents or her friends or anyone else in her day-to-day life.

Chloe: hi clyde
Clyde: hi cloworm how's you?
Chloe: good thanks, been to zoo.
Clyde: cool
Chloe: not really. How's Badger?
Clyde: Badger's mint. Worried about little Morgan tho
Chloe: why
Clyde: she's been really sick . . . colic I think, in pain and bloaty . . . wanting to lie down all the time
Chloe: o no poor morgan
Clyde: vet thought she might have to be put to sleep last night but she's much better this evening I've been walking her round and round the paddock all day since 5am
Chloe: good ole doctor clyde ☺
Clyde: think she's turned the corner bless her heart . . . now I need some sleep
Chloe: you going off line now?
Clyde: yeah, speak next week maybe
Chloe: remind me to tell you about this sister ive just found out about

Sue Cook

Clyde: what sister? your sister?
Chloe: yeah
Clyde: explain
Chloe: maybe next time. When you not sleepy.
Clyde: you've woken me up now. Really exciting. Not everyday you find you got a sister you didn't know you had

'Chloe? You still up?'

Chloe hastily shut her laptop lid as Jenny, flush-cheeked, put her head round the bedroom door.

'We had a really nice meal at that new Moroccan place. The waiters brought me a honey cake thing with a sparkler in it when we asked for the bill and sang happy birthday.'

'How embarrassing.'

'Yes, you'd have hated it.' Jenny perched on the edge of Chloe's desk.

'I'm just getting ready for bed,' said Chloe irritably.

'Have you been OK while we were out?'

'Course.'

'And you didn't answer the door?'

'No, Mum,' Chloe sighed with exaggerated patience. 'Nobody rang on the doorbell and the phone didn't ring either so no one knows your guilty secret.'

'What guilty secret?'

'That you left me home all by myself on a Saturday night. Poor lonely neglected child that I am.'

'Hey, we wanted you to come with us but you wouldn't.'

'Just joking. I was fine.'

'And you should be in bed by now.'

'Well, the quicker you leave me alone the quicker I'll be there.'

'I'm not allowed to see you getting ready for bed any more then?'

'I don't think that's necessary these days, do you?' said Chloe stiffly.

'We used to be such good mates.'

'Oh Mum. I just need my own space a bit sometimes.'

Jenny bent and kissed her daughter first on the forehead and then on each cheek. 'OK. I understand.' She went back to the doorway. 'Goodnight then, sweetheart.'

'OK . . . Mum?'

'Yes?'

'Love you.'

'I love you too, darling.'

When Chloe opened her laptop again, Clyde had gone offline. She scrambled into her pyjamas, washed and cleaned her teeth in the bathroom and negotiated her way past discarded shoes, clothes, books and papers to get into bed. She switched off her bedside lamp, pulled her pony-covered duvet up to her chin and lay staring at the glow-in-the-dark stars on her ceiling.

After a minute or two, she switched the lamp back on again and looked at her watch. It felt more like half past nine than half past eleven. She didn't feel the least bit tired. Clyde was right. It was exciting to think she had a sister. A real full-on sister. A twin sister almost.

It was funny, she'd always felt deep down that she wasn't an only child in the world; that a part of her was missing. Something that should have been there wasn't there. Maybe it was found now. Maybe it was Leonie.

She squirmed out from under the duvet, picked up her laptop and brought it back to bed with her.

Leonie Keegan . . . There she was. *The Lion Princess*. Blue striped jumper. Earnest green–grey eyes looking straight out into hers. A frizz of red-brown hair around her face. 'Last updated an hour ago,' it said under her picture.

So Leonie had been up quite late herself, for an eleven-year-old.

'47 friends'

Chloe clicked on some of the names: 'Lovely Lady Lucy', Little Miss Fairy Lights', 'Dotty Lottie' . . . normal eleven- and twelve-year-old preoccupations: teachers disliked, birthday parties, films, music, TV programmes.

It was so much better looking her up without Emma making fun of everything.

She clicked on a series of photos entitled 'making cakes at amy's'. Three small girls wearing aprons over their jeans and T-shirts, one of them stirring something in a large mixing bowl while the other two grinned at the photographer . . . close-ups of little cakes dotted with clumsy splodges of pink icing and silver balls.

Another, entitled 'school outing at national portrait gallery', showed classmates eating sandwiches, hanging on to each other, acting up for the camera.

Chloe trawled for pictures of Leonie herself but there were frustratingly few of her; presumably it was she who had taken most of the photos. The ones she did find, she pored over greedily. Unlike many of Chloe's friends and schoolmates, who loved to pout and posture and stick their tongues out for their Bebo and MySpace pictures, Leonie was always smiling: open, unselfconscious.

It was strange to be staring at the face of a girl who was actually your younger sister and yet had no idea you existed. Chloe felt a tightness around her heart. It surely couldn't be real, could it, this surge of warmth towards an eleven-year-old girl she'd never met, even if she was, supposedly, her sister?

What messages had she received this last couple of days?

hi lioness hope you got home ok the other night. I got tania's cold now. Can't stop snuffling and sneezing. Think I'll just tie a toilet roll round my face and keep it there. See you in geography xxxxx

Chloe smiled.

Wot's this julip pony thing you're asking for lion?

said the next one.

Never heard of em. Try ebay xxx

Julip thing? Wow. Leonie collected Julip ponies too! Chloe strained to make out some of the words on the screen against the busy pink star-spangled background.

Calling all Julip lovers – Anyone got Christie and Black Diamond?
This is the only one I haven't got out of the six sets and I finally saved up enough money only to find it's sold out! I got various things I could swap. Call me or msn me and we could negosiate.

Chloe had only recently managed to complete the full collection herself. There they all were, looking at her from the smart acrylic display case Mum had brought back from some house she had been redesigning.

Black Diamond was the latest addition to the catalogue and her favourite, with his glossy black coat and the white diamond on his forehead. Resplendent in purple socks and saddle, he took pride of place on the shelf amongst Dandelion, Conker, Pandora, Montana and their riders. Black Diamond's rider, Christie, stood next to him in her matching purple show jacket, proudly holding his bridle.

Parting with them would be a wrench, and difficult to replace, being a limited edition. They weren't cheap either; the pair of them had set her back the best part of thirty pounds. He'd be a good excuse to contact Leonie though.

But then, did she *want* to contact Leonie? Did she dare? Mum and Dad wouldn't be pleased. They had said it was against the law or something. Well, that didn't make sense. How could it be against the law to speak to your own sister?

Her parents really didn't seem to have the first clue on how to cope with the situation, apart from bickering with each other about it. She closed the laptop lid and turned off the light.

Chapter Thirty-Two

Starbucks at Waterloo was noisy and crowded. Finding a stool to perch on at a high circular table beside two business men in suits, Chloe was beginning to regret suggesting this as a rendezvous point. This meeting was nerve-racking enough without it being almost impossible to hear each other speak.

At least she wasn't worried about recognising Leonie. She'd studied her pictures enough. She still wasn't prepared for the physical shock of seeing her younger sister in the flesh though. She looked so like Chloe herself had looked a year ago.

Leonie looked surprised when she saw Chloe too. Not that she knew the truth of her relationship to the older girl, of course. Chloe had simply made contact on the strength of Black Diamond.

In her message, she hadn't exactly said she would sell him, but that she *might consider* selling. She wasn't sure which was the truth. Leonie had replied within ten minutes.

'Yay! Fantastic! Please please please can I see him? Can I meet up with you somewhere after school?'

Waterloo station had seemed to Chloe the best place, being easy for them both to get to by public transport.

Chloe's next few days had passed in a state of nervous

apprehension. She hadn't told a soul. Much as she loved Emma and Rosie, they wouldn't understand. They'd have gone blabbing all round the school about it, making it seem like the end of the world and trivial at the same time. This was too important to be bandied about the place like a piece of juicy gossip. And if her parents had got to find out about it, that would have been the end of it for certain.

As Leonie walked towards her in her school uniform, unruly auburn hair escaping on all sides from a navy blue headband, carrying a backpack in brown corduroy with a pony's head appliquéd on to it, Chloe wasn't sure even now whether she'd done the right thing. She certainly didn't know how the conversation would go after they'd done the deal over Black Diamond. If they did a deal. Would they even like each other?

'Chloe.' It wasn't a question. Leonie would have seen Chloe's picture on MySpace of course, when she'd sent that first message about Black Diamond.

'I'm sorry,' blurted Chloe, 'but there's only one stool between us and I wasn't sure what you'd want to drink so I got us both a hot chocolate but if you rather have something different I'll have them both and I'll get you something else.'

'No, hot chocolate is my very favourite. Thanks. And I don't mind standing up,' said Leonie. She sounded confident enough, but Chloe instinctively felt it was a front she was working hard to present.

At a low rectangular table flanked by two bucket-shaped leatherette seats, a couple of women stood up to leave.

'Quick!' Chloe nudged Leonie so hard, it was almost a push. 'Bag that table!'

Leonie made a dive for the two chairs, flinging her bag on to one and herself on to the other, getting there just ahead of a balding man with a paunch. Chloe followed more cautiously, balancing her own bag on one shoulder while trying not to spill the drinks. They settled themselves in, giggling, conspiratorial in victory.

Sipping at their hot chocolates, each sized up the other over her cup. She looks a lot like Mummy! thought Chloe – the roundish face shape and the dimples either side of her mouth when she smiles. The little gap in her front teeth is exactly the same as Dad's. Aloud, she said, 'So, you're the Lion Princess.'

Leonie nodded shyly, tracing patterns in the dollop of whipped cream on her drink with her wooden stirrer.

'Oh. Sorry. Silly me!' Chloe unzipped her backpack. 'Here he is.' She placed Black Diamond carefully on the table between them and bent over to fish inside the bag again for his rider.

'Can I hold him?' asked Leonie.

'Of course.' Chloe picked the horse up, both hands under his belly, and held him out towards the other girl.

Leonie fondled the long glossy mane and tail. 'The mane isn't as thick as Conker's. I like it better.'

'I know. Me too. Dandelion's is too long and bushy as well; a bit too much like My Little Pony, isn't it? I cut it with my mum's hairdressing scissors.'

'You didn't!' Leonie stared at her wide-eyed.

'Just shortened it a bit.'

'I tied ribbons in Conker's to make it a bit neater.'

'I did that too! Yellow ones.'

'Of course.'

They smiled shyly at each other. Both palpably relieved. They liked each other. So far so good anyway.

'So . . . Are you selling him?'

'Well . . .' Now it came to it, she couldn't let Leonie have come all this way only to snatch him back. 'I think so.'

'You need the money for something else I expect, or else you wouldn't be parting with him.'

'No. Well, yes.'

'I'll give you the full price as new. I've been saving up.' Leonie lifted the appliquéd flap at the front of her backpack, unzipped a pocket inside and brought out a heart-shaped leather purse.

'I like your bag.'

'Thanks. I've had it for about three years. I've been thinking maybe it's a bit babyish but my mum bought it for my ninth birthday.'

Chloe opened her mouth to say something sympathetic about Leonie's mother, then remembered she wasn't supposed to know anything about her and closed it again.

Leonie spilled the purse's contents on to the table. A cascade of coins and three crumpled five-pound notes.

'I like your purse too.'

'Daddy gave me this.' She turned it over. 'My name's on the other side.' She smiled, a little embarrassed, and pushed the money in Chloe's direction. 'Twenty-nine pounds fifty exactly.'

'But that's all you've got. What about getting home?'

'Oh, I've got some more money in a different purse. For coffee and things. Oh!' She widened her eyes and put her hand to her mouth. 'I owe you for the hot chocolate. I almost forgot.'

'That's OK. We might have another one anyway.'

'Yes!' She was eager to redress the balance. 'Would you like another one now?'

Chloe felt that tight feeling across her ribcage again. She had an absurd desire get up and give the younger girl a hug. She smiled. 'In a minute.'

They fidgeted, staring at each other awkwardly again.

'We look quite like each other, don't we?' hazarded Chloe at last.

'Yes, I thought that, but I didn't like to say. You mightn't have thought it was a compliment.' Suddenly self-conscious, Leonie pulled the hairband off her head and tried to smooth her recalcitrant frizz with her fingers.

'I hope you don't mind me saying, but you'll never get it to look right, flattening it down like that. I know, because my hair's really similar to yours.'

'But your hair seems to behave itself so much better than mine. You've got proper curls, nice and shiny. Mine doesn't know if it's supposed to be curly or straight, so it's a failure at both.'

'There's this great stuff that's like conditioner and styling gel at the same time. You can get it at Superdrug. I think there's one on the station here somewhere. I'll show you later if you like.'

'Oh my God, yes please. Is that what you use on your hair?'

'Yeah. It's brilliant.'

Leonie smiled her shy smile again. 'We could be sisters, almost, couldn't we?'

'Well, we . . .' As the words came out of her mouth Chloe knew they were huge. Like bricks. Like boulders. Like mountains. She should have stopped them but they'd started coming and she wasn't strong enough to hold them back. 'We *are* sisters.'

Leonie stared at her. She couldn't have heard right. She smiled blankly.

'My mum and dad are your parents too,' Chloe persevered.

'I don't understand. How can they be? I don't know what you're talking about.'

'Forget it. Never mind.' This wouldn't go well. Maybe it wasn't too late to back-pedal.

'I've got parents,' protested Leonie. 'Well, my mum's dead.

But . . .' Her voice tailed away and she looked wildly round the coffee bar as if searching for corroboration.

Chloe shuffled forward on her seat. 'It's a bit complicated. We can change the subject if you like. I just thought you ought to know. Adults seem to think we're not grown up enough to be told the truth about things.'

'What? What do I ought to know?'

'Did your mum and dad tell you they had problems having a baby?'

'No.' Leonie's clear, sea-coloured eyes were filling with tears. Dad's eyes.

'Well they, did. And my mum and dad had problems too.' Chloe was wishing with all her heart that she'd never started this. 'They ended up having to . . . well . . . you know about the facts of life and stuff, don't you . . .'

'Yes.'

'. . . the mother's egg meets the father's sperm and all that.'

Leonie was looking down at her heart-shaped purse, turning it over and over in her hands. Some remote part of Chloe's brain observed that her nails needed a scrub and the cuticles pushing back.

'Anyway, sometimes the doctors have to do that bit in the laboratory – which seems a better idea to me anyway.' It was no use trying to joke. Leonie looked devastated. Stricken. Chloe soldiered on. 'You know what an embryo is?' A hint of a nod. 'So the doctors made my mum and dad's embryos in the laboratory. I was one of them and you were another one. I don't know how many there were altogether.' Leonie's face had flushed a hot, bright red. 'The embryo that was me was planted in *my* mum's womb and the one that turned out to be you was planted in *your* mum's womb. There may have been some planted in other people's wombs for all we know. Wait a minute.'

Leonie was scrambling to her feet.

'Please don't go. I'm so sorry.' Chloe's face had turned the same colour as Leonie's. 'I was upset when I found out as well. My parents only told *me* a couple of weeks ago.' Leonie was desperately trying to edge her way out between her chair and the table, dragging her backpack behind her. 'Close your bag, Leonie, you're losing your stuff.'

'I hate you! I just *hate* you.'

'Oh no! Leonie! Come back! I just wanted . . . I thought we might . . . Please . . .'

In her rush for the exit, Leonie ran into a tweed-coated woman looking for somewhere to sit, toppling her cup of coffee off its saucer and down the back of some man's smart suit. With a yelp of pain and surprise, he leapt to his feet, knocking his own drink on to the floor.

'I'm sorry,' whispered Chloe, more to the retreating Leonie than to the injured parties, who were too busy exclaiming and mopping themselves down to notice her anyway. She gathered up Black Diamond, standing forgotten on the table, and stowed him back into her own rucksack along with the stiffly implacable Christie.

Leonie had snatched up her little purse and two of the scrumpled-up notes, but had left the rest of the money behind. The need to escape had been more urgent than the retrieval of her savings.

Miserably, Chloe held her left hand under the edge of the table, swept the coins into it with her right and poured them into a separate compartment in her bag. How she'd get them back to Leonie, she had no idea.

Her throat felt like it had a piece of broken glass in it. She mustn't crumble now. Not here. She had to get home. Away from all these people. Then she could let the tears flow.

*

Jenny heard the scrabbling of a key at the front door followed by a slam. 'You're late home,' she called from the kitchen.

She waited for the sequence of sounds that usually accompanied her daughter's arrival back from school: the thud of the schoolbag on the hall floor, the clatter of blazer buttons on the banister finial, the heavy clump of school shoes heading for the kitchen for the obligatory raid on the fridge.

Instead, all she heard were rapid thumping footsteps up the stairs. Putting down the scissors she'd been using to trim some steak, she pulled a piece of kitchen paper off the roll to wipe her hands and wandered into the hallway.

'Chlo? Is that you?' A muffled sound from her daughter's room at least confirmed the new arrival wasn't some sort of intruder. 'You OK?' Another muffled monosyllable. 'Supper in about forty-five minutes.'

Silence.

'Oh well . . .'

Jenny shrugged and went back to the kitchen. Maybe she'd been in some sort of trouble at school. A detention or something. She'd get to the bottom of it over supper. Or try to. Chloe wasn't very forthcoming this last couple of weeks. She'd come downstairs soon enough anyway. She was always ravenous when she got home from school.

The house was in darkness, the curtains undrawn.

Odd. Dan manoeuvred the van into his usual space behind number 113's battered VW and 117's newly acquired people mover.

He looked at his watch. Nearly seven. Terror flooded his soul. Where was Leonie? She should have been home for a good two hours, even if she'd stopped for a coffee with her friend JJ. She was always here by now, homework spread out on the table, supper on the go.

It struck him that Elfick might have come back and kidnapped her. Told her everything. Persuaded her that she'd be better off with her 'real family' in Blackheath. Forgetting to lock the van, he sprinted down the side of the house to the kitchen door, Boot trotting behind him.

He turned the handle. The door wasn't locked. He flung it open so hard it crashed against the work surface behind it. The kitchen was empty. Dark and cold.

'Leonie!' he howled. 'Where are you?'

Boot trotted through into the living room and Dan thought he heard a muffled sound.

'Leo!' He flicked the light on.

Leonie was sitting huddled on the floor, back against the sofa, knees pulled up under her jumper, Boot eagerly licking her swollen, tear-streaked face.

He stooped down in front of her. 'What's happened?'

She shook her head, not looking at him.

'Sweetheart. For God's sake. Tell me what's happened.'

She put out a listless hand to stroke Boot's neck.

He took her by the shoulders. 'Leo! Look at me.'

She glanced at him with red-rimmed eyes and looked immediately away again.

Putting his hands under her armpits, he hoisted her up and on to the sofa, then sat on the edge of the seat next to her, searching her face for clues. 'Has someone hurt you?'

'You could say that.'

She spoke so softly he could barely hear her.

'Who? Who's hurt you? Tell me. I'll frigging *kill* them.'

'You.'

'I what?'

269

'*You* hurt me.'

'Me? What have I done? God, this is terrible. Leo, I've never seen you like this.' She still wouldn't look at him. Paralysed, he waited.

'All my life you've lied to me.'

'Leo . . .' He tried to stroke a strand of hair from her hot, tear-damp cheek but she flinched, shrinking away from him. 'Leo, tell me who you've been speaking to.'

'Why should you care?'

He grabbed her shoulders again, more roughly than he meant to. 'I *care*. You *know* I care.'

With a low growl, Boot jumped up on to the sofa, interposing himself between these two most important people in his life. 'It's OK, boy. It's OK.' Dan ruffled his ears and the dog aimed a comforting lick at Leonie's nose.

'Now, Leonie, angel,' Dan resumed softly, 'I need you to tell me who you've been speaking to. Was his name Mark Elfick by any chance?'

'My *sister* . . . actually.'

'Chloe?'

'Chloe Elfick. Yes.'

So. Now she knew. 'Oh God, Leo.' He flopped backwards on the sofa. How the hell . . . ? What had the girl said to her? *He* should have been the one to tell her; when the time was right.

If only he'd got her out of this place before now and over to Ireland. Now his worst nightmare had become reality.

The walls and ceiling seemed to ripple and change shape. He couldn't feel the sofa underneath him any more. Everything in the room was closing in, mocking him. The street light outside stooped to peer through the window. Somehow he got to his feet and yanked the curtains closed. He had to find a way to make everything seem normal again. His very survival was at stake.

'Leo, I don't know what you've been told. Would you like to hear the story from me?'

Chapter Thirty-Three

Leonie buried her face in Boot's neck. His fur prickled against her hot cheeks. She had a choice. She could refuse to listen to Dan ever again . . . ever to trust him again. She'd been hating him for hours now. She could just carry on hating him. No one would blame her.

She could say to him, 'Why should I want to hear your story? You're not even my real dad.' He deserved it. She allowed herself to look at him properly for the first time since she heard him come in. The look on his face frightened her. He looked a little crazy. She wiped her eyes with the heel of her hand.

'I s'pose.'

He didn't dare touch her. He didn't think he could bear it if she recoiled from him again. He yanked one of the armchairs round and sat down facing the sofa – his knees inches away from his daughter's.

'You'll have to forgive me, Leo. I'm not very good with words sometimes, 'specially when I'm trying to explain something really important.'

Leonie picked up one of the scatter cushions beside her and clutched it to her chest. Protection.

Sensing the drama of the situation had abated a little, Boot lay down on the floor at right angles to the two of them, chin on his two front paws, the whites of his eyes showing as he swivelled his gaze from one to the other.

'Darling Leo, Mummy and I loved each other to bits. And we wanted to have a baby more than anything . . . to make us a complete family. But . . . that turned out to be difficult. Mummy had a kind of woman's plumbing problem. And there was something wrong with my mechanics as well. Are you following me?'

Leonie shrugged a guarded affirmative. The last thing she wanted was for him to go into details about his and Mummy's sex life.

'So we needed help . . . from the doctor . . . who could . . .' (oh Ellie why, *why* can't you be here?) 'make the beginning bit of the process happen for us.'

'I thought that was called having sex,' muttered Leonie into the top of the cushion.

'We were all right doing that. It was actually making a baby begin that was the problem.' He paused to see if she wanted any more detail. She was avoiding eye contact, pulling at a loose thread on the cushion. He could probably move on. To what though? What next? 'Erm . . . so we went to this special doctor . . . and the doctor knew of a couple who had some . . . embryos. I'm not sure if you know what an embryo is?'

'Sort of.' Chloe had done a better job of explaining, but Leonie didn't see why she should make this easier for him.

'Well, this couple were Chloe's mummy and daddy. And they had a very special embryo – which was you. And they asked the doctor to find a really nice mummy and daddy for you. And the doctor knew Mummy and me were looking for a perfect little baby of our own to love and treasure . . . and luckily he thought we were just the right people . . . to . . . entrust you to. Luckily for us anyway.'

'So why didn't you ever tell me?'

'Well, the honest truth, Leo, is . . . from the moment the doctor put you in Mummy's tummy as a little tiny dot, we just felt you were completely ours. Mummy's tummy started getting rounder and rounder and we were so excited. We couldn't wait for you to pop out and share your life with us.'

Leonie relaxed her grip a little on the cushion.

Dan continued. 'We used to play music to you. Mummy used to sing bits of classical stuff she was learning in choir practice and I used to play my sax . . . and records of course. Eric Clapton and Dire Straits and stuff.'

'I bet you played Def Leppard and Motorhead.'

'Probably.' He smiled. 'Sorry.'

Leonie put out a foot and kicked him on the shin.

Dan dared to laugh. 'Ow. That's what you used to do in Mum's tummy. You were a great little kicker, especially in the evenings. We thought you were probably dancing.'

'I was probably saying stop that horrible noise.'

Reassured by the slight fall in the emotional temperature, Boot relinquished his post as protector of the peace and trotted into the kitchen to inspect his food and water situation.

'He'll need feeding,' commented Leonie.

'I'll see to it in a minute.' Cautiously, he leaned forward to take hold of one of her hands. It felt hot and damp. 'So you see, Leo, the doctors could have chosen a different mummy and daddy for you, but Mum and I were the lucky ones. So, so lucky. And . . . well, all I hope is that you feel the same. That Mummy and I *were* the right choice for you. All we ever wanted was for you to be happy . . . and to be the best parents in the world ever.'

Leonie watched Dan's fingers entwining with her own. 'They were talking on the news last night about something called identity theft. I feel like that's happened to me. They showed a film about this man who went to jail because he wasn't who he said he was. Well, *I've* been the wrong person ever since I was born. I don't know *who* I am now. And it's your fault. Maybe *you* should go to jail.' She took her hand away.

'Maybe I should then. I will if it means you'll forgive me. Leo, angel. I realise now it was wrong not to have told you. But it just didn't seem . . . you know . . . We were just a straightforward happy family. It's only now that the Elficks have suddenly turned up . . . They read about what happened to Mummy in the papers . . .' Dan paused. He was finding it hard to breathe, his throat hurt so much. Leonie sat in silence, hugging her cushion. Her face was wet with tears again. 'It was so soon after Mummy died, though, Leo,' he managed eventually to continue. 'How do you think you'd have felt? And . . . all right, I admit it. I was scared . . . really scared that you might not want me for your daddy any more. Now that Mummy wasn't here, you might decide you'd rather have the Elficks for your parents.' He studied her face anxiously. 'They've got more money than me, and a bigger house, and an older sister to play with. What can I offer you? I'm just a smelly old plumber.'

He stopped speaking. His voice had given up on him. And in any case, he'd said all he could think of to say. Whatever happened next was up to Leonie now. He covered his face in his hands, unsurprised to find his own cheeks soaking wet.

A moment later, something hit him in the chest – with such force that his chair shot backwards across the carpet on its casters. Leonie had thrown herself onto his lap, cushion and all, and was sobbing into his shoulder.

'I . . . miss . . . Mummy . . .'

'I know. I miss her too.'

An hour later, they were still in the chair, Leonie sleeping now in her father's arms, the occasional residual juddering sob breaking through her sleep as he held her close, stroking her hair.

Taking in the scene as he wandered enquiringly back into the living room, even though it was well past his usual supper time, Boot knew better than to interrupt. With a sigh of resignation, he flopped down on to his side by the chair and closed one eye. The other, he kept trained intently on his two owners. Maybe telepathy would do the trick.

Chloe leaned over the side of her bed and grasped Archie Bear's outstretched paw, hoisting him off the pink corduroy beanbag he shared with a variety of 'beanie' toys she'd hardly ever acknowledged.

She straightened Archie's arms inside the green woollen jumper Granny knitted for him when he was new, before she was old enough to remember, and then laid him face-up on her chest, her arms clasped round his middle, so that they could lie looking up together at the luminous stars on the ceiling.

It was a few weeks since she last cuddled him. Now he seemed the only creature in the world who loved her without question, just for herself, whatever she did, right or wrong. Even Black Diamond and Christie, back on their shelf, looked disapprovingly down at her. She'd made them into unwilling accomplices – was that the right word? – in her wrongdoing.

Had she done wrong? The difference between right and wrong wasn't always as easy to work out as adults wanted you to think. Chloe knew she'd had the best of intentions, but she'd made a real mess of things, that was for sure. She yanked the duvet from beneath her and spread it over herself, holding Archie tighter for warmth.

Why hadn't she just waited? She could have kept in contact with Googlechat messages and stuff and got to know Leonie a bit better before deciding whether or not telling her they were sisters was a good idea. She hadn't expected to like Leonie so much. And she really had liked her a lot. She was so sweet and bright and smiley; she'd wanted to take her home.

Sitting opposite her in that coffee bar, being Leonie's big sister had suddenly seemed the most important thing in her whole life. That must have been why she'd blurted out the connection between them. Turning Archie to face her, she held him out at arm's length.

'The truth is supposed to be a good thing, isn't it?'

Archie regarded her with wise little black eyes.

Mum had always said you should tell the truth no matter how hard it was at the time. It always makes things easier in the end, she used to say. Well, either she was oversimplifying things or she didn't know what she was talking about. On this occasion, telling the truth had made things a whole lot more complicated.

'It can certainly be a tricky business,' Archie agreed silently.

And what would happen if she told her parents about this afternoon? Where would the truth get her then? Into more trouble almost certainly. Mum and Dad had promised not to contact the Keegans. But that was *their* promise, wasn't it? Not Chloe's.

Archie thought perhaps she should tell them all the same. Not yet though. Not till she could trust herself not to cry. It all mattered too much at the moment. She wouldn't tell Ems or Rosie either for the same reason.

Who *could* she talk to? No one. There was the safely distant Clyde, but it was too personal to explain on MySpace. She'd have to wait till he signed in on Messenger or Google Chat. And anyway he had his worries with his horses at the moment. Auntie Annabel maybe . . . she'd want to tell Mum though.

'Never mind,' said Archie, and he wiped the tears from under her eyes with his leather-patched paw.

She put him back on her chest and hugged him close.

Chapter Thirty-Four

Leonie woke to find herself in her bed, the soft glow of the old nursery lamp on the night table casting coloured animal shapes adrift on her bedroom walls and ceiling. She was still wearing her jumper and woolly tights.

She remembered now: Dad carrying her up the stairs, taking off her shoes, tucking her in gently under the duvet next to Patchy Peter, the patchwork pony Mum made from a pattern she found in a charity shop.

Her room looked the same as it always did. And yet nothing was the same any more. If only she hadn't advertised for that Julip pony. Her chin began to tremble. No! She refused to cry any more. She'd cried a whole lifetime's worth of tears already, while she was waiting for Daddy to come home.

She turned on to her side, drawing her knees up to her chest, sucking on her thumb.

'My mum and dad are your parents too,' Chloe had said. But Chloe's mother and father hadn't brought her up, looked after her, fed her, put her to bed every night . . . they hadn't even been there when she was born! Of course they weren't her parents. But then neither were Mummy and Daddy apparently.

Whose was she then? *Who* was she? In fairy tales there were babies called 'changelings' sometimes. She'd never been sure what that meant, but it was something to do with wicked witches and evil and it didn't sound like a nice thing to be; someone no one wanted to know, no one loved. Was that what she'd been all this time?

She sucked harder on her thumb. Daddy had made things seem a bit better when he talked to her downstairs, but now, lying here alone in the silence of her room, that sick, panicky feeling was coming back. She mustn't let it. She had to try and make sense of things somehow. This was like one of those nightmares you had when you were ill . . . nothing made sense . . . normal things suddenly turned scary and sinister and unpredictable.

Wide-eyed with the dreadfulness of it all, Leonie fixed her eyes on the animal shapes from her lamp making their way across the ceiling. She picked out a squat little elephant, turning on to her back to follow its progress over to the window where it surfed in and out of the folds of the curtain before cruising on towards the wardrobe.

Logical. She must be logical. She was good at logic. Mr Lindblom said. What were they like, these . . . 'genetic' . . . parents? What did they do for a living? Dad had said they were well off. Were they strict sort of people who criticised things all the time? How old were they? What did they look like? They couldn't be as nice-looking as Mummy and Daddy.

The prominent ankle bones she'd always hated must come from the Elficks. And her sticky-out ears. Mummy and Daddy both had nice neat ears. And Mummy had had lovely hair too: long and fine and shiny. Reddish like Leonie's, but paler; more like the colour of syrup flapjacks. Leonie's was infuriatingly frizzy and, well, *gingery*. More like Chloe's hair. Except that Chloe's was prettier.

My sister Chloe. She mouthed the words round her thumb, trying them on, like someone else's T-shirt. It was amazing to have an older sister; a sister who looked so like herself that it was almost spooky.

If things had been different, they might have grown up together: gone to the same school, gone to riding stables together, lots of things. Chloe must have looked her up on Bebo specially to arrange this afternoon's meeting. She'd used Black Diamond as an excuse. Should she be angry about being deceived, or pleased that Chloe had wanted to meet her? She thought about it and decided she felt both.

What must Chloe think of her now though, getting so upset and rushing out of Starbucks like that? She must have seemed like such a baby. Chloe probably wouldn't bother contacting her again now. But they had seemed to like each other. Almost as soon as they met they'd felt like old friends. She smiled, remembering how they'd bagsied the table from that bald man.

It would be nice to have a big sister. But she'd blown it. She had run away. Well, it was probably for the best. Dad would definitely prefer it that way. That's why he hadn't told her the truth in the first place.

Mummy hadn't told her the truth either. If only she were here, she could ask her why not. She must have had a good explanation. Mummy loved her. She knew she did. *Why* wasn't she here? It wasn't fair.

Leonie squeezed her eyes shut. She'd been happy, safe in the world until Mum died. Now everything had gone wrong. Now she felt so very alone.

There was God of course. Maybe He would be able to help. Mummy and Daddy were both 'lapsed Catholics', whatever that meant, but they had taken her to church sometimes. At

Christmas usually. It felt safe in church. It smelled nice. Of polish and candle wax and oldness. And everybody singing together was nice too.

Her eyelids relaxed a little. Maybe if she could go back to sleep . . . a good long deep sleep . . . things would be better when she woke up in the morning.

Quite suddenly she felt a weird calmness spreading right through her. Like maybe God had come into her room. Or an angel? The harsh, ringing silence in her ears went velvet soft. She thought she could smell the bath stuff Mum used to use. A warm hand closed gently around hers. Leonie didn't dare open her eyes; she didn't want to make the feeling go away.

Chloe's bedroom door opened.

'Are you still asleep?' Chloe felt the mattress give as Jenny sat on the edge of her bed. 'It's past suppertime. I came up before but I didn't have the heart to wake you.'

'Mm . . .' Chloe opened her eyes slowly.

'You're looking flushed, darling.' Jenny's hand pushed Chloe's fringe off her forehead to test her temperature. Her fingers smelt of potato peelings. 'You do feel a bit warm. Are you not feeling well?'

'I'm OK.' Actually, Chloe realised, she was hungry. She hadn't eaten since midday, and even then she'd only picked at her school lunch, too excited at the prospect of meeting Leonie. 'I'll come down in a minute.'

'Are you sure you're all right? It's not like you to go straight up to your room after school.'

'I wasn't feeling so good when I got back. I thought maybe I was getting a cold or something.'

'Why didn't you tell me? I'd have brought you up a hot lemon drink or something.'

'I didn't want to bother you.'

'Don't be silly. That's what mothers are for.' Jenny rubbed her daughter's back and shoulders under the duvet. 'And why were you so late back? Oh, who's this? Hello, Archie.' Chloe was fishing Archie out from under the duvet to put him back on his beanbag. 'Tell you what, I can bring your supper up on a tray if you like. Just for once. It's shepherd's pie so it's easy to manage.'

'OK, that would be good, thanks, Mum. I've got a history essay to write so I can start thinking about that while I'm eating.' And she didn't want her Dad asking the same questions all over again across the dinner table.

As her mother's footsteps receded downstairs in the direction of the kitchen, Chloe got off the bed, unsteady after her hour's sleep, and plodded across to her desk to switch the laptop on.

She looked at her watch. It was gone eight. Rosie and Emma would be wondering why she wasn't online. She'd promised to help Rosie with 'Ratios and Proportions' in return for Rosie's help finishing her essay on Neville Chamberlain and Appeasement. It should have been handed in two days ago. She'd be in trouble with Miss Knapman again.

Leonie's Guardian Angel clock showed nearly nine o'clock. She could only have been asleep for an hour but it felt like longer. The house was very quiet. Usually at this time of night she'd hear the muffled boom of the telly from downstairs or the beat of one of Dad's CDs. He must have gone to bed early too. Being upset did that. It made you feel really, really tired.

Her eyes began to close again. Then opened wide. Homework! Oops. She sat up in bed, scrabbled her feet around the floor until they found her slippers, and with the duvet draped around her shoulders for warmth, quietly opened her bedroom door and padded out on to the landing where Dad's computer sat blank-eyed on a table in a niche under the eaves.

She nudged the mouse and the screen came to life. Putting Patchy Peter next to the keyboard, Leonie wriggled on to the chair and tapped out her log-in details.

Daisy, Marcus, Tom, JJ and Manjit were still online. More importantly, Chloe was too. There she was. A mouse click away.

Chapter Thirty-Five

Finishing her shepherd's pie, Chloe put the plate on the floor for Vulcan to lick and opened her history text book at the chapter on British foreign policy in 1938.

Checking her computer, she could see Rosie and Emma were both online. So was Clyde. And now, so was Leonie. The Lion Princess. Chloe's tummy went melty, like it did on the bus to school sometimes when she saw the tall thin boy with the spiky brown hair who'd smiled at her once and now seemed not to notice her. So Leonie had got home all right then.

How would she be feeling now? She must be reasonably OK if she was on her computer. Perhaps she hadn't spoken to her dad yet. That would be quite some conversation.

She typed 'are you ok?', then her hand hovered uncertainly on the mouse. Leonie probably hated her guts after what she'd told her. She stabbed at the 'delete' key and clicked on Rosie's name instead. If Leonie wanted to make contact she would.

Chloe took a tissue from the box behind her computer and blew her nose. She'd better pull herself together and make a start on this essay. If she didn't get the thing handed in tomorrow, Miss Knapman would make her do it after school and there'd be no Rosie to help her then.

*

'What are you doing, Leo?'

Leonie jumped. She hadn't heard her father's bedroom door open. 'Sorry, Dad. Did I wake you up? I was trying to be really quiet.'

'You shouldn't be on the computer now, sweetheart. What are you doing?'

'Nothing.'

Dan came to stand behind her, resting his hands on her shoulders. 'Are you in touch with Chloe Elfick on that Messenger thing?'

'I haven't spoken to anyone at all yet. I've only just gone online.'

'It's much too late for online chatting. I didn't get us on this Wi-Fi thing so that you could chat to your friends at all times of day and night you know.'

'OK.'

'How often have you been exchanging messages with Chloe Elfick?'

'Not much really . . . just about this Julip horse she had for sale.'

'I think it's best if you don't try to speak to her any more, don't you?'

'I haven't.'

'Well, that's good.'

'She is my sister though. I should be able to speak to her if I want, shouldn't I?'

'Leo, don't. Trust me. I can't expect you to understand now and I will explain some time but not tonight. It's late and we've both been through enough emotions for one night.'

'You shouldn't worry so much, Dad. It's not as if I'm going to suddenly choose to go and live with them instead of you, is it? I don't even know them.'

'Of course you wouldn't. I know that really. It's just . . . I'd rather not encourage them, that's all. They need to lead their own lives and leave us to lead ours. They're just . . . well . . . not our sort of people.'

'I liked her though, Dad.'

'And that's another thing, young lady: I want you to promise me you'll never go off meeting someone you've met on the internet – whoever they say they are – without telling me first. I want to know exactly where you're going, and who it is you want to meet before I give you my permission. Is that clear?'

'I know, but . . . she had this Julip horse.'

'I don't care what the reason was. You must never, ever, arrange to meet a stranger; someone you've only got to know on the internet. You know that, for goodness' sake, Leo. You're a sensible girl.'

'Yes.' Leonie couldn't resist a sideways glance at the computer screen. Chloe was still online.

Dan stretched a bare foot towards the computer's control box under the desk and pressed the 'off' button with his big toe.

'Look at me, Leonie. I want your solemn promise that you'll never meet anyone outside school without telling me again.'

Leonie sighed. 'Yes, Dad. It's the only time I've ever done it.'

'Well, let it be the last time. I just want you to keep safe, that's all.'

Leonie slid off the chair, picked up Patchy Peter and waddled back towards her bedroom, trying not to trip on the ends of her duvet.

'And I've been thinking, Leo. I'm going to get you a mobile phone.'

'You don't have to. I don't mind not having one. It's just something else to worry about being stolen.'

'Just to have in your bag; in case you need it ever. Anyway, I might want to call you sometimes . . . find out what you're making me for supper.'

Leonie made a wry face.

'Just joking, angel. And Leo?' He followed her to her bedroom door.

'Yes?'

'You do know how much I love you, don't you?'

'I love you too, Dad. And I'll never leave you. OK?'

'OK.'

'So you needn't worry.'

Watching his daughter scramble into bed, Dan hoped she couldn't see the fight he was having to keep his mouth and chin from trembling. To cover them up, he put his hand to his lips and blew her a kiss.

'Night night, light of my life.'

'Night, Daddy.'

Chapter Thirty-Six

Dan drummed his fingers on the steering wheel, counterpointing the regular thump of the windscreen wipers.

'Sorry, Leo. You'd have done better going under your own steam like you usually do. I forgot how bad the frigging traffic is this time in the morning. This is why I don't usually leave home till nine.'

Leonie sat dwarfed in the van's passenger seat, school bag on her lap. 'Don't worry. If I'm late I'll tell Mr Lindblom it's all your fault.'

Her eyes were puffy and dark-ringed. He felt a pang of guilt arc across his solar plexus. He squeezed her leg under the navy school trousers.

'Are you sure you're OK?'

'Yes, Dad! For the tenth time.'

Of course she wasn't OK. But she wasn't going to confide in him this morning. There was a different atmosphere between them now. Nothing would be quite the same again. Why would he expect otherwise? Sneaking another look at her set little face, she seemed indefinably older. The child in her had grown up overnight. He suppressed a sigh of despair, immediately prompting an anxious glance from Leonie. He punched the horn.

'Bloody traffic! Come on! What are you waiting for, you silly old bugger?'

Leonie looked down at the little electric car in front of them. 'Keep your pants on, Daddy.'

'Shall we watch a DVD over supper this evening, angel? Celebrate it being Friday?'

'OK. Why not?'

'Are you angry with me?'

She turned to look at him properly for the first time that morning. 'No, Dad. I'm not angry with you. At least I don't think I am. I've just got a lot of things in my head that need tidying up, so my brain's a bit busy.'

He laughed drily. 'I know exactly what you mean.'

'Why are you wearing your nice trousers, Dad? Aren't you working today?'

'Yes, but it's more of a site meeting this morning . . . not hands on – or hands in you might say. That's why I can give you a lift. Not that it's been much of a help to you.'

'Oh, that's OK.' She turned her gaze back to the window.

'Hey. Things are looking up.' He pushed the gear stick forward. 'Third gear.'

To his own surprise, his first waking emotion that morning had been one of profound relief. At least now Leonie knew the truth. She'd let him explain everything. And she hadn't rejected him. She'd told him she loved him; that she wouldn't want to leave him. What an insecure idiot he was.

He should have had more trust in her maturity, her no-nonsense, practical way of looking at things. So often Ellie had accused him of getting things out of proportion; getting 'all Irish and maudlin', she called it. 'Just let things take their natural course,' she'd say. 'The universe is unfolding as it should, you know.'

That was the trouble with loving people though. You got so shit scared of losing them, your heart being broken. Like he'd lost Ellie . . .

'I'll walk the rest of the way, Dad.'

They were a hundred yards away from the school now, in near-standstill traffic.

'But you haven't got an umbrella.'

'I'll be OK.'

'See you later then, sweetheart. At least it's the weekend tomorrow. We can chill.'

Leonie jumped down from the van. 'Yeah, whatever.'

Slamming the door shut, she hoisted her bag on one shoulder and set off at a run towards the school gate, the clip in her ponytail sliding increasingly askew.

'Have a good day,' he called out of the window as the van edged forward in the queue of cars, almost catching up with her.

Without turning round, she lifted a hand in acknowledgement and disappeared from view.

At the next side road, Daniel turned off and parked the van in a Pay and Display bay. He glanced at his watch. Five minutes to nine. Leonie would just have made it in time for assembly. That left half an hour before lessons started and the headmistress got back to her office.

After Ellie's death she'd written him a polite letter saying how sorry she was and that she'd keep a 'discreet but watchful eye' on Leonie. She'd added at the end that her 'door was always open' if he ever needed to talk to her.

She'd written another letter after the incident with Elfick outside the school, saying again that she'd be only too pleased to see him should he need 'a chat about things'. He'd never got round to replying, so he hoped she hadn't forgotten.

He locked the van and found some change for the parking

machine. There was enough time to grab a coffee at the place up the road and think about what he was going to say.

Andrea Hamilton looked up in surprise as her secretary ushered Dan into her office.

'Mr Keegan to see you. Leonie Keegan's father.'

'Thank you, Pauline.'

The door closed leaving Dan standing awkwardly in the centre of the room. He opened his mouth to explain his unheralded arrival, but this was the headmistress's territory. She took charge smoothly.

'Mr Keegan.' She stood, stretching a welcoming hand across her desk. He stepped forward to clasp it briefly. 'Sit down, please.'

She was tall and athletic-looking, wearing a plain grey suit over a cream polo neck sweater; short, almost white-blond hair tucked neatly behind her ears. Dan perched uneasily on the edge of one of two light-coloured wooden chairs his side of the desk.

'Sorry to er . . . I should have made an appointment.'

She waved his apology away. 'Any excuse to avoid this infernal paperwork.'

She pushed two piles of papers to one side of her desk, angled the computer's flat screen away from her line of vision and stacked the keyboard and mouse on top of one another in a grey plastic tray marked 'out'.

'Oh. Just a moment. I'll tell Pauline not to disturb us.' As she walked briskly on smart, low heels towards the doorway of the connecting office, Dan caught himself observing that she had rather good legs. From the other side of the door he could hear her talking to the secretary in quiet, confidential tones.

He glanced nervously around the room. Children's paintings and drawings covered one wall; calendars and timetables papered another. On a sheet of white A4, Blue-tacked in the middle of them, was printed:

INTELLIGENCE PLUS CHARACTER – THAT IS THE GOAL OF TRUE
EDUCATION

Martin Luther King

A photograph in a stand on the desk in front of him showed Mrs Hamilton in full mountaineering gear against a backdrop of rugged, rocky scenery. She was laughing into the camera, her blond hair blowing about her face. He put out a hand towards it for a closer look.

'Three peaks challenge.'

Dan jumped, knocking the picture flat. Mrs Hamilton smiled.

'Not to worry.' She picked it up and peered at it with an air of proud amusement. 'Summer before last. Ben Nevis, Scafell Pike and Snowdon in thirty-six hours. For Meningitis Research.'

'Looks dangerous.'

'Not dangerous really, but pretty exhausting. And extremely windy.' She set it back in its original position. 'Wonderful fun though.' She sat down and wheeled her chair close enough to the desk to rest her elbows on it, her pale grey eyes looking directly into his. 'Now, Mr Keegan. Tell me about you and Leonie. How have you been managing?'

'Well, it hasn't been easy. Not at all easy, in fact.'

His throat tightened. He hadn't expected sympathy. He hadn't expected anything personal really. He usually managed to parry any concerned advances from people, but this had taken him by surprise.

'You got my letters, I hope?'

'Yes. Thank you.'

'After Mr Elfick was arrested outside school a few weeks ago, I must say I was quite anxious about Leonie for a while. About both of you actually. But the police and social services seem to think he's harmless, so . . .'

'Leonie still doesn't know about that incident.'

'I know. The social worker told me what the situation was.'

'There was just too much to explain . . . so soon after her mother . . . you know.'

She smiled gently. 'Of course. But I must say she seems to have coped magnificently with everything, doesn't she? My colleagues tell me she's a delight to teach. She's a really special little girl. You must be proud of her.'

He nodded his head stiffly. 'She is. I am. For sure.'

'You certainly have had a lot to cope with.'

A slightly protrusive lower jaw gave her a gentle lisp. Dan liked it. The imperfection made her more approachable. He usually felt intimidated by the teaching staff at Leonie's schools. Probably to do with his own schooling back in County Kerry in the seventies, when far too often he'd found himself on the wrong side of trivial rules and regulations, with painful consequences.

Andrea Hamilton was regarding him sympathetically, her head tilted a little to one side. 'So, tell me how I can help.'

'I'm afraid I'm going to have to take Leonie away from Hawkshill Park.'

'Really? Oh dear. I'm sorry to hear that. Very sorry indeed. May I ask why?'

'I've decided we should move back to Killarney, my home town in County Kerry. My sister still lives there and she's got a little boy, Fergal, quite close in age to Leonie, who goes to a pretty decent Catholic school in the town. I was hoping you might be able to pull some strings to get her a place there.'

'I hope you don't mind my asking, Mr Keegan, and do tell me

if this is too personal, but how much does Leonie know about her . . . um . . . family circumstances?'

'As of last night she now knows everything. Well, broadly everything. The Elfick family's daughter got in touch with Leonie on the internet.'

'As of last night? I see.' She waited for more details. None came. 'And her reaction?'

'Well, it was a shock. I had intended to wait for a while longer before telling her. But . . . matters were taken out of my hands.' He found a tissue in one of the pockets of his scuffed brown leather jacket and wiped his nose. 'We had a long talk last night. And she's got some thinking to do obviously . . . but she's already coming to terms with everything. She's an amazing kid.'

'And so that's what's made Leonie want to move, is it?'

'It's made *me* want us to move. She's had enough emotional upheaval now. We both have. Ireland will be a fresh start.'

'But *Leonie* wants to move?' the headmistress persisted gently.

'She'll love it once we're there.'

'Won't that be . . .' Andrea Hamilton hesitated, taking a pencil from the Simpsons mug on her desk and turning it absently in her fingers, 'yet another major upheaval for her to cope with?'

Looking up sharply, Dan Keegan met her gaze.

'With respect, Mrs Hamilton, I know my own daughter. Leonie is a level-headed, practical kind of girl. She'll see the sense of it. It'll be a fresh start, after all the sh— stuff . . . we've had to deal with. It's a beautiful part of the world and she'll have a kind of mother-figure in her life again with my sister close by.'

Mrs Hamilton drew a deep breath. 'It seems you've made your mind up, Mr Keegan. When are you thinking of moving?'

'As soon as possible. The week after next maybe.'

She raised a well-groomed eyebrow. 'You've sold your house already then?'

'I'm going to put it on the market this afternoon. We can move in with my sister until we find a place of our own.'

'From Leonie's point of view it could be quite difficult, you know, taking her away in the middle of term at such short notice. She won't have the right uniform, the syllabus will be different . . . She could feel very adrift.'

'It's not ideal, I know. But, as I said, she's a resourceful kid.'

'I don't think any new school will be too keen on taking a child mid-term either, for the same reasons. It's far from ideal for the child and disruptive for the class as a whole.'

'But if you were to explain the urgency of the situation . . .'

'What *is* the urgency of the situation, Mr Keegan? Why is waiting until the end of term so very difficult? It's half-term the week after next and after that there's only four weeks to go till the Christmas break.'

'I don't want her to have any more contact with the Elfick family. It could really destabilise her. And they just don't seem to understand that. They won't leave us alone.'

'You could get an injunction.'

'Mrs Hamilton, these things take time. And lawyers. And money probably. I've just had enough. I don't want to fight any more. I just want to go home to Ireland.'

The headmistress swivelled her chair a few degrees to gaze pensively out of the rain-streaked window. A few late stragglers were scampering towards the science block, bags held above their heads to keep their hair dry. 'All right. We'll just have to make sure we handle things as sensitively as possible.' She met Dan's eyes again. 'Make the transition as easy on her as we can.'

'Of course.' He nodded his head.

'Here's an idea. It's half-term next week. Rather than confronting her with a fait accompli straight away, why not first of all suggest to Leonie that the two of you take a few days' break in Ireland?'

'Do a selling job on her first, you mean?'

'Exactly. Really make the visit fun . . . as I'm sure you would do anyway of course. But plan it out – lots of trips and treats . . . Maybe even let her bring a friend with her if you could bear it. She's thick as thieves with little Jessica Jackman, isn't she? What about that? Would your sister be able to put you up?'

'Oh yes. She's invited us often enough. That's not at all a bad idea.' Dan's face softened for the first time since he'd entered her office. 'It's not a bad idea at all,' he repeated. 'I'll suggest it this evening.'

'She's had more than her fair share of shocks and surprises lately. Perhaps we should try and go a bit gently on this one.'

Dan nodded his head. 'Point taken. Thank you.'

'And if you can let me have the details of the school you mentioned, I'll give them a call and see what their situation is. Start paving the way.'

'St Benedict's, yes. I'll phone my sister this afternoon and get the details.'

'And the name of the head teacher would be useful.'

'Sure.'

'But whatever happens, I do advise you most strongly to give Leonie the rest of the term here and wait for the new term to begin before she starts at a new school.'

'All right, Mrs Hamilton, I'll give it some thought. I can see your point, I suppose.'

'We just want the best for Leonie at the end of the day, don't we?' She stood up. 'Good to meet you anyway, Mr Keegan.'

Dan stood too, returning her farewell handshake. 'Thank you for seeing me at such short notice.'

'How did Leonie seem this morning after the events of yesterday evening, by the way?'

'A bit battered I think – metaphorically speaking of course. Perhaps you could just alert the teachers to check on her from time to time during the day.'

'Of course I will. Bless her heart.'

'And I'll be in touch with those details.'

'Goodbye, Mr Keegan.' The door closed, leaving Mrs Hamilton frowning into the middle distance.

Chloe checked her list of Messenger contacts on the laptop. A line of blue icons, their mad screen names studded with smileys, stars, rainbows and flowers, was a reassuring indication of how many of her friends were stuck at home, as she was, in front of their computers.

The Lion Princess's icon was still greyed out, offline. What might she be doing this evening? A birthday party to go to maybe. Or watching something on TV.

Within a minute or two, Chloe had six or seven conversations on the go at the same time. She put her hand up to her mouth and giggled quietly to herself. She'd just typed the answer to one friend's question in another friend's dialogue box by mistake. Everyone did that sometimes.

Halfway through a rapid-fire conversation with Rosie about Sophie's new spaniel puppy, Chloe's fingers stopped tapping mid-sentence. The Lion Princess had signed in. Should she or shouldn't she say something? What did she have to lose? She abandoned Rosie and her puppy talk and typed:

Sorry about yesterday. I shouldn't have said anything

Chloe hesitated, then pressed 'send'.

She waited. No reply. Rosie kept on sending message after message. So did Emma. She ignored them. Was that it then? Disappointed, Chloe pushed her laptop away. Well, what had she expected?

Leonie: Sorry I ran away

Chloe grabbed the laptop back and typed:

Don't be. Its ok

Another pause. Then,

You still want to sell Black Diamond?

Chloe realised she was grinning broadly to herself.

Sure. If you're still interested

Dad must be feeling happier. Sitting at the computer on the landing, Leonie could hear him in the kitchen below, busking along with his Keith Gemmell backing track CD. Maybe it was the thought of the few days he was planning at Auntie Bernie's in Ireland.

She hadn't been too enthusiastic about the idea when he suggested it. But she could see how much he wanted to go, and she didn't want him worrying she didn't love him any more. So she'd agreed. It would only be for a few days.

Dad's playing was getting louder. He was really getting into it. She loved hearing him play. It was quite a while since he had opened that battered old saxophone case of his. Mummy's funeral was the last time. Leonie swallowed and then spluttered with quiet laughter as he messed up a twiddly bit and used the 'f' word.

Music always made him come to life: listening to it, but especially playing it. He said it was the Irish blood in him. She resolved to persuade him to get an iPod at Christmas. As a present to himself. He could gradually transfer his music collection on to it. She liked some of his stuff herself. It would all go on the computer and she could add some of it to her own playlist.

Come to think of it, Leonie was feeling happier herself. What had seemed like a disaster last Thursday, now didn't seem quite so bad. Not now that Chloe had messaged her. She felt a thrill of guilty excitement inside. Chloe did want to keep in touch after all.

Dad would come round eventually. He was usually so understanding. He just needed a bit of time. Not too much time, though, she hoped. She didn't like keeping secrets from him. She'd go and watch him play in a moment. After she'd checked the emails.

Dan turned the reed around in his mouth a few times and slotted it back into the mouthpiece. Once more from the top and he'd get this note-perfect. It was coming back to him now.

This time he put his whole being into it. This time he made it sublimely to the end, right up to the last phrase, bending and curling, stretching and caressing the last few bars until it felt like the soul of the world was calling out his name . . . but completely forgot to take in the lungful of air he needed for the final, lingering note.

His climax plunged like a dying lark, from the heights of ecstasy to a pathetic squeak. He let the sax fall round his neck, with a curse of frustration. It was only then that he realised his cheeks were wet. Goddammit, he'd cried more tears this last sixteen weeks than in the whole of the rest of his life put together. But these were good tears: creative, productive, therapeutic.

One more time. He filled his lungs again.

Leonie opened her dad's Outlook programme. She often checked his emails for him. He didn't get that many. He wasn't much of a computer man. He needed educating. Once he got that iPod . . .

There were none for her, but that wasn't surprising. She did most of her communicating through Windows Messenger and Google chats.

Dad had one from the Institute of Plumbing and Heating Engineers inviting him to their annual conference next year. June 2009! How could anybody think that far ahead? Some spam stuff; one about saving your money by changing your credit card, another selling cut-price Viagra and there was the local cinema's weekly newsletter that she'd signed him up to herself. Leonie deleted them for him. Save him the trouble.

She was about to log off, when the computer announced the arrival of a new message. Hey! Auntie Bernie. She opened it up. This would be about their visit at half-term.

```
Hi Danny
I hope you're feeling a bit less fraught now.
What great news you and Leo are coming over.
We'll all do our best to persuade her what a
fantastic idea it is to live here. We might
even take her to see St Benedict's. Fergal can
show her round. His half-term is the week after
Leonie's. I'm lining up a couple of places for
```

you to see while you're here. What do you think of this one? Let me know if you want me to make an appointment.

Bernie had cut and pasted an ad:

> **For Sale by Private Treaty**
> Detached bungalow
> 3 Bedrooms, 1 Bathroom
> Investment Opportunity
> Beautiful countryside views
> Region €250,000

Chapter Thirty-Eight

'But Leo, it's the most beautiful county in Ireland. In the world! The Lakes of Killarney . . . the mountains . . . acres of national park . . . all on the doorstep. And Dingle Bay just a stone's throw away. We'll be able to swim with Fungi the dolphin. Wouldn't that be magical? It's paradise compared with here. Really. No air pollution, noise pollution. Quite honestly we should have moved there years ago. I can't tell you how much I wish we had.'

'I do not want to move house. This is my home. Here.'

'Well nothing's finalised. Of course it isn't. If you really don't want to go, we won't. But I want you to think long and hard about it, Leo. See how you feel after you've had a couple of days at Auntie Bernie's next week. You were so young last time we were over there you probably don't remember how lovely it is.'

'No, but I remember what a pain Fergal was when they came over after Mum died. Obsessed with what knickers I was wearing all the time.'

'Oh yes, but that's a passing phase. He's an eleven-year-old boy. He'll soon grow out of that. Probably has already.'

'And I like my school. All my friends are there.'

'You'd soon make new ones. Everyone's so friendly in Ireland.'

'You're making it seem that my feelings don't matter, Dad. My friends are important to me. So is this house. There's so much of Mummy in this house – she decorated my bedroom, she made my curtains and the blinds in the kitchen . . . nearly everything in the garden, Mum planted. I don't want to leave. I won't.'

'But we could make the new house our special home as well. We can take Mum's curtains with us. And some of the plants maybe too. There's much more space between the houses there; everyone has bigger gardens. We might even be able to get you a pony.'

'That's blackmail, Dad.'

'No, really. It is a real possibility. Auntie Bernie would be around to help look after it. And look after us as well. She's already said she'd be more than happy to have us as neighbours and she'd be able to get the shopping in for us and do some of the cooking. It would save you doing so much domestic work. You shouldn't be having to do as much as you do, you know, Leo. You've got your school work to think of.'

'I know what this is really all about, Dad. It's about keeping me away from Chloe's family. Why can't you just chill and let them talk to us sometimes if they want?'

Dan was silent, trying to find a way to answer that one. He couldn't tell her what he really thought. It was that Elfick man. He was never going to let go. Dan was sure of it. The guy would be tracking him and Leonie through everything they did; every stage of life they went through.

Given half a chance he'd be checking up on Leo's GCSE results, wanting a say in what university she went to, what career she was thinking of . . . When she got married he'd be there, spectre at the bloody feast. And then of course he'd want to be co-grandfather of Leonie's children.

The further ahead he thought, the more his heart filled with dread. He didn't want to share Leonie. Didn't want to share her now and didn't want to share her future. Was that so very wicked? Whether it was or not, he couldn't help the way he felt. And the only hope of getting shot of the Elficks was to get as far away from them as possible.

But he couldn't say any of this to Leonie. She wouldn't understand. Not at the moment anyway.

'We can't move Mummy's grave though, can we?' Leonie was continuing. 'I like to go there on my way to the shops. I pick flowers to put on it and . . . I tell her stuff. We can't just abandon her there, all by herself.'

She was weeping silently now, utterly wretched. How could this be happening? This was the last thing he wanted to do to her.

He wanted to bellow like a bull in frustration and despair. He pulled himself together. 'Leo, darlin'. Please don't cry. I love you so much I can't bear to see you so upset. Let's forget the whole moving house thing. We can still go to Ireland next week though, can't we? Just have fun?'

She wouldn't look at him. 'I don't believe anything you say any more.'

'Oh Leo . . .'

'You made this really important decision without even asking me. You told Auntie Bernie to look for houses and everything. What else haven't you told me?'

'Look, you've got to let me talk things through with other adults, Leo. Please try to understand.'

'What other adults? Who else have you talked to about us then?'

For a moment, it crossed his mind to keep the truth to himself, but there'd been enough lying by omission. And if she found out, the damage to the trust between them might go too deep to repair. 'I had a little chat to Mrs Hamilton this morning.'

'Mrs Hamilton!' She stared at him incredulously. 'So that was the site meeting, was it?'

'Yes. I'm sorry, Leo.'

'And what did she say?'

'Lots of nice things about you.'

'And?'

'Well of course I mentioned the possibility of going to Ireland, and she said she'd find some information about St Benedict's where Fergal goes in Killarney. She said the school would be sorry to lose you.'

'Dad! I don't want the school to lose me either! I've told you.'

'I know, I know . . . I've got the message.'

'I'm going upstairs to do some homework. I don't want to talk to you any more.'

'Leonie?'

Already at the doorway, she half turned towards him. 'Yes?'

'You won't . . .'

'I won't what?'

'Never mind.'

'I know what you wanted to say,' Leonie muttered as she stomped up the stairs. 'You won't try to contact Chloe, will you? Well, tough.'

Chapter Thirty-Nine

'Sorry I'm a bit late.' Mark slung his jacket over the banister rail and wandered through to the kitchen, shuffling through the post he'd left too early that morning to receive.

Jenny was standing on the kitchen work surface arranging the collection of dried herbs and roses she kept on top of the cabinets for decoration. 'I'd be more surprised if you *weren't* late.' She jumped down to the floor via a chair. 'These are all getting a bit dusty. They're due for a complete change soon.'

'Well, you'll be pleased to know you've got me all weekend. Ian's going to take charge—' He interrupted himself. 'I *hope* you'll be pleased anyway.'

'Of course I'm pleased. In fact I'd sort of hoped to persuade you to take Monday off as well.'

'That could be tricky. Why?'

'It's half-term.'

'Oh God. Yes. I'd forgotten.'

'I despair of you sometimes, Mark, honestly. We had a whole conversation about it the other evening . . . about Chloe seeming a bit down lately and planning some treats for her while she's off school this week.'

'Oh yes, I remember. Of course.'

'I might have guessed you weren't really paying attention. You had half an eye on the football.'

'It was Charlton, though, wasn't it? It's so rare to see one of their games on the telly. Anyway, what did you have in mind?'

'One thing I thought we could do is go to the IMAX at Waterloo.'

'Yeah. Brilliant idea. I've always wanted to go there.'

'I Googled it this morning. The screen's twenty-six metres long and the sound's supposed to be incredible.'

Mark opened the fridge, scanning the shelves for something to snack on.

'What's on?'

'A thing about sea monsters, which sounds amazing actually. All in 3D. It feels like you're really in the ocean, swimming with sharks and things.'

He plumped for a tub of hummus and a packet of pitta bread. 'She might want to bring Emma or someone.'

'I'll go ahead and book it then. How about Wednesday or Thursday afternoon?'

'Fine. You book it and I'll make sure I'm free. You want some of this?'

'No thanks.'

He dropped a piece of pitta in the toaster. 'Where is Chloe by the way?'

'Not back yet.' Jenny glanced up at the kitchen clock. 'Oh God, it's nearly eight o'clock. I hadn't realised the time.'

'She should be back from school by now, surely.'

'She did warn me she'd be back late. They were all going to stop off at Costa Coffee for cake and goodies. A birthday thing – for Georgia I think she said – and celebrating the start of half-term.'

'What's the plan for tonight then, when she does deign to come home?'

'I thought we might take her round the corner for a pizza. Or a Chinese if she prefers it.'

'Assuming she's hungry after stuffing her face with chocolate muffins.'

'Well if she's not, there's a lasagne in the freezer. We'll have a quiet family night in.'

Mark looked at the clock again. 'I don't like her coming home on her own after dark. The clocks go back at the end of the month and it'll get dark even sooner.'

'She refuses to let me come and pick her up in the car. She'd rather have a good giggle on the bus with her mates.'

'I think maybe it's time she had a mobile phone of her own. It's not too spoilt bratty, is it?'

'I've been thinking exactly the same. For our own peace of mind if nothing else. And a lot of her friends seem to be getting them now.'

'Right. Decision taken then. I'll make sure we get her—'

The doorbell shrilled across his words, followed by thumping on the knocker and then another blast on the bell.

Mark ran to the front door and wrenched it open, his expression a mixture of annoyance and apprehension. 'Oh, it's you!'

Dan Keegan shoved past him into the hall. 'Where's my daughter?' he growled.

Mark was left standing at the front door, not sure whether to close it or not. 'I . . . how should *we* know?'

'She's here, isn't she?'

'No!' exclaimed Jenny, coming out into the hall to confront him. 'Your daughter is not here. Of course she isn't.'

'Where's *your* daughter then?'

'Chloe's not here at the moment. Why?'

'Where is she then?'

Jenny's brain was coming up with so many possible answers that she couldn't think which to articulate first.

Mark came to the rescue. 'She's not back from school yet. What is your problem, Daniel?'

Standing in the hallway, Dan was giving a passable impression of a robot with circuitry difficulties, stepping one way and then another and finally turning a complete circle.

'Look, Daniel.' Jenny grasped his arm. 'Why don't you come in to the living room and have a drink? You look like you could do with one. Come on. In here.'

Mark closed the front door and followed them. Dan sank into the armchair he'd occupied last time he was there.

Opening a glass-fronted mahogany corner cabinet, Mark took out a bottle of Jameson's whiskey and three glasses. 'I assume you like this – from your part of the world?'

Dan nodded distractedly.

'Now,' said Mark, pouring out the whiskey, 'what made you think your daughter was here?'

'She hasn't come home.'

'Maybe she's gone to a friend's house.'

He shook his head. 'I've checked. In any case, she wouldn't go off somewhere without telling me. It's only ever happened once . . . when she went up to Waterloo to meet your daughter.'

Mark froze, bottle in hand. 'She *what*?'

'The two of them have been in touch with each other ever since. About ten days ago.'

'No!' Jenny looked from Mark to Dan, equally thunderstruck. 'Are you sure? Where?' She turned to Mark again. 'Surely she'd have told us?'

'They met at Starbucks on Waterloo station.' Trying to keep his hand still, Dan accepted the glass Mark held out to him. 'Your

Chloe told her the whole story, about the family connection . . . the embryo donation.'

'My God. How did she take it?' enquired Jenny.

'You can probably imagine that for yourself. It was a bolt from the blue, obviously. All I care about right now is where she is. She should have been home four hours ago. She's only eleven.' Dan swirled the last few drops of whiskey round in his glass. He'd drunk most of it in one hit. 'Has Chloe got a mobile phone?'

'No, dammit,' groaned Mark. 'Funnily enough, we were talking about getting her one, just before you arrived. Has Leonie?'

Dan's shoulders sank. 'No. I was going to get her one at Christmas.'

Jenny got up. 'I'll go and see if there are any clues in Chloe's room.'

She left Mark and Dan sitting in silence, trying to marshal their thoughts. 'At least if they're together we know they haven't been abducted or something.' Mark hoped he sounded reassuring.

Dan threw him a contemptuous glance. 'Well, you got what you wanted, didn't you. And this is where it's got us.'

Mark let out a long slow breath as a little flame of excitement flared inside him. It was all out in the open now. All this secrecy and paranoia and yearning . . . Over. Finished.

Dan stood up. 'There's no point me hanging around here. Leonie might have got back by now.'

'Wouldn't she ring you if she'd arrived home?'

'I left a note, yes. All the same . . .'

'Do you think they might have met at Waterloo again?'

'Maybe. I intend to have a look there on my way back.'

'What made them choose Waterloo?'

'Because it's fairly easy for them both to get to, I suppose.'

Jenny burst back into the room. 'Chloe's new jeans have gone. So has her washbag: toothbrush and everything!'

Sue Cook

'Are you quite sure she's not with Emma?'

'No, I just spoke to her mother. She's not at Rosie's either. They were home two hours ago or more.'

'I can't believe she'd do this to us.'

'Well it looks like she has,' said Jenny. 'And it looks like the two of them are together, doesn't it? We'd better call the police.'

'Just wait a moment and see if we can think this through.'

Dan glanced across at Mark. 'Not too keen on the cops then?'

Mark shot him a hostile look. 'I mean it makes sense first of all to think of all the possible people they might decide to stay the night with. They won't be booking into a hotel, will they? And it's too cold to sleep outdoors.'

'Oh.' Dan's face flushed and then paled again, leaving behind a mottled blotch of colour on each cheek. 'Dear God, Leo might have taken our little hiking tent.' He began pacing in front of the fireplace. 'I found her with the bag in her room yesterday and she said she was checking the pins were all there in case we took it to Ireland on Wednesday. I told her it would be much too cold for camping and she put it back in the cupboard. I didn't think any more of it. I bet she's taken it. That settles it. I'm calling the police. Who knows what danger they are putting themselves in, sleeping out in a tent who-knows-where?'

'I'll do it,' said Jenny.

'No, I'll do it,' said Dan.

'OK, you do it,' said Mark. 'Do you want to use our phone?'

'I'll use my mobile in case Chloe rings on your line. And then I'm going to Waterloo.'

Mark stood up. 'I'm coming with you.'

Dan looked about to protest, then thought better of it. He opened his phone.

'I'll go back to Chloe's room,' said Jenny grimly. 'See if I can

314

find some clue to where they were planning to go.'

The two girls had talked almost non-stop through the two-hour train journey.

'What do you want to be when you grow up?'

'I want to be on the stage,' Chloe had asserted solemnly.

'I want to be a teacher,' said Leonie, equally earnestly. 'A nice sort of teacher . . . who makes kids feel confident and encourages them.'

From there, the conversation had moved on to favourite authors, favourite films, TV programmes, animals, foods and finally, over cheese and onion Pringles and a can of Sprite, holidays.

'What's the best holiday you've ever had?' asked Chloe.

'I used to go camping a lot with my mum and dad. We went to Cornwall twice and Wales twice and some other places I can't remember now. When I was eight we went abroad. To France. The campsites there were so cool.'

'I've been to France too. Not camping though. We always get a villa somewhere sunny every year and I spend most of my time in the swimming pool while Mummy and Daddy read books and go to sleep. When I was young I used to go to summer camp though.'

'So did I!' enthused Leonie. 'PGL. Parents Get Lost.'

'I used to go to PGL too,' exclaimed Chloe. 'We could have met!'

'Hey yes. Which ones did you go to?' asked Leonie, eyes shining.

'We couldn't have though. I think we'd have noticed each other,' Chloe had quickly reflected. 'They were good fun though, weren't they? When we were young.'

'Yeah, I used to be homesick for the first day and then by the end I didn't want to go home. I went every summer for three years and then I broke my arm.' Leonie rubbed her left wrist at the memory.

'How did you do that?'

'I was climbing a tree and a branch broke under my foot. I got told off because I should have made sure I was supervised.'

'How old were you?'

'Nine.'

'I broke *my* left wrist when I was nine, too,' said Chloe. 'I fell off this pony called Cozmo at the stables one day. He was so sweet but he could be a bit nervous and something spooked him at this jump. Probably a wasp or something. It was only a low jump but he stopped really suddenly and stepped backwards and I ended up on the ground with a mouthful of mud. I didn't even realise I'd broken my wrist at first.'

'I wonder if there's anything else that's happened to both of us,' Leonie mused. 'People say that happens with twins, don't they? We'll probably both end up getting married when we're twenty-seven to a man called Tom or something and have babies at exactly the same time.'

The catering trolley trundled towards them again.

'What's your favourite sandwich?'

Chapter Forty

'Jen!' Mark shouted upstairs. 'We're going to Waterloo. I'm taking Chloe's school photo from the mantelpiece. The police are sending someone round. You OK staying here?'

'All right, Mark,' Jenny called back from Chloe's bedroom. 'If Chloe rings I'll get you on the mobile.'

'Of course. And obviously I'll call you if we turn up anything.'

He returned to Dan, who was standing motionless in the living room, still clutching his phone, wide-eyed with anxiety.

'We'll take my car, shall we? More space for them to sit than your van, I think – if we find them.'

'Sure. Let's hope it's not if, but when.'

Inside the shopping centre, Chloe and Leonie had bought themselves a doughnut each before finding a bench to sit down on while they decided what to do next.

'All we have to do is look for Birchwood Crescent,' Chloe said thickly through a mouthful of doughnut. 'It's near the beach.'

'So we just look for the sea.' Leonie's mouth was full of doughnut too. 'That can't be difficult. And then ask someone.'

'Let's have a look round first anyway. I love the seaside.'

'Yeah, me too.'

*

'British Transport Police. Can I help you?' The voice was indistinct through the entryphone speaker, the more so for having to compete with the continual station announcements.

Uncertainly, Mark put his mouth close to the speaker. 'I – we – want to report two missing children.'

There was a clattering noise on the microphone and a long pause. Someone may have been speaking at a distance from the microphone. It was hard to tell.

'Maybe they didn't hear you properly,' muttered Dan, his gaze still fixed on the comings and goings around them.

'Two young girls . . .' Mark stooped to speak into the louvred metal mouthpiece again, his mouth almost touching it this time. 'We are the parents of two young girls who have gone missing.'

Another clatter, then, 'Wait there, sir. Someone will come down to see you in a few moments.' Dan and Mark exchanged helpless shrugs, their eyes darting nervously around Waterloo station concourse.

'I wonder how long "a few moments" is.'

Mark's mobile phone burbled, making both men jump. In his fumble to get it out of his inside jacket pocket it slipped out of Mark's left hand. Somehow, his right hand shot out and caught it around knee level. Sheer, desperate reflex. 'Jenny! Have you heard from her?'

'No, nothing. But I'm calling to tell you . . .'

Mark shook his head at Dan's questioning face. 'They haven't called,' he murmured. Dan went back to his surveillance of the station.

'. . . they definitely went to Waterloo station,' Jenny was continuing. 'I've been looking at Chloe's chat history on her computer. It wasn't difficult. Her password for everything is

318

Popeye, her favourite pony's name. They arranged to meet at three fifteen and the plan was to change out of their school uniform in the Ladies' loo on the station concourse.'

'And then what?'

'I don't think they knew.'

'You mean they didn't know where they were going?'

'If they did, it's not in any of the correspondence I've read so far. There's something here about a book Leonie read once where the main character went to an airport and decided to go to the most attractive-sounding place name on the indicator board. It sounds as though they were thinking of doing that at Waterloo.'

'So we look for pretty-sounding place names,' Mark groaned. 'I can't believe they hadn't worked out where they were going.' He looked at his watch. 'Three fifteen. That was six and a half hours ago.'

'Have you looked everywhere? It's a big station.'

'Jenny, believe me, we've been to every single coffee bar twice, ground level and upper level . . . every single shop . . . We even persuaded a woman to go down to the Ladies' loo to see if they were there. We've shown their photos to the clerks at all eight ticket office windows and three information desks . . . and no one has seen them.

'You'd think someone would remember two red-headed kids who look so like each other.'

'Yes but they might have used one of the machines to buy their tickets of course. And some of the ticket clerks have gone off duty now, so we might have to come back tomorrow.'

'So what are you going to do now?'

'Right now we're in a corner of the station waiting for some guy from British Transport Police to come down and see us. Maybe they can alert all the stations, you know, put out an APB

319

if they still call it that. And maybe we can have a look at their CCTV recordings.'

'Good luck then. I'll get back to Chloe's computer. They've been—'

'Sorry, Jen,' Mark cut in. 'I've got to go.'

A tall, middle-aged officer in a yellow reflective jacket was pushing open the heavy door of the British Transport Police station and Dan was thrusting his picture of Leonie in front of his face.

'How long do you think you'll be, Mark?' inquired Jenny's voice from the phone.

'I really don't know, darling. I might have a better idea in a few minutes. I'll get back to you.

'Is this the beach?' Leonie had sounded disappointed. 'There's no sand.'

'I suppose it must count as the beach. Maybe the tide's in. Excuse me.' Chloe bounced up to a pleasant-looking middle-aged woman in a grey quilted coat getting out of her car.

'Is this the beach?'

'It's the nearest we've got to a beach round here, love, unless you go five miles along the coast,' she waved a vague hand, 'up that way or down that way. This is the quayside.' She eyed the two girls and their bulging rucksacks curiously. 'Your first visit here, is it?'

'Yes. We're staying with a friend. We just wondered. Thank you anyway.'

Sauntering back to Leonie, Chloe put her arm around the younger girl's shoulders, steering her purposefully towards the waterfront. 'Look confident,' she hissed. 'Just don't look lost. She looks like the interfering type.'

'What if she calls the police?'

'I don't think she will.'

A hundred yards further on, they'd stopped, pretending to watch a group of older boys performing tricks on BMX bikes beside the harbour wall. Chloe glanced furtively back the way they had come.

'It's OK. She's gone.'

'Hello, girls,' smirked one of the bikers.

'Hello, boy,' replied Leonie with dignity.

'Come on.' Chloe tugged at Leonie's arm. 'There's an amusement arcade over there.'

'I'm sorry, sir; it'd be like looking for a needle in a haystack. We have two thousand CCTV cameras in operation at London stations round the clock, and all of them feed directly through to the control room at Victoria. We don't monitor the footage here. And even if we did, literally thousands of people pass through every day. It just isn't possible.'

'But we know they were here shortly after three,' interposed Mark, 'so that narrows it down, doesn't it?'

'Sir, even if we did take some officers off normal duties to trawl through all the CCTV footage, and let's just say we did spot your girls here on the station, it wouldn't tell us where they went next, would it?'

'You don't seem the least bit sympathetic,' exploded Dan.

'I am sympathetic, gentlemen, believe me. But you have to understand that in the course of today alone, the number of children who've gone missing across the South-East will probably rack up into the hundreds. And I can assure you the majority of them will reappear safe and sound within the next twenty-four hours. One night is usually enough, especially this time of year.'

'Well can you at least tell all your officers to keep an eye out for them?' asked Mark.

'Gentlemen, I'd like to be able to tell you we'll put a message out to every station in the area but it simply isn't feasible. Waterloo station covers destinations across the whole of the South-East. Imagine if we did that for every one of the hundreds of kids that go awol every day. The service would seize up.'

'So that's the best you can do, is it?' fulminated Mark. 'Nothing.'

'If anyone sees two young girls looking a bit lost or uncertain on one of our stations, they are likely to report it to the police. If they do, we'll be notified here and we'll get in touch with you straight away. If not . . . I realise it's disappointing for you to hear this, gentlemen, but from what you've told me, the bottom line is that these two girls have planned this trip together. It's a conscious decision they've made. They haven't been lured away by some malevolent third party and we have no reason to think they are in any danger.'

'All right then, at what point *do* we start worrying, in your opinion?' demanded Dan.

'That's right,' Mark weighed in. 'How long do we have to sweat and chew our fingers to the bone before you decide to take this seriously and start pulling out the stops to look for them?'

'If after twenty-four hours, there's still no sign of your daughters, then yes, perhaps we'll start the job of looking through the security film. But, in any case, it's not up to the Transport Police to initiate that. Any investigation will be in the hands of your local police station. They'll be the ones to call on us if and when the need arises.'

'So what the hell do we do now?' Dan's voice was hoarse with anxiety and frustration. 'Go home and have a nice cosy sleep?'

'That's about the size of it, sir. Go home and think of every possible lead or link . . . friends, relatives . . . anywhere they might have gone. That's much more likely to bear fruit than anything we can do here. And keep in touch with your local police. Believe me, it's home the girls will want to return to when they've found out the world isn't the warm, friendly place they thought it was.'

The temperature had been dropping as rapidly as the watery October evening sun and the amusement arcade offered a welcome warm retreat.

They'd pounced first on the Dance Dance Revolution machine, spending twenty minutes and three pound coins frantically trying to make their feet on the illuminated dance platform follow the pattern of arrows on the video screen in time to the disco beat. After that, hanging on to each other and staggering with mock exhaustion, they had moved on to the slot machines, wasting several five-pence pieces each on a machine that looked as though the very next coin would push a five-pound note over the edge and into the receptacle below.

'It's not fair. I think it's glued on,' wailed Leonie.

'We'd better not spend too much,' Chloe warned. 'You never know when we might need some for food or bus fares or something.'

'I've got a hundred and two pounds, nineteen pence,' stated Leonie proudly. 'I took all my savings out of my money box at home. All my birthday money, Christmas money, pocket money that I've been given for years. I don't spend very much really.'

'You've got more than me!'

Leonie smiled naughtily at Chloe. 'Of course I would have twenty-nine pounds fifty less if I'd bought Black Diamond off someone.'

'Just as well you didn't then,' Chloe laughed, prodding her in the ribs.

'Ooh, look over there.' Leonie was pointing at what looked

like a passport photo booth. '*"Gogh's workroom"*,' she read. '*"Have your picture drawn the way great artists would have drawn them."* Can we, Chloe?' pleaded Leonie, as if Chloe had been her big sister all her life.

Chapter Forty-One

'So what do you want to do now?'

'Apart from punching your lights out, I don't know.' Dan slammed the passenger door of Mark's car as hard as he could.

'Hey. That's not fair. I couldn't have predicted this. I didn't suggest to Chloe she get in touch with Leonie. And don't take this the wrong way, but if Leonie had known about the way she began life in this world, what Chloe told her wouldn't have come as such a shock.'

'And if you'd been bigger than your ego – and that's saying something – you'd have left us alone. And we wouldn't be going through any of this.'

Mark started the engine. 'We could hurl blame at each other all night. Where's it going to get us? Now's not the time anyway.'

Dan grunted, turning his face to the window. 'I hope they've found somewhere warm and dry, wherever they are.' A light rain was beginning to spatter the glass.

'For what it's worth, Daniel, I'm sorry. I really am.'

Dan made no reply, his head turned implacably away from him. Had he even heard? Or had he retreated into his own private world of angst and recrimination?

Mark exhaled. 'I'll take you back to our place, shall I? Your van's there.'

'I suppose you'll have to.'

Mark changed up the gears and merged into the line of traffic heading south towards the A2.

'Make sure your faces are central in the circle,' the mechanical male voice barked in its American accent.

In high spirits, cheeks pressed together, the two girls watched the screen in front of them as an unseen, scribbling hand gradually gave shape to their grinning faces.

'Which one's you and which one's me?' laughed Chloe when the booth dispensed the black and white sketch a minute or two later.

'It's printed the opposite way round,' said Leonie, as they pored over it. 'I'm the one on the left. Look, you can tell by my hair slide.'

'We'll have to do another one so we can both have one to put on our walls,' said Chloe.

'My turn.' Leonie took a pound coin from her purse, put it in the slot and they giggled their way through the process again.

Jenny watched from the window as the two men got out of Mark's car, leaving it parked in the driveway, and trudged towards the front door, their faces set and pale.

'I've just put a lasagne in the oven. I thought you might be hungry,' she said hesitantly as they wiped their feet on the mat.

Dan managed a faint, polite smile in her direction. 'I don't think I could manage to eat anything right now.'

'I don't think I could either, darling,' added Mark. 'A coffee would go down well though.'

'OK. I'll turn the oven off. Coffee for you, Daniel?'

'I'd better get home in case Leonie comes back. And I want to start phoning everyone and anyone who might know where they've gone.'

'I can tell you they're not planning to come back tonight,' said Jenny quietly. 'I've been looking at Chloe's computer and reading some of the correspondence between the two of them over the past couple of weeks. They've been planning this.'

'Do you know where they are then? What do they say? What the hell do they think they're doing?'

'I haven't had a chance to read everything yet; I had two policemen from Lewisham here for the best part of an hour, asking questions about our family life and searching the house. They seemed to think they'd find them hiding in the wardrobe or something!'

'I don't get this at all. It's all so out of character,' said Mark. 'Chloe may be stroppy at times but she's never been really rebellious. She's certainly never knowingly worried us before.'

'It's out of character for Leonie, too, believe me. She wouldn't have done this without encouragement.'

'I think you'll find their Google chats quite an eye-opener. Both of you.' Jenny threw a questioning glance at Dan. 'Can you stick around for half an hour or so longer?'

'Of course. If it means I'm going to find out what's going on.'

'All right. You make the coffee, Mark, and I'll go upstairs and print off what seem to be the most significant conversations.'

'Print all of it,' Dan called after her.

'I usually see Popeye on Saturdays. He'll wonder where I am tomorrow.'

They were demolishing toasted ham and cheese sandwiches and a hot chocolate each in a coffee bar next to the amusement arcade. The waitress had started stacking chairs on the tables around them. Chloe looked at her watch. It was five minutes to nine.

'I hope Dad's OK.' Leonie nibbled the edge of a dried-up slice of cucumber decorating the side of the plate. 'He's hopeless on his own.'

'Shouldn't you have thought of that before? This was your idea.'

'I know. It's just . . . we had such a big argument last night.'

'What did you argue about?'

'Going to Ireland. Again. He seems to think I have to do what he says and I suppose I do. But I can't change the way I feel. I screamed at him that he'd have to go without me and I'd rather kill myself than go and live in Ireland. Then I shut myself in my bedroom and put the chair against the door to stop him coming in. I wouldn't say good night to him or anything. I hope he doesn't think I've really killed myself. He'll be really worried, Chloe.'

'Isn't that the whole point of running away? To *make* them worried. Make them see we should be with each other whenever we want. Show them we're capable of managing our own lives, and they have to treat us with respect.'

'Yes, but I feel bad now.'

'Do you think our parents will have talked to each other when they realised we weren't' coming home?'

'I don't know.' Chloe shrugged. 'Probably not. Our dads don't like each other, do they?'

'Do you think they'll get the police looking for us?'

'They might.'

'We might be on the news.'

Chloe gasped, 'Oh Leo! Do you think they'll put our pictures on the TV?' She glanced up at the screen above the café's display cabinet, half expecting to see their photographs and the caption: Have you seen these missing children?

'They might. We might be in the *Daily Mail* as well.'

'Look, Leonie. Perhaps we'd better not sleep out tonight. I haven't seen anywhere to pitch your tent anyway. We could try somebody's garden but they might call the police. It's a bit cold as well.'

'Have you finished? We're closing now, sorry.' The waitress didn't look much older than they were. She had a silver stud in her nose and henna-streaked hair and she spoke with a foreign accent. Leonie popped the last crust of her half-sandwich into her mouth and they stood up, hauling and shrugging their rucksacks onto their shoulders.

Leonie peered at the scrap of paper that was the bill. 'Four pounds eighty. Should we leave a tip?'

'Have you got a fiver, Leo?'

'Yes.' She pulled her pink heart-shaped purse out of her pocket.

'Well that will be enough. I'll owe you two pounds fifty. Can I give it to you later?'

'Sure.' Leonie looked only too pleased to seem to be the more responsible of the two of them.

''Bye, thank you.'

''Bye.'

Outside, they stood looking both ways along the road between the café and the harbour wall, while the waitress locked the door behind them.

When Jenny came down from Chloe's room, several sheets of paper in her hand, Mark and Dan were sitting facing each other in silence in the kitchen, their eyes fixed on four phones lying in a row on the table – the Elficks' landline and three mobiles belonging to Mark, Dan and Jenny.

'No news then,' she commented superfluously.

Mark got to his feet. 'I'll pour the coffee.'

Jenny sat down at the head of the table, and solemnly spread the papers out in front of her. 'I'm not sure where to start here. It seems they've been planning this for the last few days.'

'Dan tells me they've been in touch for a couple of weeks now,' said Mark, resuming his seat with the coffee pot and three mugs. 'Chloe must have found Leonie's Bebo entry.'

'She answered Leonie's ad for a Julip horse she'd been desperate for,' Dan cut in. It was pleasing to know more than the Elficks for once. 'That's how they came to meet up at Starbucks.'

'And it seems they've been in touch on a daily basis pretty much ever since,' said Jenny. She held up one of the pieces of paper for Mark and Dan to see. 'They read a bit like the dialogue in a stage play or something. Here's one of the early ones. It must be shortly after that meeting at Waterloo. It starts off with Leonie saying "I'm really annoyed with my dad" . . . Chloe asks why and she says, "He thinks I don't understand why he didn't tell me I was an embryo baby. But I do. I'm not stupid. I can see why he and Mum might think it was too complicated to tell me when I was very little, but then they never got round to telling me later."

'And then Chloe asks why she's annoyed with him. And Leonie says, "Because he didn't want me to know about you. I wouldn't have known at all if it wasn't for you. I got a perfect right to know I've got a sister and he doesn't see that. He says I'm not allowed to speak to you. If he catches me online with you he'll probably ban me from using the computer."'

Mark glanced at Dan from under his eyebrows. 'And Chloe knew she shouldn't be contacting Leonie either.'

Jenny continued. 'Chloe then says to Leonie, "Maybe your dad is frightened of losing you." And Leonie replies, "Why would he lose me? Der!" Then Chloe says, "my mum coming. Speak later."'

Dan seemed to be inspecting his knuckles.

'What next?' Jenny leafed through the papers. 'I didn't write the dates on these. They're on the computer but they haven't printed out. There's a fair amount of stuff comparing notes on their teachers and what set books they've been doing at school . . .' She looked up at Dan. 'Is Boot the name of your dog?'

'Yes.'

'There's a lot about him.' She turned over another page. 'And Chloe talking about Vulcan . . . Oh, here Leonie says, "I don't understand why they don't want us to see each other. It doesn't make sense." And Chloe's reply is "No it doesn't." And Leonie says, "My dad says it's against the law. He says your dad broke the law." To which Chloe says, "My dad lives in a world of his own. He doesn't know what day of the week it is most of the time."'

'That's a bit much,' interrupted Mark. 'What does she mean by that?'

'Your daughter's perception of you. Ask her,' returned Jenny tersely, continuing, 'Chloe then says, "And my mum is more interested in keeping the peace than understanding my point of view."' Jenny winced and shuffled to another page. 'Oh, this is where they start planning to run away together by the looks of it. This conversation starts with Leonie saying "I'm thinking of running away." Chloe naturally asks why and Leonie says, "My dad wants us to move . . ."' Jenny looked up at Dan, her eyebrows raised, '". . . to *Ireland*."' She continued incredulously, 'Chloe says, "When? Why?" And Leonie answers, "Before Christmas probably."'

Jenny stopped and stared at Dan again.

Mark was gaping at him too. 'So you were going to run away with her,' he exclaimed, 'to make sure we lost track of her.'

Dan put his elbows on the table and buried his face in his hands. 'It seemed like the best solution.'

'Why, for God's sake? I told you we wouldn't get in touch with her without your permission!'

'How did you expect me to believe that? Once your daughter got her claws into her that was it. It was the only thing I could do.'

'But . . . that's sheer paranoia!' spluttered Mark.

Jenny kicked him under the table.

'Why, Daniel?' she asked quietly. 'Tell me why should Leonie befriending Chloe be such a dreadful thing?'

'I'm not sure any more.' His hands, still covering his face, muffled his voice. 'All I wanted was a new beginning for the two of us. We'd been through so much . . .'

Jenny and Mark waited. Daniel didn't seem about to say any more on the subject.

Tensely, Jenny went back to the page she'd just been reading from. 'Leonie says here, "Dad says I'll be happier in Ireland, but I won't. He knows I won't. It's because he wants to take me away from *you*. That's the real reason. He hates your dad and so he doesn't want me to have anything to do with you." Chloe replies, "He can't do that. It's not fair." And Leonie says, "I've got no choice." Jenny turned another page. 'Leonie then talks about her home being where she lived with her mum and she feels her mum's spirit is still there. She says here, "I'm sick of all these secrets. I don't trust my dad any more." And Chloe says, "Ditto", with a line of exclamation marks.'

The two men exchanged mortified glances across the table.

'Chloe asks Leonie, "If you run away, where will you go?" And Leonie says, "I don't know yet. I'll think of somewhere. It's the only way to make my dad realise he can't make me go to Ireland." Chloe then says, "I'll come with you," and Leonie says, "But you've got no reason to run away." Chloe says, "I have! I'm as fed up with the secrets and lies as you. Anyway I'm your big sister. I should look after you." Then Chloe says . . .' Jenny stopped. 'Oh God . . .'

'What?' demanded Mark.

'She says, "We could go and see my friend Clyde."'

'Who the hell's Clyde?'

'Wait,' Jenny continued. 'Leonie asks, "Who's Clyde?" and Chloe's reply is "He looks after horses at a place in Yorkshire, near the sea." Then Leonie asks, "What's he like?" And Chloe says, "I met him on a MySpace group called Crayzee about Horses. He's really nice and intelligent and understanding. He loves horses and all animals."'

'Christ!' Dan was half standing, reaching for his phone. 'We've got to tell the police. And look up that group on MySpace; find out where he is.'

'Hold on a minute, Daniel.' Jenny put out a restraining hand in Dan's direction. 'Leonie, to her credit, says, "I don't think we should go and stay with someone we've never met." She goes on to say, "He's a stranger, even if you have talked loads on the internet." Chloe says, "I s'pose. But he lives by the seaside. Think of all those horses. We could help look after them and have free rides." And Leonie says, "If you haven't actually met him in person I don't think we should just turn up and expect him to look after us. And he might not be as nice as you think."' Jenny smiled wryly at Dan. 'She's got her head screwed on, hasn't she? And then – this is the bit I told you about before – they talk about some book Leonie read once where the heroine packed her bags, left home and decided where to go by choosing a place name she liked the sound of. They decide to meet at Starbucks on Waterloo station again . . . quarter past three . . . look at the list of destinations on the board and choose where to go. Leonie talks about packing this lightweight tent she's got in case they need it . . . they decide to empty their rucksacks of their school books and put changes of clothes and shoes in instead so none of the parents will notice when they leave for school in the morning.'

'So we're none the wiser as to where they've gone,' said Mark bitterly.

Dan was clutching his phone. 'I want to tell the police about this Clyde character your daughter was proposing they go and see.'

'Trains don't go to Yorkshire from Waterloo, do they?' asked Jenny.

'No,' argued Dan, 'but they could have taken the Tube to another mainline station from there.'

'Yes, you're right,' said Jenny. 'Better safe than sorry.' She took a business card from her skirt pocket. 'I've got the direct line number for the officers who came round earlier. They should get on the trail of this Clyde character right now.

'I don't like it round here any more.' Chloe shivered. 'It's a bit dark and deserted. Even the amusement arcade looks empty.'

'We could get a taxi,' suggested Leonie. 'Let's start walking back towards the shopping centre and find a phone box. It can't cost that much, can it?'

Rucksacks bumping against their backs, they set off back the way they'd come from the station.

'Hello, young ladies.'

They hadn't noticed the car slowing down behind them.

'You're out rather late, aren't you, you two? Are you lost?'

The man leaning across the passenger seat, calling to them through the half-opened window, had dark, greasy hair and his teeth were uneven, but he seemed friendly enough.

'Do you know where Birchwood Crescent is?' ventured Chloe.

'Birchwood Crescent. Hmm . . .'

'It's near the beach.'

'The beach? Ah . . . Well . . . the beach is a bit of a way from here but I'm not in a particular hurry. I'll give you both a lift if you like.'

'No, it's all right,' said Leonie. 'Thank you anyway. We can walk, if you just tell us where it is.'

'Two nice young ladies like you shouldn't be walking all that way. With those heavy bags as well. I wouldn't want daughters of mine walking round the coast road in the dark. You don't know who you might meet. You get some funny people around here at night, you know.'

'Well . . . how many miles is it?' began Chloe doubtfully.

'It's OK, it doesn't matter,' cut in Leonie, grabbing her arm. 'I've just seen our friend Peter over there. Come on, Chloe. Let's go.'

'Who's Peter?'

'Chloe!' muttered Leonie through clenched teeth, 'I don't like him. Come on!'

The man had got out of his car now and was walking round to the passenger side, opening both the front and the rear doors. His jeans were ill-fitting and oil-stained. 'Come on then, get in. It'll only take a jiffy in the car. You'll be nice and warm in here too. I've got the heater on.'

'No thank you,' said Chloe over her shoulder as they turned away, trying to make her voice sound firm and unconcerned. 'We're all right.' Clutching each other's arms, they began walking as quickly as they could without running, towards the entrance to the shopping centre about two hundred yards away.

'So . . . maybe this isn't all my fault.' Mark refilled their three coffee mugs and thrust Dan's aggressively across at him, slopping some of it on to the table. 'It seems to me the real reason they've run away is that Leonie doesn't want to be railroaded into moving to Ireland.'

'How dare you!' countered Dan angrily. 'I wouldn't even have thought about moving to Ireland if it wasn't for you!'

'Well, going to Ireland because of us is frankly ridiculous,' rejoined Mark. 'What were you going to do? Lock her up in a tower and throw away the key? How possessive can you get? Doesn't she get a say in things?'

'Shut up!' shouted Jenny walking back into the kitchen. 'That's enough, both of you. You're both in the wrong. All the way through this, you've both managed to see things only from your own points of view. Now our two children could be in danger – and why? Because neither of you could see beyond your own selfish interests.'

'That's not fair,' objected Mark.

'Listen, there's only been one person's welfare uppermost in my mind and that's Leonie's,' shouted Dan.

'And doesn't that show how little emotional intelligence you have!' Jenny shouted back. 'You've both lied. You've both kept secrets. You've both tried to manipulate things to suit your own agendas. And Chloe and Leonie have seen through you. I don't mean they don't love you. Of course they love their dads. But their trust has been badly dented.'

The two men were looking up at her like scolded schoolboys as she stood glaring at them from the end of the table.

'They've felt powerless with you fighting and arguing over their heads. That's why they've run away. It's the only way they can show us how they feel ... and ... regain some sense of control over their lives. They're not babies any more. They're young adults. Very bright young adults at that. They deserve to be treated as such. And you have treated them like ... possessions.' Stunned into silence, the two men stared at the table.

Jenny took a moment to fight back the tears. 'And I'm to blame too. Chloe's right. I try too damned hard to please everyone. I'm too willing to take the line of least resistance. I should have had the courage and the sense to step in and put a stop to all this nonsense. The bottom line is, the girls have found each other. We can't break them up now. It's frankly ridiculous to even think of it. I just hope it's not too late to tell them that.'

'That's all I ever wanted from the start,' said Mark as Jenny took a tissue from her pocket and blew her nose. 'It truly is. I never, ever wanted to lay any claim to Leonie. You are her father, Daniel. You brought her up. And you've done a brilliant job of it. I just wanted those two girls to be part of each other's lives.'

'It's all very well to say that now, Mark,' said Jenny, 'and I'm sure that's the truth. But look at all the deception that's been going on. I've lost count of how many times you've lied to me. Right from the start, when Lionel told you about Leonie and her parents, I had months of secrets and lies. And then it started again when Daniel's wife died. If I hadn't read the story in the papers myself, you wouldn't have told me.'

'I would. I just would have waited a bit, that's all, until I knew what was happening.'

'And then there was that incident at the school . . . and engineering that meeting with Daniel . . . I could go on.'

'I know. I did realise I was being devious a lot of the time, but I couldn't see any other way forward,' said Mark.

'And like father, like daughter, your Chloe resorted to devious tactics herself, luring my daughter into meeting her under false pretences.' contributed Dan primly.

Jenny turned to face him. 'So you think you've been straight as a dye, do you?'

'Well . . .'

'I can understand how difficult it must have been to find the right time to broach the subject of Leonie being a donor-conceived child, but once you knew she had a sister, couldn't you have had the courage to tell her then?'

'I wanted to pick the right time.'

'And what if you'd never got round to it? What if she'd found out by accident in her twenties or thirties? The odds are that she would have, you know. How do you think she'd have felt?'

'Betrayed, I guess,' mumbled Dan. 'Cheated.'

'Isn't it much better that she's learned the truth now while she's young, and the bond between you is close and loving and trusting?'

Dan nodded. 'Actually, it's been a relief, to my surprise.'

'And what about this great escape to Ireland. Didn't Leonie have a right to be consulted?'

'All I can say is . . . like Mark, I thought I was doing the best for Leonie. I thought Mark was the selfish shit in all this. And I was the victim. I have to admit, I've been selfish too.' He looked at Mark reluctantly. 'I'm sorry.'

'I didn't want to take her away from you, Dan,' said Mark gently, 'I wouldn't have stood a chance anyway.' His voice cracked. 'All I ever wanted was . . . God, it sounds so pathetic . . . I just wanted us all to get along together. Accept each other.'

'Meanwhile,' Jenny's voice had taken on a hard edge, 'all this has made our two children feel forced to leave their homes. They're out there somewhere in the cold and dark, who knows where, thinking that they've been the cause of all this hostility and aggression between you two. Which they have been of course. Do you think now, assuming our prayers are granted that is, and they come back to us safe and sound, we might be able to show them that we're bigger than the petty, selfish, possessive, quarrelling parents they thought we were?'

*

Annabel selected a wide, round-ended brush from the clay pot on the table beside the easel and dragged it across the glossy purple snake she'd just squeezed on to her palette. Cobalt violet was just about the most expensive pigment you could buy, but this was going to be worth it. Such a wonderful vibrant colour.

A little turpentine . . . she breathed in . . . she loved that smell . . . but not too much of it; the paint should be laid on thickly . . . lavishly.

On the three-foot-wide canvas in front of her, an enormous exotic bird was beginning to materialise; his feathers curling and swirling in rich viridian greens and blues against a flaming sky of alizarin red and cadmium yellow.

She'd added a smudge of silver-streaked indigo in the top right-hand corner to suggest a hint of menace, but the bird himself was triumphant in his wild, vivid beauty.

Pleased with her handiwork, she put down the wide brush and picked up a fine-tipped one, dipping it into the blob of zinc white on her palette . . . add a gleam to his eye.

Her studio was bathed in light from the old photographer's lamp an ex-boyfriend had given her. In its sound-dock, her iPod was playing her favourite Doors track, 'Riders on the Storm'. Life simply didn't get any better than this.

Her brush hovering just above the bird's shiny, blue-black eye, she became aware of a thudding noise. She cocked her head to one side and listened. There it was again.

She turned the music down. Someone was at the front door, using the door knocker instead of the bell for some reason. And using it with some vigour.

She glanced at the clock. It was after midnight. She always lost all track of time when she was working. Who would be hammering on the door at this time of night?

Aware of her heartbeat moving up a gear, she wiped her hands on her denim overalls and padded down the two flights of stairs to her front door. She realised she was holding the little paintbrush as if it were a club and smiled at herself. How ridiculous. She bent down to the letter box.

'OK, tell me who's there or I'll paint you to death!'

'Auntie Annabel, it's Chloe.'

'Chloe?'

Annabel fumbled to release the safety chain, slid back a bolt, and yanked open the door. 'Chloe! What are you . . . ?' She took in the two little faces looking up at her hopefully, pale and pinched in the darkness, and for a just a moment looked bemused.

Then she beamed, first at Chloe and then at Leonie. 'And I think I know who *you* are. How absolutely super! Come in, come in.'

She bent to re-bolt the door and then flung her arms wide enough to envelop both of them in a hug that smelled of oil paint and warm lavender. 'I bet you could both murder a cup of hot chocolate. And I just bought a tin of extremely naughty chocolate biscuits. My subconscious must have known you were coming.'

'I thought we might have heard something by now.' Dan's face was grey; lined with worry. 'I think maybe I'd better go home. It's getting on for one o'clock.'

The three of them had moved back to the living room and turned the gas fire on. They had been taking it in turns to go to the toilet every twenty minutes or so, they'd drunk so much coffee. All three of them could have used something stronger but there was the chance that at any moment the police would ring to say the girls had been found and they'd have to drive somewhere to collect them.

'You can stay the night if you like,' said Jenny. 'We've got a spare bedroom.'

'I don't know whether to stay here in case the police ring with any news, or go back home in case Leonie turns up there. I think it's unlikely, but that's where my instincts tell me I should be.'

'I don't think any of us will be sleeping much tonight anyway.' Mark, too, seemed to have aged ten years. 'I keep thinking of them out alone in the cold in some strange town. And praying to God they're OK. And making all sorts of pacts with the devil at the same time. I'd give anything—'

The phone rang. Jenny actually screamed. Mark grabbed it first. 'Yes, hello . . . Annabel!'

Jenny's head jerked up in surprise. 'Annabel?' She looked at Dan. 'My oldest friend,' she mouthed.

Dan raised a surprised eyebrow and they both fixed their gaze back on Mark.

'What? They're with you! Both of them! Oh. Oh, thank God.'

Jenny and Dan could only hear the faint twitter of Annabel's voice, but the look on Mark's face gave them the answer to the only question that mattered. The girls were safe. They were fine. All the other questions could come later. Without thinking, Jenny flung her arms round Dan's neck, her sobs muffled in his shirt. Dan's own shoulders were shaking with emotion.

'They're having biscuits and hot chocolate . . .' Mark's voice was high-pitched, almost hysterical with relief. 'Thanks so much, Annabel. Hang on to them then. It shouldn't take too long to get to you this time of night. Oh . . . Yes . . . I see . . . Yes, I suppose that makes sense. I'll just tell Jenny and Dan.'

He covered the mouthpiece lightly for a moment.

'She says she's going to put them in a nice warm bath and then tuck them into bed. It's late. And they're both exhausted apparently. OK, Annabel, that's fine . . . Tomorrow morning then. About ten o'clock? Wonderful.' He took the receiver away from his face. 'She wants to know which of us is coming to get them.' His eyes met Dan's.

Slowly, holding Mark's gaze, Dan nodded his head.

Mark put the phone back to his ear. 'Tell the girls we love them . . . and tell them . . . their parents will be coming to collect them in the morning.' He returned Dan's smile. 'Yes, that's right. All three of us.'